in the weeds

Garrett County Press

Printed in the United States of America

First edition 2018

ISBN: 9781939430205

Designed by Kevin Stone

Garrett County Press books are distributed to the trade by National Book Network, 800-462-6420.

www.gcpress.com

in the weeds

Daniel Browne

Garrett County Press

Beforehand (this had begun with his childhood and kept growing until he was completely adult) when he had tried to do something for the good of everyone, for mankind, for Russia, for the whole village, he would notice that thinking about it was agreeable, but that the activity itself was always incoherent...

– Leo Tolstoy, *Anna Karenina*

Hello, Brooklyn, how you doing? Where you going?
And can I come too?

– Jay-Z, "Hello Brooklyn 2.0"

Under the Lunch Bus

The chairman was slung low in his seat, his long legs crossed at the ankles, pink, manicured fingers folded over a soft knoll of belly. "We're not paying them off," he said. "Not happening."

I hadn't even gotten the words "financial compensation" out of my mouth. The meeting was off to a bad start, but what else was new?

We'd come to that colorless conference room to discuss the construction of the Second Avenue subway, a hundred-year boondoggle recently revived. Vivienne had been getting complaints from her constituents on the Upper East Side. Blast excavation was sending up plumes of smoke and debris right on their doorsteps. Drilling was shaking their foundations; scaffolding obscured their signs. Business was down by half, the end nowhere in sight. It was my job to come up with recommendations to ease their plight. Ever watch a public hearing on TV and notice a youngish person in a wrinkled suit discreetly passing notes to the official on the dais? That rumpled note-passer was me.

This was my last chance to do something useful for the people before Vivienne left the city council. A well-known Park Avenue socialite, she'd been fundraising for liberal causes and candidates, serving on boards and blue ribbon commissions, for thirty years. Her friends—Ralph as in Lauren, Bill as in Clinton—were always needling her about running for office, and after her older husband, a legendary white-shoe lawyer, died on the tennis court, she finally felt bored enough to do it. Turns out, though, she didn't like the job much, found it sordid, throwing elbows at the same people she rubbed shoulders with at the Century Club, grubbing for headlines in papers that referred to her only as "Viv" or "Vanderbilt confidante." When Bloomberg made his controversial push to change the law so he could run for a third term, she was quick to announce that, as a matter of principle, she would bow out at the end of her second.

By the time we got on the MTA chairman's calendar, we were deep in running-out-the-clock mode. Vivienne's lunch meetings were getting longer, the invitees more likely to be gossip columnists and tennis pros than PR consultants and pollsters. Daily briefings were increasingly held at the hair salon. Still, I had my talking points committed to memory and a folder full of supporting documents at hand. I'd already passed out copies of some letters of complaint we'd received from Second Avenue business owners. Now I mentioned that in Portland the city had backed loans to small businesses affected by an extension of the municipal light rail system.

The chairman gave his flunky—a moonfaced lunk with Addams Family hair plastered to his forehead—a quick eye-roll. I'd heard he was halfway out the door himself, looking to break into the international consulting racket, and clearly he felt no need to keep up appearances.

"This ain't Portland," he said.

Vivienne held out her hand as if to stop my next suggestion before it reached the chairman's ear. "No one's saying we're Portland. Anyway, we have ideas that don't involve money. Right, Will?"

I shuffled my stack of papers. "There are ways of mitigating the loss of business. We did a scan of best practices."

"Well, isn't that enterprising," the chairman said. He flapped his fingers in a bring-it-on gesture. "What've you got?"

My eye fell to the top of my stack. "Seattle has a lunch bus program."

"What's a lunch bus? Is that like a food truck?"

"What's a food truck?" Vivienne asked.

"No food trucks on Park Avenue yet, Viv? You should talk to your pal Danny about doing one up there. The kids are crazy for them."

I could hear the hinge of my jaw pop as I tried to cut in. "Once a week," I said, "the city of Seattle provides a shuttle to its employees so they can visit an area affected by construction and have lunch at the restaurants there."

The chairman glanced over at the lunk and then at Vivienne as if he expected one of them to reveal the hidden camera, let him in on the prank.

"You're kidding, right?"

The lunk suppressed a grin.

"It's considered a successful program," I said.

"How many employees do we have?" the chairman asked.

"Forty-eight thousand," the lunk said, without looking up. He was now lost in his screen, probably texting his fellow transit drones, letting them know they were missing amateur hour.

"In how many locations?"

"Dozens."

The chairman turned his palms up, voila. "And I'm supposed to get them all up to Vinny's Pizza in rush hour traffic, spend who knows how much on logistics so they can shell out a buck-fifty on a slice?"

"We're not talking about every transit employee in the city. Think of it as more of a goodwill gesture."

The chairman cocked a sandy eyebrow. "With all due respect, we're moving more than five million passengers a day. We don't do gestures."

Vivienne snickered. "You have to admit, Will, it sounds pretty silly."

For a moment, there was silence. Blood rushed to my ears; my throat went dry. Even the chairman seemed stunned by how quickly she'd thrown me under the bus.

Strong-arming done for the day, his tone shifted. "Look, we're really not the ones you want to talk to. My job is to get this damn tunnel built before another hundred years goes by. That's the mayor's priority. We've got Small Business Services to help out mom and pop."

Vivienne nodded, apparently missing the condescension in this little civics lesson.

"But I understand you've got to go back to your people with something, so how about this: On Monday, we're going to launch a website for the businesses in the corridor, let people know they're still open, do regular updates on any promotions or special offers they're running, maybe spotlight a different business every week. Have I got that right?"

"It's more of a web*page* than a web*site*," the lunk said.

"Site, page, what do I know? The point is, we're dedicating MTA staff time and resources to addressing this issue."

"How is anyone going to know this webpage exists?" I asked.

"We'll do the usual song and dance, press release, e-blast…press conference?"

The lunk shook his head, a mortician who's been asked about the possibility of an open casket.

"OK, no press conference. Unless, of course, you want to do one, take a little credit. How does that sound?"

"It sounds like you want us to do your PR for you."

"Really? Because I think we're going above and beyond here."

A year or two ago, I might have just moved on to the next paper in my folder, kept throwing out proposals—sales tax holiday? off-street parking for construction vehicles?—till the chairman was so sick of me he'd promise something, if only a follow-up meeting. That, I figured, was what they meant by "incremental progress." Now I was just burning to get outside. It occurred to me, not for the first time, that I'd spent the better part of my young adulthood in government conference rooms and government conference rooms never had windows.

The chairman turned to Vivienne. She stood and offered him her pallid, ring-studded hand. "You've been more than generous."

I glared at her. I couldn't help it.

"With your time," she added quickly.

The chairman unfolded himself like a mantis and engulfed her hand in his florid executive pincer. I was forced to press flesh with the lunk, who was, inevitably, clammy as a dog's nose.

Meeting over. And so, I decided at that moment, was my career in politics.

The chairman held the door for Vivienne. "This wasn't your last official business, was it?"

"You know, I'm not sure. We've got a few days left till the winter break, but after that it's my successor's problem. No one can believe I'm walking away, but I had to take a stand."

"Will I be seeing you in St. Barts?"

She made a curlicue in the air with her hand. "I'm trying to carve out some time to myself, but there's been a flood of offers." Sigh for emphasis. "Whatever will be will be."

The chairman mimicked the flutter of her hand, giving it a little extra zazz. "Always leave 'em wanting more, right?"

* * *

Back in the Viv-mobile—black SUV, plusher than the mayor's, to hear her tell it—I was brooding over what the chairman had said about a Park Avenue food truck. Could that be my next move? After the meeting we'd just left, the notion of dishing out Waldorf salads from a to-go window had its appeal. I could call it the Ladies Who Lunch Truck. Maybe I was just hungry. Other than a damp tuna sandwich before the meeting, I hadn't eaten all day. Tricia was doing her monthly evening shift, so I texted Elliot to see if he was free for dinner.

Vivienne, meanwhile, was buoyant. "Feels good to be going out on a high note."

My face must have given me away.

"Come on," she said. "Don't be so hard on yourself. We got the website."

"Webpage."

"Do you think the guy who owns Vinny's Pizza knows the difference?"

"I don't think there is a Vinny's Pizza. That was a rhetorical flourish."

Vivienne swatted away my gloom. "We did what we could."

"We could have threatened to go to the press, tell them the Second Avenue subway is killing small businesses and the MTA won't do anything to help."

"Will, you know the press won't pay attention if you're not running for something. That's what I get for taking a stand, right?"

"Right." For everyone's safety, I aimed my death-stare out the window.

In the reflection, I watched her fish a compact from her purse and take a gander. "You have to admit, the bus thing is pretty goofy. I mean, New York imitating Portland? Can you imagine?"

Savory Brooklyn

As soon as I set foot in Rita's, I was hit with its distinctive smell, a mix of fresh basil and bathroom sex. The place was packed as always, never mind it was a Tuesday night. The regulars were yowling along to AC/DC. I was the only one dressed like I'd come from the office.

Vivienne was wrong, part wrong anyway. Manhattan, with its glass and steel towers, its greenery largely confined to Central Park, could never be Portland, a modestly proportioned town surrounded by forest, a kind of nature preserve for the young and the restless, tattoo artists and furniture makers, freelance video game designers and adventure sports enthusiasts. Brooklyn, on the other hand, was looking more like Portland—more organic, more handcrafted, hairier—every day.

In 2009, Brooklyn was about two-thirds of the way through its evolution into Brooklyn™. The Hasids, the Poles, the Puerto Ricans, the Dominicans, the old-school Italians—they were all still around. Traders had been bunking down in Brooklyn Heights for a while, taking the R train two stops to "the street." The artists, already zoned out of the warehouses in Williamsburg, were taking their perpetual 1978 to the

Queens border. Some of them were old enough to have seen this movie play out across the bridge in Soho and Tribeca.

Then there were the ones like me—white people with inessential degrees, no church or temple but maybe a yoga practice, some posters nice enough to frame. Fifteen years ago, we wouldn't even have considered living in Brooklyn. Now, it was just what you did. The financial collapse was supposed to drag down rents in Manhattan, but if that happened, I missed it. In any case, I'd already landed in Brooklyn by then. It didn't take me long to realize it was more than just a place to crash after a day's work in "the city." Once people left behind the high-rises and the tourist hordes, it seemed to open up the possibility of a whole new lifestyle. I knew that lifestyle existed because I saw it in the pages of *Savory Brooklyn*.

Savory Brooklyn was a free magazine stocked in the gourmet stores and wine shops that dotted my neighborhood of Park Slope, its cover graced with luminous photos of crusty loaves and tattooed artisans in flour-dusted aprons. The text inside adhered to a set of tropes I came to recognize after a few issues: Subject X had been toiling away in [finance/academia/PR/fashion] but felt unfulfilled. On a trip to [Asia/the deep South/a clandestine supper club], he/she was moved by the humble yet sophisticated foodstuffs on offer, steeped in history and meaning, so different from the anonymous fare we've been conditioned to expect from our rootless, industrial monoculture. He/she began making his/her own [pickled watermelon rind/quinoa dosa/foraged elderflower-infused gin] as a hobby and giving it away to friends at [dinner parties/the holidays]. The first time one of those friends said, "This is amazing. You need to bottle this stuff and go into business!" he/she laughed it off as hyperbole, but eventually the revelation set in: *This* is what brings me happiness, not [making even more money for the one percent/elucidating some abstruse point of theory/perpetuating the tyranny of body image]. Why keep at it when I could be working with my hands, giving a little piece of myself to others, bringing a smile to their faces, turning them on to the simple power of a good thing crafted with love?

Fortunately, he/she had set a little money aside. Even better, one of his/her loyal "customers" turned out to be a venture capitalist with an itch to give back. Fate was speaking loud and clear: time to go professional. It was tough finding a suitable production space (shout-out to the transgender art collective that was looking to get out of its lease), and moving from a home kitchen to an industrial one wasn't without its headaches—he/she's become a regular MacGyver when it comes to repairs!—but by far the biggest challenge has been keeping up with demand. In fact, the only way to source enough raw ingredients of the quality and provenance the famously discerning Brooklyn clientele has come to expect is to cultivate his/her own sustainable [greenhouse/apiary/chicken run], a whole new adventure, more than that, an opportunity to learn about one's place in the eternal circle of life—and leave Brooklyn a little greener than he/she found it. And to think, none of it would ever have come to pass if he/she hadn't taken that first plucky step into the unknown!

I read this story in all its many manifestations dozens of times that year; I couldn't get enough. Flipping through the pages of *Savory Brooklyn*—not glossy but of a weighty, sumptuous stock—gave me a whisper of the feeling I used to get from watching *The West Wing* as a crusading student council president.

But no tale of reinvention made a stronger impression on me than the legend of Rita's.

People who knew things said that John Cardini, Rita's principal owner, had been an international security contractor who'd earned his nut supervising ransom drop-offs, training dictators' bodyguards, that kind of thing. When he returned, he had money but no particular plan. On a whim, he bought an abandoned factory on a grim industrial block in Bushwick and used it as a clubhouse for his friends: bikers, metalheads, stoners, a wide assortment of ne'er-do-wells and extreme bohemians. One late night, John's boys were complaining about the long walk to the nearest taco stand, and someone mentioned that what he could really go for was his grandfather's pizza. His Nonno Arturo had a restaurant in Sicily, and you just couldn't find anything like his pies in the States, not even at di Fara's or Lombardi's. Something about the brick oven, a whole fading way of life baked into its cracks. The shame of it was Nonno Arturo was retiring; soon you wouldn't be able to get his mind-altering pizza in Sicily either.

John's vision came to him then and there. Just hours later he was shouting at Nonno Arturo, the connection patchy, making a godfather offer for his mystical oven. It took months of back and forth, protracted consultations with the shipping company and customs, but eventually the ancient heap arrived more or less intact on the doorstep of his clubhouse, which from that moment forward was a pizzeria. He did all the necessary renovations without permits, taking electrical shocks from frayed wires and giving out bribes to city inspectors with equal stoicism. He didn't decorate, just left the space raw, cinderblock walls, chicken wire over the front window. He and the guys hewed the long plank tables and benches in the backyard. For the bar, they salvaged metal and wood from the scrap yard around the corner. He never told anyone who Rita was.

John had never been much of a cook, but a number of his buddies were professionals, speed freaks who crashed headlong into his place at two in the morning, raged till dawn, and then headed right back into work, knives sharp, nails clean. John hired them all away from their jobs in Manhattan, promising them freedom not only to come up with their own menu (as long as it started with pizza) but to make the place their own. Most of the crew came from low- and mid-level establishments, your chicken Caesar, Eggs Benedict joints, but his buddy Francisco had worked the line for Daniel and Jean-Georges, so John made him chef.

It took a few months before anyone other than John's extended family of high-living lowlifes figured out that this was no Vinny's Pizza, that the food at Rita's was, in fact, excellent. The first story in the *Times* wasn't a review; it was a "get a load of this: some misfit opened a pizza parlor in the 'hood…and the kids love it!" piece. The review came next, one star, an unprecedented coup for Bushwick. The dining critic certainly played the down-and-dirty angle to the hilt: he had become addicted to the Phil Speckter (speck, quail egg, and mustard greens) and, like a debased junky, had to venture into a seedy underworld to get his fix. The third story was the real coup de grâce though: a full-page profile of John, Francisco, and the rest that doubled as a trend piece, something about how food was the new rock and roll and Rita's was the CBGB's of a new dining scene.

To be clear, I wasn't there from the beginning. Maybe I had my first Psycho Kale'er before the restaurant editor from *Bon Appétit*. Maybe I didn't. Either way, I didn't "discover" Rita's. I wasn't cool enough to be part of the scene. No, I was there because of Elliot. He was a regular, three days a week on average, and he was there, working on a beer, as I hurried in, still hot from my shaming before the MTA chairman.

"The L was a shit show," I said by way of apology for my lateness.

Elliot grinned. "Should've taken the lunch bus."

I'm not sure what his title was, although technically I was his supervisor. A galumphing sheepdog of a guy, his untended beard, brutalized boat shoes, and rotation of fraying vests—puffy, fleece, and sweater—would have been more than enough to disqualify anyone else in Vivienne's eyes. As it was, she could go on about the vests at length without much prompting. But Elliot was one of those people who somehow knows everybody, and there could be no quality more impressive to the socialite in her.

He'd been with Vivienne much longer than me and probably could have had my job if he didn't suspect it would cramp his style. Vivienne was chair of the education committee of the council, and she relied more or less completely on Elliot, a former teacher with a PhD in urban education, to run that show. But to say he was her expert on the public schools would be to radically understate his role.

Who exactly did Elliot know? Everyone on the council and their staff, for starters. Then there were his Department of Education contacts in the old Tweed Courthouse and all the superintendents, deputy superintendents, principals, assistant principals, teachers, and union reps he'd crossed paths with over the years. He was a favorite unnamed source of reporters at all the dailies, the darling wayward son of his old professors, light in the darkness for activists searching for comrades in the morass of government. And his sphere of influence went beyond the professionally useful types, encompassing all the usual New Brooklyn suspects, too: craft brewers, burlesque dancers, graying skate rats. Oh, and he was friends with John Cardini.

Loosening my tie and rolling up my sleeves somehow only made me feel more conspicuous. "I swear to god, I'm done with government."

"The chairman wasn't moved by your presentation?"

"The chairman," I said, "is an asshole."

Elliot raised his beer in the direction of the bar, pointed at it, then held up two thick fingers. "I play soccer with his son. Major stoner."

"Vivienne was in rare form."

"When someone is always in rare form can you still call it rare?"

His face was pink with booze and good cheer. Clearly, the next round was more than his second.

"Where were you all afternoon anyway?"

"Field work."

The waitress who arrived with our beers had short, pink-blonde hair, an eyebrow ring, and a polka-dot romper that looked like it belonged to a giant infant.

"Elliot, you hanging out later?" Her voice was surprisingly husky given her appearance.

"I might be. Why, what's going on?"

"I've got this tiny ukulele. We're going to take mushrooms and sing songs."

Elliot tapped his chin as if considering her proposal. "Interesting."

"Should be." She left us to imagine the scene.

"Hard to believe people like that really exist," I said.

"Hard to believe any of us exist. Pretty improbable when you think about it."

I eyed him as he took a long pull from his beer and let the suds froth in his beard. "What's with you? Why are you talking like that?"

He wiped his chin with his sleeve. "Done with government, you say?"

"Government, politics, public service. Done, done, and done."

"So what's next then?"

Given my looming unemployment, I should've had a ready answer, but I'd put off thinking about it. In the back of my mind, I knew there'd be another place for me in the council, maybe even city hall. Next time could be different. But no, clarity had come to me: I really was done. Now I'd confirmed it—out loud, in front of witnesses—and it felt too good to turn back.

"I don't know. Consulting? Maybe get paid for a change, see how that feels."

Elliot shook his big head like he was disappointed with my answer. "If you're going to be done, why not be done? With all of it."

"All of what?"

He waved his hand to take in my attire. "All of it, man. The suit and tie. The office life."

"Working for the man, man?"

"You said it, brother."

"I genuinely have no idea if you're serious."

The girls' night out seated next to us was getting a tad rowdy. They were all dressed like mimes and slamming down their empty shot glasses.

Elliot leaned across the table. "Dude, aren't you sick of trying to make things happen from behind a desk? I am. Legislation, resolutions, conference reports. It's all so *removed*."

"You thinking of getting back into teaching?"

He'd taught kindergarten at Little Red, which was that perfect oxymoron, a socialist private school. It was hard for me to picture him in *loco parentis*, responsible for all those tender young minds. Then again, the guy was in *parentis parentis* these days. Sadie was three, and so far he hadn't misplaced or corrupted her in any obvious way. He'd even organized a daycare co-op with a prize-winning war photographer, two regular contributors to *The New Yorker*, and a highly sought-after mixologist.

"The problem with teaching," he said, "is you've got to answer to everybody. Administration, parents, even the kids. And answering to people isn't exactly my style these days."

"I've noticed." I stretched my neck in search of our waitress.

"Men like us need to work for themselves," Elliot said. "Not filling out timesheets and taking webinars. We need to be out in the world, doing some good."

Men like us. Out in the world. I turned the words over in my mind, appreciating their heft.

"I hear you," I said. "In fact, I was just thinking the same thing." I was about to mention the Waldorf salad truck but thought the better of it.

"Helping people face to face, making a real difference in their lives."

"I like it."

"The Lone Ranger and Tonto."

"Wait, am I the Lone Ranger or Tonto?"

There he went, tapping his chin again. He appeared to be taking the question seriously, but like I said, it could be hard to tell with him.

"Tonto did most of the logistics, right? The scouting, the maps. LR was more of the front man. So that makes me the Lone Ranger and you Tonto, I guess. But we can switch off if you want to be the cowboy sometimes."

"Sounds like you've got our future all planned out."

Elliot killed his beer, his gaze drifting to a point over my shoulder. "I just might," he said. His eyes brightened. "There he is."

I turned around and saw John shouldering his way through the crowd towards us. Stocky and ever so slightly bow-legged with neat black hair and pink ears like perfect little shells, he didn't exactly fit the stock image of a killer, but once you knew his backstory, details started to jump out at you: the skull tattooed on the knuckle of the ring finger on his right hand, the expressive tendon in his neck. John didn't really smile as near as I could tell, but the tendon was relaxed, and he was gripping shoulders and bumping fists as he approached us, so I gathered he was in a good mood. A space on our bench appeared where none had been before. He sat down next to me and offered me his hand. It was dry and cool but carapaced with calluses, the hand of a man who calmly bends nature to his will.

"Gentlemen." His voice was low but seemed to cut straight through the noise.

"Crowded tonight," I said. Pure banality, but I realized too late it could be taken as a compliment or a complaint, depending on the hearer's inclinations. Truth is, I never knew what to say to John. You could fit the totality of our past conversations into the average commercial break.

Elliot, on the other hand, always knew what to say to everyone. "Bread and circuses, right, John?"

John nodded as if he knew exactly what Elliot meant. "Always."

"Will and I were just discussing which of us is the Lone Ranger and which of us is Tonto."

John's eyes were making a quick survey of the room, keeping tabs on his business, but the rest of his face remained impassive. "Yeah? And what did you decide?"

"That identity is fluid."

Again, John nodded. "So you haven't brought him up to speed yet?"

"Slowly but surely," Elliot said.

"Up to speed on what?" I asked.

"John and the boys are building a farm."

Elliot leaned back as if he'd laid all his cards on the table and their value was self-evident. I looked from him to John, who still wasn't giving anything away.

"Is that what you do? You 'build' a farm? I always thought you just kind of planted things in the ground, rounded up some animals."

Pedantic distinctions were a big part of my job: the difference between an economic opportunity zone and a business improvement district, a letter of interest and a letter of intent. Tough to turn it off sometimes.

John flexed his lips, but I couldn't tell if it was a smirk, a grimace, or some kind of hybrid he'd invented. "When you're doing it on a rooftop in Brooklyn, you build it."

Elliot jumped in to fill the ensuing silence. "Find the right roof and you've got enough acreage to supply the restaurant with fresh organic produce and sell to some of the other restaurants in the area."

"A real local food system that's sustainable and profitable. That's what we're doing," John said.

I stuck my lip out and nodded like a fair-goer appraising a ribbon-winning squash. "Sounds awesome." I still wasn't sure why John and Elliot considered it important that I be in the loop.

Elliot picked up the story. "So I was telling John for this thing to really have the impact he wants there needs to be a community component. A farmers market to deal with the food desert situation in the area, an education program for kids."

Food deserts were a trendy topic in the council at the time. The thinking was that poor neighborhoods had grim health statistics in part because the residents didn't have access to the right foods, particularly fresh fruits and vegetables. Bushwick, for instance, didn't have a major chain supermarket, just the usual assortment of bodegas, where "fresh" was an elastic term. In other neighborhoods, a single supermarket would take advantage of the lack of competition by gouging customers, the very people who could least afford it. I'd read a lot of the reports circulating in the council and even briefed Vivienne at one point, but food deserts weren't much of an issue on the UES, and Vivienne herself, having never set foot in a supermarket, was a tad fuzzy on the problem. "Can't they just order from FreshDirect?" was a question I fielded during our briefing.

As for education, teaching gardens were starting to become a thing, at least among the more progressive schools. The impetus for this one was that our children, growing up in a world of Lunchables and Go-GURT, were losing touch with the concept of real food—what it is, where it comes from. A survey had found that the majority of kids couldn't identify an array of common vegetables when they were shown to them in unadulterated form, and the results were even worse for poor kids. As for spending time in the kitchen learning the basics of cooking, forget it. Have you seen all the put-upon moms in fast food commercials?

The answer was to get kids down in the dirt at an early age, raising their own tomatoes and baby greens, learning to cook what they grow, and then converting their parents to the gospel of fresh, seasonal, local. Tie garden time into their biology lessons, bring out the art classes to sketch the plants at every stage of development, invite the families for a fall harvest festival—the vision was the garden as the pride and hub of the school.

John didn't look to me like a guy who cared much about food deserts or the childhood obesity epidemic, but hey, what did I know? I mean, what does a humanitarian look like anyway? Is a skull tattoo disqualifying? I told John and Elliot that a large-scale rooftop farm, responsive to community needs with ties to local schools, sounded like an excellent idea.

Elliot tapped the wing of his nose like I'd whispered the secret password. "You forgot one thing. Social entrepreneurship. Did you read that report from the small business committee? The division between for-profit and nonprofit is eroding. Every good start-up has community development as part of its mission now. Every venture capitalist wants to be a philanthropist."

"And we think that's a good thing?" I asked.

"It can be," Elliot said. "It will be for us."

I was starting to get the picture. "So are you two going to be working together?"

Elliot looked to John to answer.

"I told Elliot I've got a lot on my plate," John said. "But I like his angle. I want this thing to be good for the neighborhood. So I'm going to do what I do, which is build a business, and he's going to do what he does."

I turned to Elliot. "What is it you told him you do? I've been waiting years for this."

Elliot grinned. John didn't.

"I'm going to put together the most forward-thinking urban agriculture program for public schools anywhere in the country," Elliot said. "And I'm going to find all the money to pay for it.

Actually, kemosabe, you and I are going to do it."

"Is that right?" My stomach did a little flip, but it may just have been the hunger talking.

"Picture it," Elliot said, making a frame with his hands. "Between the two of us we've got every aspect of urban policy covered. I can pull together an expert panel tomorrow to develop a curriculum. You can draft a budget and write up a grant proposal in your sleep. This is it. Our chance to work for ourselves. No more dank offices, no more ugly ties."

He pointed at my tie, red silk with little blue ties in various stages of knotting.

"We do this right," he said, "and we're CEOs of our own nonprofit. Out in the world doing good instead of just talking about it."

Before I could think of what to say, John was standing, looking down at me. I could feel my neck getting damp under my collar.

"Listen," he said, "You should know, everything I do succeeds. Big. Look around here and you'll see a lot of people who are glad they got in when they did. Now I've got to get back to it, but I'd like to shake on this first."

John's eyes boring into me, hot as his Sicilian oven, made me want to look away, say I needed time to think it over. But really what was there to think about? I was going to be out of a job in a month, and I didn't particularly want to do any of the things my resume most qualified me to do. Now I understood why I couldn't stop reading about the people in *Savory Brooklyn*, the picklers, the foragers, the beekeepers. They were a vision of my future.

I took John's hand and tried to match the firmness of his shake. "One thing. If we're going to do this, I don't want to be stuck in the background doing budgets and grant proposals. I want to get my hands dirty, grow things, work with the kids. I want us to build this thing together."

John nodded. He didn't seem especially impressed, but he wasn't dismissive either. He may well have figured I was after a sliver of his macho glory. Maybe I was. My marriage to Tricia worked fine for the most part; we related to each other as sensible, straitlaced yuppies, your basic industrious urbanites. But her dad was a carpenter who built the house she grew up in, and while she never held me to that standard, I sometimes got the sense she wouldn't be upset if I were the kind of guy who at least knew how to fix her rusty ten-speed bike rather than putting it on Craigslist, who could assemble an IKEA shelving unit without tears. Truth is, I wouldn't have minded being that guy either. Now, in John Cardini's farm I saw an opportunity. The word "farm" itself could do wonders. I imagined telling Tricia to have dinner without me because I'd be working late on the farm, and I liked the way it sounded, though I was dimly aware that I was more likely to be working early on the farm than late.

"When do we start?" I asked.

Elliot actually rubbed his hands together. "I say we celebrate with a little feast."

I was so taken with the idea of manning up, I'd momentarily forgotten how hungry I was. Already a good sign. "What are you thinking? Phil Speckter? Hakuna Burrata?"

John made a quick chopping motion with his hand. "Forget it. It's taken care of. Just enjoy your evening, gentlemen." And with that, the throng parted for him, and he was gone.

What followed was unquestionably the greatest meal of my life, a nonstop parade of off-menu dishes. Our waitress, she of the tiny ukulele, reappeared to explain that these were the first fruits of a "new concept" Francisco and John were working on. A chickweed salad in a goat's-milk yogurt dressing, garnished with lemon zest, aged gouda, and blueberries. Seared Japanese cuttlefish heads, kind of like calamari, only served with nectarine nectar, purple basil, and jalapeño instead of cocktail sauce. Wagyu beef carpaccio dabbed with caviar on a bed of gooseberries and watercress. Not everything was so out there. There was a simple plate of house-cured prosciutto that was unlike any I'd ever tasted—"creamy" was the word that came to mind. Most remarkable of all was just a bowl of corn kernels mixed with a bit of basil, scallion, and tomato. It would be a cliché to rave about the sweetness, even more of a cliché to say Francisco had captured the essence of corn. So let's just say I would have traded all my Wagyu and caviar for Elliot's bowl. I briefly considered plucking the last kernel from his beard.

He said, "Now imagine this dish made with corn grown up the block, planted and picked by kids from the neighborhood."

I tried to imagine it, but I was having trouble. Corn grown on a roof in Bushwick couldn't possibly taste this good, could it? Here was a simple, perfect thing, created to provide a moment's enjoyment with no need for analysis or ambivalence and then... gone. The idea that I could be a part of a process so elemental was frankly overwhelming. I knew I should just savor the moment, but the overachiever in me was ready to take over.

"How much?"

Elliot barely looked up from his plate. "Don't worry. John said he was taking care of it."

"I mean the farm."

He looked like he wanted to pinch my cheek. "All business. That's why you and I are the perfect team."

"Just give me your back-of-the-napkin estimate."

He let his head bobble slightly from side to side as if he were rolling the numbers around in there. "Depends. To do it right? It'll take an upfront investment, for sure. At the same time, if we want this to be a model program, it has to cost-effective."

"And what about us? Do we get paid?"

"We're professionals, aren't we? We're the ones who are going to be doing all the work."

I let Elliot's tone, his cool confidence, sink into my gray matter.

"Look at it this way," he said. "John wants this thing to be sustainable. You can't even say the word 'farm' anymore without adding the word 'sustainable.' How can a farm be sustainable if the people working on it can't make a living?"

I did a quick calculation. "So we're talking six figures. Two hundred?"

"Maybe more, but yeah, that's a good goal."

"And how much time do we have?"

"Well, growing season starts in April. Drop dead for seeds in the ground is sometime in May. So four, five months or we have to wait till next year, and I know John isn't going to want to hear that."

"Four months?" I was already halfway out of my seat. "I've got to talk to Tricia. Now."

"Hold on." Elliot reached across the table to stop me.

I stopped. He laced his fingers behind his head.

"I heard something about a cheese course," he said.

Save the Chickens

Tricia got home about an hour after me, still in her purple scrubs, hair pulled back with a rubber band. She was a vet, and I often envied the straightforwardness of her work. It's not like she was rolling around, Eskimo-kissing puppies all day; all those hours on her feet took a toll, and most of the critters she dealt with wanted nothing to do with her and her Vaseline-slicked finger. At the same time, she didn't have to question whether keeping people's treasured dogs and cats alive was a worthwhile way to make a living. She provided a service her community needed. Whereas I had spent many a Sunday representing Team Viv in a politically significant walkathon or preparing talking points for a last-minute presser, wondering if any of it made a difference to anyone at all.

Tricia always heard me out when I needed to vent, but she didn't feed my doubts. I'd been working for Vivienne since we got together, and as far as she was concerned, it was a respectable, decent-paying job, maybe even a prestigious one, looked at in a certain light. For all I knew, her acceptance of me was conditional on my remaining a go-getter with a promising career in politics, an upstanding professional with a city pension plan, vested after an unfathomable thirty years. Which is to say, I had no idea how she would react to what I had to tell her.

As she ducked into the fridge for a beer, I let her know I had to call Elliot in an hour.

"Don't you two ever get enough of each other?"

I let her settle down next to me on the couch and drape her legs across my lap. Rubbing her feet, I laid it all out for her, just as Elliot had for me. She listened without commenting, winding her hair around her hand, her eyes tired but attentive. When I was finished, she took a thoughtful pull from her beer.

"Do you think it can work?"

"Elliot likes our chances."

"But what about you?"

I gave myself a moment to consider. "There are a bunch of details to work out, but we've got a lot going for us. Contacts, expertise, the restaurant everyone's talking about."

"Charm and good looks."

"Am I crazy to want to do this?"

"Because you've never even kept a house plant?"

My face fell. Tricia set her beer on the floor and squeezed my knee.

"Sorry. You're not crazy to want to do something different. You're not."

"This could be a whole new start for me. *If* you're on board..."

Tricia cocked her head to the side. "Why wouldn't I be on board?"

"I don't know. It's a risk. There might not be a steady paycheck for a while."

She shrugged. "We're not in any rush to have a kid. The landlord won't even let us get a dog. If you want to take a risk, I'd say now's the time."

"No summer cabin in the Catskills."

"We'll kick it here. Summer in the Slope."

"I may not be around much. They need me to be super hands-on."

She slung her arms around my neck. For a second, I thought she was going to say, "And so do I." What she actually said was, "You're not having a midlife crisis, are you? Because that would be a little ahead of schedule."

"A little?"

"So you're not?"

"I honestly don't think that's what this is."

"Because if you really want this, you're the one who's going to have to make it happen."

"It's about time I made something happen."

"Then I say, go for it. I want you to be happy."

What can you say about a woman like that? I reached for her waist, but she pulled away.

"Don't you have work to do?"

Elliot picked up on the fourth ring. I could make out "Dirty Deeds Done Dirt Cheap" in the background.

"I'm in," I said. "What do we do now?"

Elliot enunciated thickly. It was that phase of the evening. "I think it's time to deploy our secret weapon."

"Our secret weapon?"

"We have an advantage no other baby nonprofit could even dream of."

He waited for me to catch up.

"Oh, no," I said. "Don't tell me."

"Got to keep it in the family, right?"

Vivienne. She was our secret weapon.

* * *

Vivienne wasn't lying when she told the MTA chairman the offers were pouring in. Every pol who still had a future in the city wanted her to chair their re-election committee. She was the board member of every museum and hospital's wet dream. Her late husband's law firm wanted her on the payroll to help with some business they had before the city. But Elliot and I could offer her something none of her other suitors could: the chance to stay connected to her favorite staffers, the feisty comers who, in her own words, kept her young. It took more to convince me she should be our rainmaker than to convince her.

"A farm?"

We were in her district office on 93rd Street, packing up boxes of beer koozies with her name on them. The koozies had proven to be undesirable campaign swag on the Upper East Side. Vivienne herself never quite wrapped her mind around the idea that people drank beer straight out of the can.

"Like with chickens?"

Elliot aimed a pair of finger guns at her. "You want chickens, Viv, we'll get you some chickens."

"Did I say I wanted chickens?"

"The kids would probably go crazy for chickens."

I looked up from an old leaflet—the top ten most dangerous intersections in the district. "Let's save the chickens for Phase II."

"And why Brooklyn?" Vivienne asked. "If we did it right here, we could probably use whatever's left in the discretionary fund."

I don't know, I thought, maybe because there aren't as many people deprived of fresh food on Park Avenue? I let, Elliot, the Viv Whisperer, give a more diplomatic answer, involving proximity to Rita's.

Vivienne narrowed her eyes. "Never heard of it. Will, I thought you said there was no Rita's Pizza."

"I said there was no Vinny's Pizza."

Elliot spun a koozie on his finger. "Isn't there a Vinny's in the Village, near St. Mark's?"

I gave him the sign to drop it. Like a cell phone signal on the subway, Vivienne's attention was not to be squandered.

"Have you found a location yet?" she asked.

Elliot explained that John knew most of the landlords in the area and was looking into some of the nearby warehouses, but nothing was set in stone.

Vivienne pecked at the screen of her phone. "What we need to do is talk to Arthur and Barbara."

At first, all I heard was that mellifluous "we." Vivienne was in, which meant we were officially in business. As she found what she was looking for in her phone and held it up to her ear, it occurred to me she might actually be calling the aforementioned Arthur and Barbara right then and there. In Vivienne's world, a quick phone call to a friend was usually enough to make things happen. I figured I'd better ask who Arthur and Barbara were. Elliot, of course, already knew.

"Arthur and Barbara Schlosser. Founded the Begin to Win Charter School. One of the pioneers in the city."

Vivienne covered the phone with her hand. "I helped them get it off the ground. I'm sure they'll be interested."

I summoned Elliot to an impromptu strategy session with a tilt of my head. He ambled over to where I was standing beside a life-size cutout of Vivienne and slung an arm over its corrugated shoulder.

"Is this a good idea?" I whispered.

"The Schlossers are loaded. And they owe Viv. Sounds good to me."

"I wasn't picturing a charter school." Elliot had conditioned me to blame charters for siphoning off the brightest kids and most with-it parents, hastening the downward spiral of neighborhood schools.

"I wouldn't call Begin to Win progressive," he said, "but it could be worse. No uniforms, no silence in the halls. And if we partner with a charter, we can steer clear of Tweed."

He had a point. Vivienne's position as head of the education committee had made her a go-to critic of the bureaucratic death star that was the Department of Education. Vivienne may not have seemed like a natural ally of the teachers' union and parent activists, but she got along better with them than the swashbuckling b-school grads Bloomberg had installed at Tweed. To her, they were the political equivalent of nouveau riche. To them, her long history of service meant nothing. Elliot somehow managed to buddy up with the enemy, drinking with them after even the nastiest hearings, but collegiality only went so far, and if we were to partner with a regular public school, the DOE, out of sheer pettiness, might asphyxiate us with red tape. Best-case scenario, they would let us do our thing and then bogart the credit.

Still, I was suspicious of Begin to Win. I didn't want to be a naysayer, but Vivienne and Elliot needed adult supervision and that had always been my job.

"Is Begin to Win even in Brooklyn?" I asked.

"Pretty close to Rita's, actually. Do you know where the old Pfizer factory is?"

I didn't, though I'd lived in Brooklyn for several years.

"It's on their property," Elliot said. "Near Woodhull Hospital and a bunch of projects. Marcy, Tompkins..."

I nodded, but I couldn't actually picture it. My working knowledge of the Marcy Houses came entirely from Jay-Z songs.

"Aren't we supposed to be serving the community? The kids are probably bused from all over the city."

"Fifty-fifty local and bused, if I'm not mistaken. Anyway, the farmers market can be the community piece."

"Racial-ethnic mix?"

"Respectable. And get this, Begin to Win is co-located with a public school...District 75."

Elliot said this last part slowly, with raised eyebrows, clearly expecting a big reaction, but all I could do was blink back at him. I knew "co-located"—it wasn't uncommon in Bloomberg's New York for charters to share a building with traditional schools—but I was drawing a blank on District 75. Elliot rolled his eyes.

"District 75...as in special education. We're talking about seventeen-year-olds in the fifth grade."

"But wouldn't that put us back on the DOE's radar? I thought we're trying to keep our distance."

"We'll already be in the building. If we can make this work with a respected charter school *and* come up with an awesome curriculum for special ed, we'll have the DOE eating out of our hand."

Vivienne waved her phone for attention.

"We're on. Arthur and Barbara want to meet with us tomorrow."

Elliot extended his fist for a celebratory bump. I obliged, but my mind was already swarming with logistical considerations.

"I don't think we can invite them to the office. Misuse of public resources."

Now it was Vivienne's turn to roll her eyes at me. "Duh. I told them we could do it over dinner. At your friend's restaurant."

Elliot looked like he'd touched a staticky doorknob. "You sure, Viv? Rita's may not be the Schlosser's speed. Pretty hipster."

Vivienne lowered her glasses. "Elliot, please. Arthur and Barbara have a standing reservation at every fashionable restaurant in town. They practically live at The Waverly Inn. They even have a table at Rao's."

How to explain the concept of the hipster to someone like Vivienne? I could barely put it into words at all. More of a know-it-when-you-see-it kind of thing. Then I remembered our intern, Kat, with the granny glasses and the tattoo of crows flying up her arm.

"Picture a roomful of Kats," I told her.

"Cats? In a restaurant?"

"No. Kat, the intern. A roomful of people like her."

"Who?"

Never mind, then. Actually, I couldn't say for sure Kat even was a hipster. I remember seeing her get excited about the new Harry Potter movie and thinking she was kind of a dork.

"You know what? It's fine. It's perfect. Rita's is an experience. They can tell their friends about it."

"Just make sure you have your pitch down," Vivienne said. "With people like this, you only get one opportunity."

With one meaty hand still draped over cardboard Vivienne's shoulder, Elliot laid the other on mine. "We're on it. Will and I will talk tonight and jam through a quick one-pager."

It was happening now. I had a date to ask an old rich couple for their blessing to start my new life.

* * *

Elliot and I were already waiting at one of the few private tables squeezed in along the wall when Vivienne and the Schlossers arrived at Rita's by town car. The place was crammed and roaring as always, and when she first entered, Vivienne took a step backwards as if hit by a physical force. She was wearing some kind of voluminous black shawl and diamond earrings. The Schlossers, on the other hand, were a little more Century Village than Park Avenue, Arthur in a nylon windbreaker, Barbara a cable knit sweater, both in cream-colored slacks. You'd never peg them as real estate billionaires, at least not immediately. On second glance, the total ease with which they strolled into a room where they obviously did not belong was pretty telling.

Elliot and I stood to greet them. I was wearing an oxford and tie but had decided against the full suit. I was easing into this new, make-my-own-rules existence. Elliot appeared to be wearing the same clothes as yesterday, though really, who could tell?

Barbara raised her iPhone and slowly pivoted on her heels,

taking video of the room. "Well, will you look at this. Other than graduation day, I've never seen so many people together out here. Right, Arthur?"

Arthur scratched his nose. "Peter Luger, maybe."

"You're crazy. There's never a crowd at the bar at Peter Luger. Not like this."

"I told you, it's so stimulating working with young people." Vivienne presented me and Elliot with a sweep of the hand, as if we were a dinette set on *The Price Is Right*. "They know things."

Arthur shook my hand solemnly, Barbara distractedly. She was on safari, captivated by this rare glimpse of the native wildlife in their habitat.

John was at our side before we'd even settled into our seats. Elliot made the introductions.

"Welcome to Rita's, guys. If you don't mind, our chef has a special menu in mind for you. So if you just tell me what you want to drink, we can get started."

Vivienne and Barbara decided to split a bottle of Sancerre. Arthur ordered a beer, and Elliot followed suit. I said I was fine with water. Like I said, still easing in.

"Enjoy, guys," John said, unsmiling. "We're all excited you're here."

I had my doubts about the special menu. The Schlossers didn't seem like the weeds-and-cuttlefish type. But John—no surprise—was a step ahead of me. The first course was a big wooden bowl of salad, romaine in a vinaigrette with strips of salumi (made in house, of course), candied walnuts, and Vermont blue cheese. Then came the pizzas: a Coppa Feel, a Zooey Béchamel, and a Provolone Wolf. The main was a whole pork shoulder, served on a cutting board, lustrous with drippings, if not falling off the bone then willing to part from it at the merest suggestion. Sides included roasted carrots dressed in lime and—hallelujah—that mystical, near-psychedelic corn. It was as rustic and people-pleasing a meal as the tasting menu Elliot and I had shared was refined and inscrutable.

Little was said while there was food on the table, and what words did pass between us were on the order of, "Divine," and "Have you ever…?" and "I shouldn't, but…" I decided there was no harm in ordering a beer after all. By the time the plates were cleared and the coffee served—no dessert; John *hated* dessert—our pitch was scratching my throat, itching for release. I'd done the requisite internet research earlier in the day. The local population was younger with more blacks and Hispanics, and more families living in poverty, than Brooklyn or New York as a whole. Nearly half of the elementary school children in Bushwick were either overweight or obese. That likely had something to do with the fact that 84 percent of the food stores in the neighborhood were bodegas, and only eight percent of those carried fresh vegetables. With our help, the Schlossers could tackle this problem head-on, putting the students of Begin to Win on the path to a healthy lifestyle, meeting their families' urgent nutritional needs, and lifting the spirits of the entire community. Elliot, for his part, was ready to rattle off a spiel about aligning with the school's academic goals and measuring the development of the students' social-emotional skills. Not too shabby on a day's notice, if I do say so myself.

Too bad because we didn't even get to clear our throats, let alone launch into our song and dance before Arthur tossed his napkin on the table and said, "We're not giving you any money."

"We're not asking for any money," Vivienne said before either

Elliot or I could summon a response.

I shot Elliot an urgent glance. I was pretty sure the plan was to ask for money. A lot of money. After all, Begin to Win stood to reap the PR gains from the project—on top of the benefits to the kids, who, it went without saying, came first.

Arthur raised his considerable eyebrows, an effort that seemed to involve much of the musculature of his face. "You're not?"

Vivienne waved him off as if the mere suggestion were ridiculous. "All we want from you is your roof. Leave the rest to us."

He stared into his coffee cup, searching for a sign in the dregs. "Our test scores are slipping. We've given the principal one more year to turn it around. We can't have any distractions."

"Distraction? This is going to help with your test scores. Elliot has all the data."

Elliot gave them a dazed smile. "There are some promising studies…"

The Schlossers waited, but he didn't elaborate. My turn.

"The broccoli on the pizza tonight…Imagine if it said 'Begin to Win broccoli' right on the menu."

I didn't have John's permission to put the words "Begin to Win" on his menu, but I figured I could get it more easily than Elliot could get hard data showing that a school garden could boost test scores.

Barbara laid her hand on Arthur's arm, as if to hold him back. Odd since he didn't exactly look like a man about to leap into action.

"What we need from you is help with the community," she said to us. "We've been here twenty years, but still they act like we're taking something away from them."

"Some," Arthur corrected her. "A minority."

She gave Vivienne a meaningful look. "You know how it is."

"Barbara, this is what we do," Vivienne said. "Let us help you."

I saw Barbara squeeze Arthur's arm. He let out a heavy breath, as though she'd punctured him with a fingernail.

"You'll meet the principal," he said. "If he's open to it, the roof is yours."

Vivienne nodded. "That still leaves the question of money." I thought for a moment Barbara really would need to hold Arthur back. "I told you..."

Vivienne held up her hand. "You're not giving us any. I remember. And you remember, of course, I said we're not asking. But I bet you can think of somebody, a friend of Begin to Win, who'd make a good angel investor."

I was pretty sure nonprofits have donors, not investors, but that was way beside the point. Vivienne was operating at the peak of her powers—something we rarely got to see at the council, where the people weren't her people and the horse-trading was too malodorous for her sensibilities. It was magnificent to behold. Arthur Schlosser had slumped down in his chair like a man who knows the person across the table has ways of making him talk. Barbara glanced at him and decided to put him out of his misery.

"Martin," she said.

Martin. Vivienne mouthed the word, rolling it around like the first swig of Sancerre offered by the waiter. "I didn't know you were friends."

Did anybody above a certain net worth use last names? You'd think we were talking about Madonna or Shaq.

"Oh, we've been friends forever. He's on our board."

Vivienne looked first at Elliot and then at me, her silent partners, as if we'd have something meaningful to contribute. "Well, that's it then," Vivienne said. "Martin's such a peach, I'm sure he'll be thrilled to help."

Arthur fidgeted in his seat. "Don't tell him we sicced you on him. Please."

Believe it or not, Vivienne actually pantomimed zipping her lip and throwing away the key. She was having a ball. "Of course. We just came across his name when we were looking up your board."

And that was that, more or less. We all clinked coffee cups to seal our partnership. Elliot and I rushed over to help the Schlossers to their feet and out the door, where their car was waiting. Arthur wished us luck, and Barbara added that they wanted to be kept in the loop every step of the way, but Arthur had already gotten into the car at that point, so I figured she wasn't really speaking for both of them. Vivienne told them she'd join them in a moment for the trip back to Manhattan, then turned to us with a sly, vaguely feline grin.

Elliot fake-applauded. "Amazing, Viv."

She brushed the backs of her fingers against her shawl, the international sign for hot stuff.

"Just think," she said, rolling her eyes in the direction of the car, "if those two weren't so fucking cheap, their test scores might not be in the toilet. Guess how much they paid Pfizer for that building…a dollar. I should know, I brokered the whole thing."

"We need to set up a 501c3," I said, half to myself, an epic to-do list starting to take shape in my mind.

Vivienne shook her head. "Priority number one is Martin. Come by the apartment later this week, and we'll work on a game plan."

As we watched the town car slip off toward the Williamsburg Bridge like a salmon upstream, John joined us on the curb.

"We in business?"

"We are," Elliot said.

"How soon can we get up on that roof?"

"We need to talk to the principal," I said, still in list mode.

"Aren't those two the principal's boss?"

"And they said we need to talk to him."

John glanced at Elliot before answering me. "Growing season is coming up. The way we work, we try not to get too bogged down with formalities."

His tone was so even, his face so still, I was having trouble interpreting what he'd said. "Right, I get that. But we're talking about a school here. There's going to be some coordination that has to happen."

Elliot made a motion I guessed was meant to convey the smoothing out of difficulties but looked more like petting a cat. "Nothing we can't take care of in a week or two, tops. We'll be ready for growing season."

John nodded. "The money?"

"We've got a promising lead," Elliot said.

"Well, I've got another one for you. You know Greta?"

Guess which one of us did.

"She's Tommy Brutti's assistant."

At least I knew who Tommy Brutti was. Everyone did. Ten years ago, that assertion might have sounded like big city snobbery, as in, "You mean you haven't tried the sautéed calf's brains at Brutti's Trattoria? Is your idea of Italian still veal marsala on a checkered tablecloth?" Even five years ago, you could probably find people who had never seen *Forza Brutti*, his cult classic on The Food Network, and therefore didn't have the image of Chef Tommy, a shock-haired volcano in trademark cargo shorts and mismatched Converse high tops, delivering a mile-a-minute, stream-of-consciousness lecture on the kitchen secrets imparted to him by Ligurian grandmothers to a rapt audience featuring conspicuously inconspicuous celebrities like Sofia Coppola and The Edge. Now, though, with the campout cookbook, the line of custom spatulas, and the signature Converse, it was just a fact: the guy was everywhere.

My pulse revved. I was a fan of Chef Tommy's talk show appearances, an avid consumer of his jarred sauces. Dinner at the Trattoria was on my New York bucket list.

"He just started the Tommy Brutti Foundation, and they're looking for projects," John said. "Greta can get us a meeting next week, and I want to have it up on that roof."

John's olive-pit eyes settled on me. "That's not going to be a problem, is it?"

First Fruit

We offered to pick up Starbucks before our strategy session with Vivienne, both of us knowing full well what that meant. Vivienne's drink of choice was notorious: a "two-pump" skim chai latte. Elliot and I did rock-paper-scissors to decide who would have to place the order. It fell to me—paper. I was afraid the girl working the register would scream out the order to the barista, but instead, she just scribbled on the cup with a Sharpie and passed it along the line. Things are a little more genteel on the Upper East Side, even in Starbucks.

Vivienne lived in a venerable doorman building, but the apartment wasn't quite as luxe as you might expect. That's the secret with a lot of these places. Building staff will pick up your laundry for you, but it's not like you get a washer-dryer of your own. Or a dishwasher. Or room for a king-size bed. There was a piano in the den and some early work by a lesser Modernist on the walls, alongside the one editorial cartoon to feature Vivienne: her entire head eclipsed by outlandish sunglasses, she walks an extravagantly coiffed poodle who bears a striking resemblance to the mayor at the time, the suggestion being that this unlikely power broker (we're talking pre-council, pre-Bloomberg here) had Hizzoner on a leash. All in all, the place had a lived-in, slightly tatty feel one typically associates more with the Upper West than the Upper East Side. But that was Vivienne for you: compared to her fellow council members, she might as well have been Gloria Vanderbilt herself, but in society circles, she was a lovable eccentric, practically a Bolshevik.

Sitting in the middle of the faded Persian rug, surrounded by manila folders, was a girl with granny glasses, a knit beanie, and a Hawaiian shirt: Kat, the hipster intern. Or was she a dork? It was still a close call. She looked up as we entered the room, announced by the creak of the Knickerbocker-era wood floors.

"Hey," Kat said.

Elliot and I exchanged a look. "Hey," we said in near unison.

"Vivienne will be out in a minute. She's just finishing up a call."

We took a seat on a baroque-ish sofa with green velvet upholstery worn to a sheen. It felt like Kat should be offering us watercress sandwiches.

"So…" Elliot ventured.

"I know, right?" Kat widened her eyes and put on a little debutante drawl. "Fancy meeting you here."

Elliot pointed at her shirt. "Never seen one with volcanoes before."

She looked down as if she were noticing it for the first time. "Yeah. I'm mostly by myself here, so I figured it wouldn't matter what I wear."

"You're working here?" I asked.

Kat scrunched up her forehead, embarrassed by the lameness

of the question. Did I think she just happened to stop by?

"I was looking for a job, and Vivienne needed someone to organize her papers and appointments and stuff now that she's out of office."

It seemed rude to mention that, a few days earlier, Vivienne seemed to have no idea who she was, so I just nodded.

"Next time, we'll bring you coffee," Elliot said, holding out the paper tray.

"Are you guys working for Vivienne, too?"

Did the coffee suggest to her that we were gophers, cogs, along with her, in the vast machinery of Vivdom, one minion to do her filing, two to fetch her morning chai, a man for each pump?

"She's helping us out with a project we're doing," I said.

"A rooftop farm in Brooklyn," Elliot added.

Kat's eyes lit up. "Really? Where in Brooklyn?"

"The Broadway Triangle. It's this kind of no man's land where Bed-Stuy, Bushwick, and East Williamsburg all meet."

"Cool. I've been living in Crown Heights since I moved here." Turns out she was from Oregon, near Eugene, and had grown up on a farm—more of a hippie commune, really—but they'd raised their own vegetables, and there were goats and bees. She'd come to New York to study urban planning, just about the only form of rebellion she had available to her, but jobs were scarce, so she figured she'd bide her time with Vivienne, pick up whatever connections and tidbits of Gotham lore she could. I probably should've known all this already, having worked in the same office with Kat all summer, but after a while, the constant parade of interns passing through our doors started to look like an undifferentiated mass of C students with politically connected uncles.

"You know, you guys are totally on-trend," she said. "One of my classmates at the New School is raising tilapia now."

"As a job?" I tried to picture it, but I wasn't sure what tilapia looked like in its un-filleted state.

"Fuck yeah, as a job. Sustainable urban aquaculture, Holmes."

A crafty look had come over Elliot's face. "How many hours are you putting in for Viv?"

Kat gave a one-shoulder shrug. "Whatever she needs. About two-and-a-half days a week?"

"You want to go back to the land with us?"

I could see it coming, and I could already hear Elliot's post-facto rationalization. An urban planning background plus real (albeit hippie-derived) farming experience plus an extra voice in Vivienne's ear to keep her on task? How could we afford not to bring her aboard?

She laid a finger along the severe taper of her chin, weighing the offer. "What does it pay?"

"Nothing," I said.

If he weren't holding a tray of coffee and tea, Elliot would've elbowed me in the ribs. "We're still hammering out the budget. We've got a line on a couple of big donors. Do you know Tommy Brutti?"

"I'm not a hick."

"Well, he's interested. Once the donations start coming in, we'll be able to discuss compensation. Right now, this is an opportunity to get in on the ground floor."

"I thought it was supposed to be a rooftop farm."

"What Elliot means is…"

Kat rolled her eyes. "I'm in."

Before I could make even more of a pompous ass of myself, Vivienne dashed in, a phone in each hand.

"It's not working. You're going to have to go there and do it in person."

We stood. Vivienne reached reflexively for her chai, then remembered both her hands were occupied. A little ballet ensued as she swung around to hand the phones to Kat, who couldn't quite reach them from the floor. I stepped between them to facilitate the transfer while Elliot shuffled over to Vivienne's side so she wouldn't have to turn back around for her drink.

Vivienne took a sip of her chai and grimaced. "The council wants its crummy Blackberry back, so we've been trying to transfer all my contacts to my iPhone, but the fucker won't cooperate."

"Which fucker?" Elliot asked.

"The Blackberry, obviously. I begged those creeps in IT for an iPhone, remember? They said the city had an exclusive contract with Blackberry. Somebody should investigate that!"

Actually, Vivienne had demanded that I investigate it, but I just ignored her, figuring she'd forget about it. Which she had.

Kat held up the two phones like she was about to start juggling them. "I'll take care of it."

"Good because we have to go. I got us onto Martin's calendar for this afternoon. We'll strategize in the car."

The car was still driven by Rick, the impassive ex-cop. Most members of the council didn't have an entourage that included a personal driver. By and large, they took the subway. Vivienne just called Rick campaign staff and held an annual fundraiser to pay him, known to the inner circle as the Rick-a-thon. Wondering where his checks were coming from now, I had an urge to remind Vivienne she could only dip into the campaign funds if she was, you know, running for something, but then I had the positively liberating realization that it was none of my business anymore. Instead, I turned my attention to another mystery.

"So you do know who Kat is after all," I said.

"Who?"

"The girl you left in your apartment with all your valuables and personal information."

"Oh, you mean Katherine? Don't worry about her. She came highly recommended."

"Really? She says she's from a farm in Oregon."

"Don't be a snob, Will. She interned for the planning commission. They raved about her."

"She interned for you, too, you know."

"You're kidding."

I looked to Elliot for back-up. He gave me the old hand across the throat sign.

"So, strategy. How formal a meeting is this? Will he mind us calling him Martin? Or should we go with Mr. …" He trailed off. At least I wasn't the only one who didn't know who we were on our way to meet.

Vivienne sniffed. "Well, considering you're dressed like a hobo, I'd say that formal isn't an option. Just follow my lead."

Not exactly fair, given that the meeting was sprung on us at the last minute, but even with a month's notice, Elliot probably would have shown up in the same baggy corduroy pants and half-tucked denim shirt.

"He must be pretty excited about the project to schedule us so quickly," I said.

"He's going to Israel next Tuesday, and he won't be back till September. I practically had to beg to get us in. We're lucky John is able to make it."

I was just starting to mentally cross-reference the Israel clue when the mention of John made my brain lock up.

"Wait. John from Rita's? He's coming?"

"He was so good with Arthur and Barbara. And since we don't have time to take Martin to Brooklyn, I thought we'd bring Brooklyn to him."

Elliot let his fingers root around in the tangle of hair above his collar. "So you two have been in touch?"

"He asked for my number at the restaurant. And then yesterday he called. He wanted to see if I could help him sort out a problem with the Department of Buildings."

I tried to picture when, over the course of that evening, John had the opportunity to hit Vivienne up for her number, but my memory was shrouded in food fuzz.

"And could you?" Elliot asked, aiming for just-out-of-curiosity. "Help, I mean."

"What do you think? It was just some silliness over permits."

"Hector Contreras couldn't handle it?"

Hector Contreras was the councilman in Rita's neck of the woods. A real backslapper. Front row center at every presser and rally. Great suits.

"Hector Contreras doesn't know anybody at DOB. That's the problem with these grassroots types. Big talk, but they don't know how to get anything done."

Or maybe he just wasn't inclined to call in this particular favor (which, for Vivienne's sake, I hoped wasn't too dodgy). Hector's political base wasn't exactly teeming with guys like John Cardini.

John was waiting for us when we pulled up to our destination, one of those all-glass Midtown towers you can't take in from street level. It was unclear from his attire—red checked flannel and chinos, leather work boots—whether he'd attempted to dress up for the occasion. He nodded silently as we joined him.

"So we hear Vivienne has been pulling strings for you," I said while we waited for security to print out our visitor badges.

John's eyes narrowed slightly. "That's a different project. We're building a radio station on the back patio."

I bopped my head as if I were already picking up the signal. "Cool. Just let us know if there's anything else we can do to help."

"I think we've got it under control for now." John stepped aside so Vivienne could be first on the elevator. He was right behind her; Elliot and I piled in last.

Martin turned out to be Martin Gollick, as in the Gollick School of Business, the Gollick Institute for Jewish Culture, and Gollick Media, publisher of several of the city's community weeklies. One of the original hedge fund whiz kids, he was probably best known as the founder of Next Year in Jerusalem, which promises every assimilated Jewish teen in America a free trip to the Holy Land and inevitably sends them back wearing yarmulkes and hassling their moms about the bacon bits in the salad.

I vaguely remembered a story about him circulating at the council. A reporter we all knew had scored a rare interview and tour of his Westchester estate. Gollick was keen to show her around his private zoo and insisted she pet his favorite camel. No one consulted the camel, though; it bit straight through her arm. She had to be airlifted to the nearest hospital. More upsetting to Gollick, the camel had to be killed on the spot. Apparently, the only way to tell if it had rabies was to examine its brain.

So now we knew: this was the guy people like Vivienne and the Schlossers turned to when they needed a little financial aid.

His office was like a modest wing in a venerable museum of antiquities. Relics were scattered around on pedestals and book shelves: bronze urns, shards of pottery imprinted with what I took to be cuneiform. The floor-to-ceiling windows were shaded, the overhead lighting diffuse. Gollick himself was seated behind a glass oval desk, his paunch visibly pressing against the underside as he tucked into a vast chopped salad. With his buck teeth, round specs, and capacious crescent of mustache, his pink suspenders unhitched, he looked like a cross between Teddy Roosevelt and Jackie Mason. He waved us over to the leather sofa opposite him.

"Vivvy, you don't call, you don't write. Must be all these young men you're spending time with." His breathing was labored, his voice a rumble that sounded painful to produce.

Vivienne made a little moue. "Maybe if you got out more, we'd run into each other."

Listening to them flirt like teenagers somehow made me feel like a toddler. I crossed my legs, wishing I'd hit the bathroom before we sat down.

"I'm worried if I get out they'll never let me back in." A phlegmy crackle followed, Gollick appreciating his own joke. We each chipped in with our own not-quite laugh, except for John, of course, who may have lifted one corner of his mouth a fraction of an inch.

Gollick crumpled his napkin and dropped it into the remains of his salad. "We better get down to it. I don't want to have to cut you off in the middle."

We got down to it. Vivienne talked up the enthusiasm of the Schlossers. Elliot rhapsodized about being a model for schools across the country. I chipped in my bullet points on obesity and bodegas. It was hard to tell how much he was taking in. His milky eyes wandered to the ceiling and, from time to time, closed altogether for what felt like long intervals. We wrapped up with the Year One budget. In the car, Vivienne had insisted that, when dealing with a man like Martin, you had to bring hard numbers to the table. All we had was the back-of-the-napkin guesstimate we'd come up with that first night at Rita's: two hundred thousand.

"Three hundred fifty thousand to get us up and running," Vivienne said with finality.

A flicker crossed Gollick's face, a mere tremor of an eyelid, which I imagined was amusement at the paltry sum on which our fates depended. Just one of his ancient potsherds would have been more than enough to bankroll our rich and fulfilling new lives.

"I don't care about Year One," he croaked. "What's your sustainability plan?"

I looked at Elliot who looked at Vivienne. She squared her shoulders. "We were hoping to get your advice on that very thing."

Another amused tremor. "You want my advice? Figure out

how to make money selling veggies in the ghetto. Because I'm not bankrolling you in perpetuity. In fact, I'm not bankrolling you at all till you show me how this thing starts to pay for itself."

There followed a pause filled only by the sound of Gollick's breathing. It's not that we were unfamiliar with the concept of a sustainability plan. But events had been moving so quickly, there'd been no time to come up with one.

"I can field this." It was John, speaking for the first time since he'd introduced himself.

Gollick sized him up, throwing his whole head into it. "You're the pizza man."

John didn't flinch. "I'm a businessman. And I can tell you, businessman to businessman, we don't expect the farm to pay for itself."

"You don't?"

I uncrossed my legs again, knocking knees with Elliot, who stared at the tasseled scimitar in a case on the wall. Wondering, I figured, whether he'd need to use it on John. Vivienne's face was frozen in a grin as if anticipating the punchline of a joke.

"We don't expect it to pay for itself. We expect it to turn a profit."

Gollick coughed, as if John's answer had gone down the wrong tube, like a wayward crouton. "You'll have to excuse an old man. I thought we were talking about a not-for-profit."

"We are," I said.

"My partners," John lifted his chin in our direction. "They're do-gooders. Nothing wrong with that. Me, I'm a capitalist. I've got a need at my restaurant. Customers want to see the words 'locally grown' on the menu, and they want it to mean 'grown in New York City,' not the Hudson Valley or Connecticut. And I figure, if this is a need at my restaurant, it's a need at other restaurants, too. I want to be the one to fill that need. I *know* there's money, lots of money, to be made filling that need, if we do it right. And if we can do some good for kids in the community while we're making money, all the better, as far as I'm concerned."

We braced ourselves while Gollick mulled John's speech—or took another micro-nap, hard to say. When he finally spoke, the words seemed to come from a deeper, more serene place inside him.

"Do you know what *fraise de bois* are?" he asked.

I spoke up when it was clear no one else was going to. "Isn't *fraise* French for strawberry?"

He gave his mustache a pensive stroke. "It is. But the French strawberry is a completely different experience from the tasteless junk you find in supermarkets here. When I was living in Paris in my twenties, one of the old women in the market let me try one. I couldn't believe it. That intense flavor. Like going from black-and-white to Technicolor. My first thought was that if I could grow strawberries like that back home, I could make a fortune.

"So that's what I did. I sweet-talked the old woman into introducing me to her supplier, and I convinced him to sell me a cutting from one of his bushes. I smuggled the plant back to the States in my coat and brought it to my summer house upstate, where I'd have space to cultivate on a commercial scale. I consulted horticulture experts from Cornell to figure out exactly the right conditions: temperature, soil, exposure to sunlight. When the first fruiting came, I was so nervous, more than when I started my company. The flavor was there, maybe not quite as vibrant as the original, but miles beyond anything you could get anywhere else in North America at the time. I was certain of that.

"So Jeannie—that's my late wife—and I loaded our crop into the bed of an old pickup truck I'd restored, and we drove it down to the city bright and early. We went to all our favorite restaurants, we insisted on speaking to the head chef, and we wouldn't leave until they tried our *fraise de bois*. Every last one of them had the same reaction I had in Paris. They couldn't believe what they were tasting. This was when *nouvelle cuisine* was starting to take over New York. Strawberries weren't just for dessert anymore. We could name our price.

"The problem was the demand was insatiable. We were waking up at four in the morning every morning to haul another batch of those damned berries to the city. At a certain point, it wasn't practical anymore. I had my business to run. Jeannie had the kids. I suppose we could've hired people to handle it for us, but I didn't see the point. From the beginning, this was a labor of love.

"I realized the only solution was to grow them in the city, so we could cut out the back and forth. I found an old warehouse and converted it into a greenhouse. I brought in the Cornell people again, poured close to a million dollars into the thing. It was an obsession. No matter what I did, though, I couldn't get the same flavor here as I did upstate. The berries were just as bland as the imposters from the supermarket. The restaurants lost interest, and I had to give the whole thing up."

Gollick paused to let his story sink in or maybe just catch his breath. We sat in silence, mesmerized. The epilogue was aimed straight at John.

"So, my fellow businessman, my question for you is this: are you confident that what you grow on a rooftop in Brooklyn will be good enough to serve in a four-star Manhattan restaurant?"

John met his wavering gaze and held it. "No doubt."

"He can even grow your *fraise de bois* for you if you want," I heard myself say.

John's back stiffened, but he kept his eyes on Gollick. I spotted a faint movement beneath the old man's mustache, but I couldn't tell if he was smirking skeptically or smacking his lips at the memory.

"In that case, you've got my support. Because if you can do that, you're going to be sitting on a gold mine."

It took Gollick struggling to dislodge himself from his desk for me to comprehend that the meeting was over and we were leaving with a commitment. Even when we were back on the street, divested of our visitor badges, it was unclear what exactly he had committed to. A donation? An investment? Did he expect to see a return?

"Was all that true?" I asked John. "We're going to make a profit on this?"

John watched the traffic like it was a mighty river in which he alone could discern the elusive nature of truth. "It depends."

"Depends on what?"

"The margin on fucking *fraise de bois*."

I gave him a cold smile. "Maybe we're a nonprofit after all."

Elliot eased himself between us. "We are whatever we want to be, right, guys?"

"Until we file the paperwork," I said.

"Forget the paperwork," Vivienne chimed in as she rummaged through her purse. "Martin wants to see you *do* something. That's what men like him respect. So that's what we're going to do. Damn it, where did I put my phone?"

"You gave both your phones to Kat."

"Who?"

I took a deep breath and thought, so this is what an adventure feels like. I was starting to have fun.

A Farm Without Grit

It turned out to be harder to get an audience with the principal of Begin to Win than with the mighty Martin Gollick. Finally, after nearly a week of noodging, we were in. He was a man straight out of '80s teen movie central casting: colorless hair cut close to the scalp, wire-rimmed glasses, khakis. He seemed edgy, distracted, and not all that enthused about the prospect of a vegetable farm on his roof. He reeled off a fuzzy spiel about the school's new focus on "literacy and numeracy," but once we conveyed how excited about the project the Schlossers were, all the fight went out of him. He introduced us to Edgar, the weather-beaten head of maintenance. Call ahead anytime we needed access to the roof, the principal told us, and Edgar would take care of it. Meanwhile, he would round up some teachers to work with Elliot on the curriculum. Basically, he arranged matters so he wouldn't have to talk to us again. Elliot made a bland comment about coordinating with the District 75 school. That set off a round of sputtering about "efficient allocation of resources" and "respecting autonomy." We let it go and left him rearranging stacks of papers in his office.

Our meeting with Tommy Brutti was set for the following day. Vivienne was sitting this one out. She'd graced Begin to Win with her presence one time—the grand opening twenty years ago—and said that was enough for her. Her understanding of our powwow with Gollick was that he had tacitly agreed to cover our entire first-year budget, and while there was no harm in adding to the kitty, she'd essentially done the heavy lifting for us.

So the welcome committee consisted of John, Elliot, and me, along with Edgar, the maintenance guy, who inspected the blacktop roof with a proprietary eye.

"So you guys really putting a garden up here?" he asked.

"A farm," I said, using my hand as a visor, the very picture of a man with a vision.

The view from the roof was less than majestic. I could make out a sliver of the BQE in the near distance. Behind us loomed the hulk of Woodhull Hospital. The scenery at ground-level wasn't much of an improvement. Most of the acre or so outside the doors of Begin to Win was taken up by a car lot; among the teachers' dingy compacts were a couple of beaters, apparently abandoned, and a carpet cleaning van, probably taking advantage of the free parking.

Alongside the lot was a scruffy playground with a faded jungle gym and merry-go-round—not the kind with ponies and music, the kind that's just a metal disc on a spindle with a few bars to hang onto—pale, anemic pines poking out of the perimeter swale. Adjacent to the playground was a handball court, its concrete spiderwebbed with cracks. The scene was desolate, despite the neat brick row houses lining the street opposite the playground (formerly Pfizer worker housing) and the projects whose outer edge faced the handball court on the other side of the block. Suffice to say, the space wasn't a neighborhood hub.

Not exactly inspiring, but taking it all in, I felt like I was getting somewhere. Just a few days ago, I'd been trapped in a windowless conference room, yearning for the outdoors. Now here I was. One small step for Will, but I'd take it.

"A farm," Edgar said. "So, like with chickens?"

"Maybe," I said. "Eventually. But for now just vegetables."

"In boxes?"

John answered, his back to the rest of us. "No boxes. Just a layer of gravel and a layer of soil. Better yield that way."

Edgar crouched down as if the roof, his roof, wanted to tell him something. "That's a lot of weight."

I said, "We're going to hire a structural engineer to make sure it's safe." I'd been looking into it. "That reminds me, do you have access to the building plans?"

He squinted as if my question were a beam of light. "Access? Yeah, but I got to remember where they are. What vegetables you going to grow, anyway?"

We turned to John. "Tomatoes, lettuce, herbs, zucchini…"

"Fraise de bois," I said.

John may have grunted, or he may not have reacted at all.

Edgar shook his head. "You got to grow chilies, tomatillo, *calabaza*. That's what people eat around here."

"You garden, Edgar?" Elliot asked.

"Oh, sure. I've got a garden for the kids around back."

I'd been gazing at the crummy view, but now my head snapped

in his direction. "Wait, this school already has a garden?"

"Oh, sure. Been doing it for years. It's not a farm or nothing, just a few beds, but the kids seem to like it."

"Principal Jenner didn't mention it to us."

"No disrespect, but Principal Jenner doesn't have the best idea of what goes on around here. Anyway, it's mostly the other kids who come out to help. The special kids."

Elliot held out his arms as if to literally embrace this unforeseen development. "That's great, Edgar. You could be like the Yoda of this whole thing. I say we join forces, move your plants up here, and learn from each other. John?"

"Chilies, tomatillo we can work with. Not much of a market for calabaza." John's cell rang—Iron Maiden, "Number of the Beast"—and he stepped to the edge of the roof.

Edgar said, "I doubt they're going to let them special kids come all the way up here, to be honest with you. It'd be a lot for them to deal with—the kids and the teachers."

I kneaded my jaw. "We can't have a state-of-the-art rooftop farm for the charter school and a handicapped garden round back."

John rejoined the rest of us. "Tommy can't make it. He had to spend an extra day in Vegas hammering out a deal. Greta's on her way up. She'll check it out and report back."

"We're just kicking around a problem," Elliot told him. "The special ed students can't come up to the roof."

A moment passed. I couldn't tell if the information had pierced the air around him.

"That sucks," he said after a while. "It would have been a cool thing for them."

I wanted to tell him he didn't appreciate the implication of the news, but I knew that would drag us off track. "There's got to be a way to make it work. Small groups, extra adults, guardrails maybe. We'll figure it out."

John nodded vaguely. "Good." He didn't sound especially concerned one way or the other.

A head popped out of the open roof hatch. "Is this where the party's at?"

Pink-blonde hair, eyebrow ring—it was the waitress from Rita's, the tiny ukulele player. My frustration with John was mounting. Didn't he know better than to invite his hangers-on to a business meeting?

"Hey, Greta," Elliot said, lurching in for a hug.

She fist-bumped John even as she threw her other arm around Elliot. When she noticed me, she closed one eye and pointed. "Hey, I know you."

"I thought you worked at Rita's," I said.

"I help out at night because John's my dude. But running shit for Tommy is my official gig."

Now that she mentioned it, she did seem to be dressed in a Williamsburg version of business attire: high-waisted slacks, formless blazer over a Public Image Ltd T-shirt.

Greta spun around on her heel. "So this is it, huh? The next outpost of the Rita's empire."

"We look at it as more of a community project," I said.

"Right, the kids." She held out her phone and continued swiveling around as she spoke, taking video. "Tommy's foundation is going to be all about helping kids. But he's not interested in what everyone's already doing—book drives, mentoring, wishes. He's looking for projects that fit his brand—bold, innovative…and fun. Fun is important to Tommy, for the kids and for him. Because if it's not fun, then why bother, right?"

"Seems like a fun guy," Elliot said.

Greta flashed her ring and index fingers: devil's horns. "Work hard, play hard."

Elliot mirrored the gesture, getting into the Tommy Brutti spirit. "At a school like Begin to Win, so much of what the students do all day is test prep, drill and kill," he said. "Our program is going to help the teachers do their job, but at the same time, it's going to make the kids excited to show up in the morning. Like, 'we get to grow the tomatoes that go on our pizza? How cool is that?'"

Greta pulled her face free from her phone, a glint in her eyes. "So the kids get to eat the food?"

Elliot gave John a careful look. I decided to cut in. "A portion of it, sure. Eating is a part of the learning experience. We're talking to the principal about incorporating some of the fresh ingredients into the lunch menu. That's the nutrition piece of the puzzle."

I made a mental note to send the principal an email broaching the subject as soon as we were back on the ground.

"John, what do you think of Francisco doing a cooking demo with the kids at harvest time?" I asked.

John forced the breath out of his nose like a bull. "It's doable."

Edgar had been standing silently with his hands behind his back like a secret service agent trained not to listen to what doesn't concern him.

"Edgar, what do you do with the vegetables from your garden?"

Elliot asked him.

"Mostly just give them away to parents, my neighbors. I tried giving them to the cafeteria for the kids' lunch, but they said it was against regulation. They got to use the stuff they buy from the district, all that frozen crap, because it's been approved by the inspectors."

"I think we can handle a little red tape," I said. "Right, Elliot?"

"We eat red tape for breakfast."

"Once things are really up and running and we're getting the yield we want, the next step is a farmers market," I pressed on. "That's how we bring in the parents and the neighbors."

"And we get to add an economics piece to the curriculum," Elliot added. "Entrepreneurship, what it takes to run a business."

Greta gave the screen of her phone a series of spirited jabs. "Innovative. See, that's why this is a perfect project for Tommy. You've got the Rita's connection, and John, you know Tommy loves you guys. Then you've got the kids, growing the food, learning the science, eating it, selling it. And it's all happening in this reclaimed space nobody uses. I mean, think about how many rooftops there are. Just the schools alone..."

"We're thinking of this as a pilot," I said. "The idea is to design the program so it can be scaled up to schools all over the city."

Finally, I'd said something that met with John's approval.

"Every restaurant in the city could get their produce within walking distance," he said. "Fuck the supply chain." The way he was staring past us, it was as if he were laying claim to the virgin rooftops of all New York's 1,700 schools.

"Word." Greta's eyes were glued to her phone. "So I sent some video to Tommy while we were talking. He's in. I mean, not officially till he's back in town and we can get it all on paper. But he's giving this the green light."

Headrush. This "yes" was even more improbable in its swiftness than Gollick's. He, at least, had to be persuaded in person. I was used to budget negotiations at the council; the haggling over a single line item could drag on for months. So this was how the other half lived.

Greta forged ahead. "Listen, I know this is probably going to be disappointing, but the foundation isn't exactly flush at the moment. Tommy's got a big fundraiser coming up at South Beach Food & Wine, but that isn't until next winter. For now, the ceiling on grants is fifty thousand. And since Tommy's new at this, he's only doing matching gifts. He doesn't want to throw money into something unless there's at least one other big commitment."

Elliot was smiling so hard, it looked like it hurt. "We understand completely. We've already got a big anchor donor, so we can just match Tommy's gift against that."

I heard myself say, "No."

Elliot's smile froze. "No?"

I had the group's undivided attention.

"That would be a waste," I said. "What we need to do is make a big announcement—'Tommy Brutti Pledges $50,000 Matching Gift'—and use that as leverage to bring in more."

Elliot remained still for a beat. Then, like someone had pressed "un-pause," he clamped down on my shoulder.

His eyes bounced from Greta to John. "What have I been telling you? We've got the master strategizer right here." He gave me a little shake.

"Tommy's all for big announcements," Greta said. "I think he's going to enjoy doing business with you gentlemen."

She said she'd be in touch when Tommy was ready for us to sign the agreement. And with that, she raised a fist still adorned with last night's club stamp, drawled, "Viva la revolucion!" and disappeared down the hatch from whence she came. I thought I heard Edgar say something in Spanish under his breath, but when I looked at him he didn't look back.

* * *

We called Vivienne to tell her the good news. She said to call back on her iPhone so my contact info would be stored. I did as instructed, and Kat answered.

"Oh, yeah, the farm boys."

"You couldn't get them to transfer her contacts?"

"I did. She just doesn't know how to find them. Hang on. I think she's on her Blackberry."

We muddled through this little comedy of errors for another minute or two before we were able to commandeer Vivienne's attention and ask her who to hit up for the match money. She sighed, a woman wearied by the burden of so much wisdom.

"You're not going to like this, but I think it's time."

She was talking about the Prometheus Foundation, the 800-pound gorilla of the nonprofit sector. The name referred to the myth of the Titan who stole the secret of fire from the gods and gave it to mankind, a grave personal sacrifice that allowed civilization to advance and prosper. In other words, the first philanthropic grant. Laying claim to the capital—intellectual and actual—of society's powerful ruling class and using it to make life better for the less fortunate: that was the foundation's mission, and counterintuitively, it seemed to go over well with its intended victims.

Prometheus had become the go-to tax write-off for New York's upper crust, best known for its star-studded annual gala. "Turning guilt into *gelt*" was the catchphrase coined by last year's host, a political comedian widely beloved by coastal elites. Every major anti-poverty initiative in the city had Prometheus money flowing through it.

So what made Vivienne think we wouldn't want to target them for our next big ask? Well, as sterling as Prometheus's reputation with the gentry was, it was less so among the beneficiaries of its largess, the food banks and clinics and tutoring centers that received the grants. For years, there'd been horror stories going around about the infamous "Prometheus trial by fire," their insistence on micromanaging every aspect of the work they funded. Most of the nonprofit leaders I'd met just wanted someone to pay the ConEd bill so they could get on with the endless work of triaging their clients' needs—food, shelter, medical care, counseling—but that wasn't the deal with Prometheus. I'd heard that, in one extreme case, a modest after school arts program gratefully accepted the foundation's offer to pay off their mounting debt; within two years, it had been transformed into "a pilot initiative to align enrichment instruction with the STEM curriculum." There may have been interpretive dance involved. Could be an urban legend, but still...gives a whole new meaning to doing the robot.

To me, it was inevitable that Prometheus would want to get all up in its grantees' business. After all, its board of directors was made up of captains of industry, corporate titans—as opposed to the original Greek variety. Their worldview, as I understood it, was that every problem up to and including child hunger and adult illiteracy was a symptom of poor management. Handouts were easy, but what the kind-hearted schlubs ladling out the soup and flashing the flash cards really needed was someone to show them how to maximize efficiency, create economies of scale, use metrics to drive continuous performance improvement—you know, the important stuff.

"Can't we just go to another one of your friends?" Elliot couldn't keep the whine out of his voice.

"We *can,*" Vivienne said, "but we don't want all our eggs in one basket. We've already got a big-time private donor and a famous name. What we need is credibility. Right now, this is still just a cute little project. If Prometheus gives us their seal of approval, that makes it real."

"Do you think they'll go for it?" I asked.

"Martin and this Chef Tommy of yours will be enough to get us a meeting. Beyond that, I don't know. But one thing I've learned, boys, there's no shame in asking. At least, I've never felt any."

Elliot got a kick out of that. "Ain't too proud to beg, Viv?"

"Excuse me?"

We talked it over and decided she was right. The Prometheus imprimatur had value far beyond the $50,000 we were seeking. And we figured a couple of savvy political operatives such as ourselves had to be better equipped to deal with the dreaded trial by fire than your typical frazzled community nonprofit director. Besides, maybe they'd have some useful ideas for us. They did have more than two dozen PhDs on staff. In any case, Vivienne, having come up with the suggestion, was likely to set up the meeting whether we assented or not.

That settled, there was something else on my mind. I told Elliot I didn't want to invite John. My argument was that this wasn't his crowd. There was no denying his maverick capitalist shtick had done the trick with Martin Gollick, and Tommy Brutti was his contact from the get-go, but Prometheus was a different animal, a haven for policy wonks and "mission-driven change agents." If John were to murk up the waters again, raising questions about our collective intent and even our nonprofit status, we'd blow it for sure. To my surprise, Elliot didn't object. I wondered if he'd been secretly hoping I'd make the case for excluding John, if, like me, he was concerned we were becoming a subsidiary of John Cardini, Inc.

The Prometheus offices were sleek and silent. A screen behind the front desk advertised various activities taking place that day—a "Social Innovation Laboratory" in the Fire Room, a live-streaming TED Talk in the Clay Room (a reference, I took it, to the story of Prometheus molding the first humans out of clay). We were led to a curvaceous, glass-walled conference room and provided bottles of spring water. The back wall was decked out top-to-bottom with jittery crayon drawings on construction paper, an incongruous gallery of children's art, from Lascaux-like pets to abstract expressionist splatters.

I'd seen similar stuff on display before, but always in the offices of organizations that worked directly with children. The longer we waited for our hosts to join us, the more questions came to mind: How did all that art find its way here? Was it part of the grant agreements that Prometheus owned a percentage of all creative work produced with its support? Were bags full of glitter-and-macaroni collages arriving by courier on a daily basis? Did Prometheus display whatever it got, or did it skim the best stuff off the top, and if so, had it developed an assessment tool to measure the artistic quality of the work? Was there a discreet storage room (the Tartarus Room?) piled high with pieces that didn't make the cut?

The Prometheus team that eventually joined us was six-strong: there were program officers representing its food security and educational opportunity divisions, as well as a communications officer and a lawyer—at least, I thought he was a lawyer; he just said his name and "Legal" by way of introduction. They were a remarkably diverse bunch for such a toney outfit, about an equal mix of men and women, white, black, and Asian: (East and South). Men and women alike were in suits, distinguished only by a whimsical fluorescent sock, chunky fashion glasses, or, in one case, a gold lapel pin with the Prometheus logo: a single flame. At each of our previous meetings, I'd felt overdressed in chinos, shirt and tie. Now, I felt underdressed, although I doubt anyone noticed since I was sitting next to Elliot, who, as usual, hadn't ironed his shirt or worn a belt.

They were all about the same height (too short for professional basketball but maybe not lacrosse) and young, younger than me and Elliot, by the looks of it. Maybe that meant our proposal had only risen to the level of the B team. If so, fine with me. They were still the most impressive group I'd ever faced across a conference table.

Brad, the senior officer for food security, took the lead. "Whenever we meet new folks, we like to start with a little explanation of how we work."

His colleagues looked on with unwavering attention.

"Our grantees, when they come to us, most of them are already doing great work, but they're serving small numbers. Or they have a cool idea, but they don't know how to operationalize it. Our value add—well, it's the money, of course it's the money..."

Brad paused to allow for a soft chuckle from the group. "But we like to think it's more than that. Because the problems we're facing are huge, so huge that throwing money at them, even Prometheus money, barely makes a dent. And frankly, we're not interested in dents. We want to *demolish* those problems."

Another pause to let the words assume their full weight. Maybe this is the TED Talk, I thought. There could be a camera installed in that wall of children's art, hidden behind the lion with the paper plate face, microphone secreted between its triangle teeth.

"We don't have the satisfaction of helping jobseekers with their resumes or reading to kids on a daily basis. What gets us excited to come to work every morning is the opportunity to meet with folks like you, take a good look at what you're doing, really get under the hood, and figure out if what's working for a few dozen people in need can work for millions. How does that sound?"

All three of us—me, Elliot, Vivienne, and me —were slow to realize the question was meant to be answered.

Brad jumped into the silence before it got too awkward. "I know, it's a lot, right? Kind of like asking the centipede which leg he moves first..."

Reassuring nods from the team. Thank god they weren't the winking type.

"Being so intentional can be difficult for some organizations. Sometimes the fit just isn't there. But if it is, we'll be with you through the whole strategy development process, helping you build the muscle."

Brad checked his watch. "So I see I've taken up way too much time talking about us. Why don't you tell us a little bit about what you're doing and how you think we can help each other."

Elliot and Vivienne both turned to me. "Operationalize," "intentional," "strategy development process"—these were terms that didn't enter into their understanding of how the sausage gets made.

Brad rested his chin on steepled fingers as I carefully explained our plans, his eyes closed, as if I were a Zen monk presenting him with a kōan. They stayed closed after I finished. Somehow I could tell, though, this wasn't a Gollick situation; there was no question of him nodding off. Rather, he'd chosen to screen out all visual input, knowing it would only distract from the deep reflection underway.

"Do you have a logic model?" he asked after a while.

I only had a dim concept of what a logic model was, some kind of diagram or chart. All I could think to do in that moment was imitate the master.

"We were hoping to get your advice on that," I said.

Brad opened his eyes to share an ambiguous glance with his colleagues. "Right, let's skip the logic model for now. Can you give us a sense of what kind of impact you expect to have on food security in that section of Brooklyn?"

My mouth opened, forming words my brain rejected before my voice could get involved. I'd already burned through the bodega statistics, my best material.

"You can just ballpark it for us," Brad prompted. "Metric tons of food produced. Percentage of the local population moving from insecure to secure..."

I scanned the faces arrayed across from me—all benevolent, affable even. This was not a hazing. They were rooting for me to supply the right answer. They might even be disappointed if I didn't.

"We're thinking of the farm mainly in terms of its educational value," I said. "There is a hunger problem in the Triangle, and we believe we can make a dent..."

Out of the corner of my eye, I saw Elliot flick his hand like he was brushing dirt off the table.

"A *difference*," I caught myself. "But that's really a secondary benefit. Our main focus is on developing an innovative curriculum and giving these kids a richer learning experience."

Brad rocked back and forth in his chair, his fingertips still pressed together. He might have been giving me a little bow, one sensei to another. "You're prioritizing. That's good. Education's not really my area of expertise, though, so I'm going to turn the floor over to Kenesha."

Kenesha was the one in the sharp gray suit, curls tight against her scalp, her obelisk earrings miniature works of art. I instantly wanted her approval.

"Thanks for giving us a chance to get to know you. Such an interesting project. My questions are basically along the same lines as Brad's. What are you projecting in terms of achievement gains for the students?"

This was one question I'd seen coming. Kenesha was asking if the farm would raise test scores.

Normally, I would have let Elliot answer, but I was on a roll. "Well, this is going to be a pilot year. The plan is to work with the school to identify the students who stand to benefit the most. That's the baseline, and from there we'll be able to track achievement gains."

"But we're going to be looking at a bunch of other indicators, too," Elliot said. "Social-emotional outcomes—self-efficacy, regulation of emotion…"

Kenesha straightened up in her seat. "Grit?"

Elliot, the rascal, winked. "Can't have a farm without grit."

Everyone had a good, albeit brief, laugh over that one.

"I'm so glad to hear you're taking the noncognitive factors into consideration," Kenesha said. "You'd be surprised how many of the organizations that come to us don't do that."

"This is not your run-of-the-mill school garden," Vivienne said, responding to the vibes in the room like a plant opening up to light. "There are years and years of policy experience sitting at this table. I won't say how many of them are mine, but you get the idea."

Kenesha gave her a look like she wanted to pat her cheek. "You can understand, then, as important as those noncognitive factors are, achievement is a go-no-go threshold for us. As a rule, we just don't invest in projects that don't already have evidence of gains."

She winced as she delivered the blow. She didn't want to hurt us.

I winced back, playing along. "And that's a hard rule? Because, like Vivienne said, we feel this is a special circumstance. Not only have you got the expertise we bring to the table. There's the location, the school, the support from Martin Gollick and Chef Brutti, names I'm sure you all know. There's the involvement of Rita's, which is unique for this type of project."

Brad bolted upright. "Rita's is the restaurant you're partnering with?"

"This has been a shared vision with them from the beginning,"

I said.

"I've been wanting to get out there for months. You guys all know about Rita's, right?"

I watched their faces carefully. They seemed excited by the possibility there was any knowledge they didn't already possess.

Brad didn't wait for an answer. "From what I've read, it's a real experience. Pizzeria 2.0," he said.

Elliot threw his arms out in front of him, a genie who's just heard the magic words. "Exactly! And they don't want to be involved in anything that isn't just as innovative and entrepreneurial and, uh..."

"Cool?" Brad looked like a kid anxious to hear that teen idol X is exactly how he seems on TV.

Elliot snapped his fingers, the genie granting his wish. "That's it. They're cool guys, and they want to work on cool projects, and what we're doing is going to be the Rita's of urban agriculture."

Brad had pitched his finger tent again and redoubled his rocking. It seemed dangerous to interrupt such furious cogitation, but Elliot couldn't help pressing his luck.

"You know, if you all wanted to take a field trip out there, we could show you the site, have a late lunch..."

It was too much, not a gross lapse of ethics, judging by the reaction, but just enough of a misstep to snap Brad out of his fanboy paroxysms.

"We've got a marathon TA session after this, so I'm afraid we're going to have to pass. But I think we can all agree this is a conversation that needs to continue. Kenesha's right. We understand this is still in the pilot phase, but we can't make an investment that isn't evidence-based. That's at the core of our strategy."

Kenesha and the others nodded solemnly. But Brad wasn't finished. "What we *can* do is give you a planning grant to help you make this a really kickass program."

"Kickass" came out a tad bumpy. He seemed to have broken it out especially for the occasion.

"To be clear, you wouldn't be able to spend the money on shovels or photocopies or any other program expenses. We'd want you to go out and talk to as many people who are doing this kind of work as possible, a real deep dive. We can hook you up with some names. The idea is to take what you're learning and feed it back into the program design. Build it into your logic model. I know you said you're looking for some help with that. We've got a whole toolkit. Kick the tires, see what makes sense. It's an iterative process. Then, a year from now, if the model really works, I can guarantee you we'll be all in. How does that sound?"

Vivienne gave him a shrewd look, like he'd invited her to negotiate. "What about the matching gift from the Brutti Foundation?"

"That's between you and them. I'm sure they have their requirements, just like we have ours. But as long as they understand that the Prometheus grant can only be used for planning activities, then you won't have a problem with us."

Elliot had both palms pressed to the table like he was ready to leap up and start shaking hands. But a problem had occurred to me. "The growing season."

Brad looked at me blandly, Vivienne with a flash of irritation.

"We really appreciate this opportunity to go deep into the planning process with you," I said. "But the growing season starts in a matter of weeks now, and we have an obligation to Rita's and Begin to Win to get seeds in the ground."

I was afraid Brad would start to wobble on his axis again, but he seemed to take it in stride. Elliot and Vivienne on the other hand…one particular vein in Vivienne's temple was so taut, I could've reached out and played a note on it.

"Plant away," Brad said. "The way we see it, planning shouldn't be a dry, theoretical exercise. You've got to roll up your sleeves and get your hands dirty. In this case, literally. That's how you learn. All we ask is that you capture the learning and share it with us."

"And if we want to take what we've learned and bring it to other schools, Prometheus will back us?"

Brad smiled at my brass. "That's how we hope the process will unfold. For now, just think of the planning grant as seed money."

"But please don't spend it on seeds," said Mr. Legal. Chuckles all around.

The vein in Vivienne's temple retreated. Brad stood, and we all followed suit. Handshake time was nigh. They weren't a bad bunch, really, if you spoke their language.

Mr. Legal cleared his throat. "So, Brad or Kenesha—I'm thinking probably Kenesha—will set your paperwork in motion. I assume you're all set up as a 501c3."

Elliot and Vivienne both avoided eye contact with me. Hadn't I told them we needed to file that paperwork?

"We're exploring our options," I said. "The school is funded by a 501c3, and there's a possibility they may act as our fiscal sponsor, at least in the planning phase. We'll keep you informed."

Mr. Legal's eyes went blank as if he were inwardly scanning my words for potential improprieties. But when he resurfaced it was with a nod of approval.

Brad buttonholed us as we were shuffling out. “So, rain check on that lunch? I heard there’s all these off-menu toppings: raw-milk cheese, magic mushrooms. Is that true?”

We pled the fifth and left him with his illusions.

Building That Network

Red Hook: the first stop on our Prometheus-sponsored listening tour. A Park Sloper for as long as I'd lived in Brooklyn, Red Hook had always held a dark allure for me. Just compare the two names—one redolent of yuppie privilege, a gentle, undemanding way of life; the other vivid, sharp, evoking hard work and rough trade, meat and murder.

In truth, Red Hook wasn't exactly a salty longshoreman's paradise anymore. It was still relatively cut off from the rest of the city by a lack of public transportation, but now you could hop a free shuttle bus or ferry (if you were coming from Manhattan) to the waterfront IKEA and walk to Van Brunt Street. You could still hit the soccer fields for the best pupusas in the city (with a plastic baggie of mango and chili salt on the side), but now you'd have to spend the better part of an hour in line behind know-it-all bloggers. The Department of Health had gotten involved, so the dozen or so women with their plastic coolers and lawn chairs had been replaced by a small handful of professional-grade food trucks.

The projects still had a reputation, and there was hardly a view anywhere in the neighborhood that didn't look out onto a bus depot, but that hadn't stopped a wave of colonists—a little hardier than the typical Park Slope denizen—from gobbling up three-story townhouses near the water for the same amount they'd spend on a one-bedroom just ten minutes away. With them came the galleries and shops (or maybe the galleries and shops came first): the liquor store doing a brisk business in small-batch whiskey brewed in a distillery just up the block; the jeweler making one-of-a-kind pieces out of hemp knots, bits of rusted anchor and other detritus from Red Hook's nautical past; the incongruously elegant bar, passion project of an in-demand cocktail historian, its every fixture and floor tile worthy of its own "Talk of the Town" piece, every ice cube a geometric ideal. Frankly, Van Brunt still looked a bit blighted—weedy, graffitied, trash-flecked (even after the city deemed it well-trafficked enough to install garbage cans)—but maybe that was the way the new residents wanted it, a serene way station between a rough past and a boutique future.

Right in the middle of it all, in a prime storefront between the jeweler and the liquor store, was the office of In It Together Farms, the first serious agricultural enterprise in Brooklyn since the days when it was all pretty much one big farm. In my neighborhood, the idea of a hand-to-mouth community organization hanging out its shingle on one of the main commercial drags would have been inconceivable to realtors and landlords who were busy pushing out cobblers and used bookstores in favor of cell phone stands and yogurt chains.

I had a feeling that suited Duncan Donner, the founder of In It

Together, just fine. His was the classic people-thought-I-was-crazy story, as in, "When I first came here and said, 'I want to build a full-scale working farm on an abandoned lot in Red Hook, and I want kids from the projects to do the farming,' people thought I was crazy!" But—these stories always hinge on a "but"—Donner was relentless. And when the neighborhood's only grocery store closed down, leaving locals at the mercy of the bodegas, he started to seem less crazy. (No one could even dream of the world to come, in which the old shipping depot would become a supermarket so bounteous people from other neighborhoods would join Zipcar just to shop there.) The city stepped in with funding for a farm stand, and Heifer International—better known for donating livestock to third-world villages—got involved with the planning and startup. Donner, whose background was in juvenile justice, recruited idle teens from the Red Hook Houses, just like he said he would, promising them that the proceeds from the stand would be theirs to keep.

Ten years later, on the Venn diagram of New York City, he owned the space where the circles labeled "urban farming," "food justice," and "youth development" overlapped. Take the idea of installing scanners at city green markets so vendors could accept food stamps—the speaker of the council had lapped up the credit, but I'd heard it started with Donner. Everything Elliot and I aspired to do in the Triangle, he had done in Red Hook. And as luck would have it, he was Prometheus's go-to guru for all things vegetal.

"Between you and me, Prometheus wasn't willing to commit a dime when I needed it to get this thing off the ground," he said in a caffeinated falsetto. He sounded like a squeaky wheel rolling down a steep hill. "Now that I'm over the hump and the *Times* has been out to see us, I'm their idea of the perfect consultant. They send me starry-eyed young dudes like you every month or so. I give you the tour, report back on what I think of you, they send a check. America, right?"

I watched his ginger soul patch bob with each word. He was stomping through the office in dirt-caked work boots, cut-off jean shorts, and a black In It Together T-shirt (their logo was a pile-up of hands in gardening gloves; I could practically hear the implied "one, two, three...team!"). The floorboards groaned with every step. There were a few other people working, a pasty woman in a sunhat who seemed to be dropping off some paperwork, and a trio of black teens, all in the same T-shirt as Duncan, huddled around the one computer, which appeared to be in a state of distress. He high-fived the woman and stuck his sweaty, bald head among the teens, checking on their progress. Then he whirled around to face us.

"Don't worry. I give everyone a good review. You could be on Wall Street raping pensioners or Madison Avenue coming up with a cuter logo for rat poison…maybe put a little party hat on the skull and crossbones, I don't know. But you're here, right? And that's good enough for me. I always tell Brad and those guys, let a thousand flowers bloom, it ain't my money. Except for the consulting fee, of course.

"Let's call that Lesson Number One: you help the people who need your help. Everyone else has to pony up. You guys ready to take a walk with me? There's something I want to show you."

The farm itself was five minutes away. It wasn't until we'd come right up to it that I could see how impressive it was. While nothing much was growing, long furrows had already been dug in anticipation of the season. There was a row of chest-high compost bins, a cluster of beehives made of remaindered shelving units donated by the nearby IKEA, even a wire pen of baby goats. I expected to see more local kids doing the day's chores, but instead the farm was being tended by a gaggle of adults, middle-aged men and women in powder blue polo shirts and matching baseball caps. A small sign had been posted by the entrance gate: "In It Together Welcomes Windham-Mercer's Annual Give-Back Day."

Duncan stood with his hands on his hips, a general surveying the ranks. "They all want to come in the summer when I'm trying to break in a dozen new youth empowerment fellows and two dozen community volunteers. There isn't much for them to do now—I've got them weeding, turning compost, picking up the trash—but at least they're not getting in the way."

Indeed, many of the Windham-Mercer crew were just milling around, shooting streams of Gatorade from company-branded squeeze bottles into the space between their straight, white teeth, whipping their heads back to shake off phantom bees.

"I charge them a hundred bucks a head," Duncan said. "Call it a guilt tax. I don't even know what these guys do, but it must be pretty bad if they're willing to pay that much to do our donkey work. What line were you two in anyway?"

We told him and braced ourselves. Where did government hacks rank alongside pension rapists and poison peddlers in his rogue's gallery?

Duncan just fingered his soul patch. "Then you know a hell of a lot more about what you're getting into than I did. Probably not much I can pass on you haven't figured out already."

We assured him that we had figured out virtually nothing, that we were, in fact, hungry for his wisdom.

"Gotta show Brad you're earning that sweet grant money, right? All right. One more lesson, then I've got to get some work done. This is a big one. You ready? Talk to everybody. I mean, everybody. Every community board meeting, you're there. And I mean every meeting, not just when they put you on the agenda. Every church potluck, every school fundraiser, you're there, showing your smiling face, handing out leaflets, explaining what you're trying to do, asking for their support. But you're not just telling them what you need *from* them. You're asking what you can do *for* them. 'Oh, you need bodies for your rally protesting bus service cuts? I'm there. You need someone with fundraising experience to sit on the board of your art space? I'm there.' I've been doing it for twelve years, and half the time I'm still the honky interloper. I'm telling you, every CB meeting, there's a faction of old biddies from the Houses who say, 'Why are we wasting time on this white boy? He's not even from here'—meaning I wasn't born here—'and he ain't gonna be here when we need him.' Every time. I carry their groceries for them! You saw their grandchildren back at the office! But they get to have their say, everyone kind of rolls their eyes, and then the board backs us up. Because they know us. They know what we're about. And then, when I'm having a problem with the city, which is, like, every week, I can say to them with full confidence, 'I've got the community behind me. Are you sure you want this hassle?' That, guys, is my whole life. And that is really the lesson of lessons: be prepared to spend every waking hour, and most of your few sleeping hours, thinking about it, talking about it, worrying about it, freaking out about it—and everything will work out just fine."

I couldn't tell if Duncan's speech was meant to be a pep talk or a cautionary tale. I'd been to my share of community board meetings with Vivienne—they were epics of tedium, like the Ring Cycle if the Ring Cycle were about the placement of recycling bins and Siegfried was an ancient crank with a fraying collar, sardine breath, and an encyclopedic memory of every neighbor who ever committed a violation. Those mind-numbing evenings were reason enough to get out of politics.

But that was the Upper East Side, where activism was mostly a matter of keeping out pesky waste transfer stations and homeless shelters. The Broadway Triangle was another world, one in dire need of revitalization (or vitalization, really). Unlike Vivienne's constituents, the people there had real problems. As far as I was concerned, that could make for a nice change of pace. No question we'd have to prove ourselves, but between my diligence and Elliot's gift for putting everyone at ease, I was confident we'd manage. Didn't Duncan say we were far better prepared than he was when he started?

Duncan wished us luck and sent us off to make the world a better place. We figured The Customs House—that exquisitely conceived bar, which I now learned from the wrought-iron sign was actually a "cocktail club"—would be a quiet spot for a debrief. As it turned out, though, the place was full at three o'clock in the afternoon. On a Wednesday. Elliot and I stood in the doorway, gaping at the tableau before us. There were some single customers huddled over Macbooks, but you could find their kind at every last coffee shop and dive bar in Brooklyn. Harder to figure were the couples and families at leisure, each table its own magazine spread, the men a cross between lumberjacks (shirt, beard, build) and architects (glasses, wristwatch), the women manic pixie dream girls aging into earth mothers, the babies all dirty blonde curls and cerulean eyes, dunking Scandinavian-looking wood rattles in the bourbon milk punch.

Who were these people? What did they do for money? Were they all sculptors and chapbook publishers, as their looks and demeanors suggested? Or did they represent the latest leap in the evolution of the consultant, their brains percolating with new product names and pop-up concepts, racking up the billable hours as they nursed their Sazeracs and pisco sours? Waiting for a table to free up, I was struck by the strange realization that what separated me from them at that moment wasn't money or status or the subtle accumulation of life choices, but rather the availability of seating. If we wanted to make this place our office, drafting budgets and work plans over devilled eggs from In It Together hens and artisanal moonshine from up the block, we could. We'd just have to show up a little earlier.

I looked over at Elliot, wondering if his thoughts ran along similar lines.

"I've got to go anyway," he said. "It's my shift at the daycare."

Easy to forget the guy had a whole life, teeming with responsibilities, that I never saw. Easy to forget, really, a world outside The Customs House, outside Red Hook, existed, and most of the people in it were, right at that very moment, still at work, most likely resenting their jobs. Poor saps.

* * *

Next stop was supposed to be Gravesend to visit The Living Classroom. Duncan Donner may have been the godfather of youth farming in Brooklyn, but Linda Light was at another level of the pantheon altogether. She was the undisputed goddess of green, patron saint of slow food, queen bee of school gardens. No one associated with cuisine in America provoked stronger reactions. *Is this bitch for real?*—that was Tricia, watching Linda tell a bemused TV reporter that families in the inner city could afford to eat organic if they stopped spending all their money on cell phones and brand-name sneakers. The interview was shot in her home kitchen, and while she sounded off in an ethereal lilt, she lovingly coddled a single egg, holding it over a wood fire in a copper spoon at least two feet long. The video went viral, naturally, and the consensus seemed to be that Linda Light did not give a fuck, though opinion was divided on whether this made her a badass or a disgrace. Either way, it didn't stop the stampede to her renowned Berkeley bistro, where tables booked up months in advance, especially as April approached and the local asparagus reached the peak of its season.

Linda herself didn't spend much time at the restaurant anymore. She was busy raising awareness, and more tangibly, getting her Living Classroom project off the ground. The idea was basically that every school should have a garden, so that kids could learn how to grow, cook, and eat real, wholesome food—pretty much the same thing we were trying to do, only Linda, as near as I could tell from my research, didn't have ambitions to raise test scores, end hunger, or turn schools into restaurant suppliers. You had to hand it to her: she was admirably insistent that a fresh tomato should be an end in itself, a good so radical it justified a massive restructuring of school budgets.

Because that, in effect, was what she was advocating. Her vision for a 21st century school garden, much like her wood oven and copper spoon, didn't come cheap. The flagship Living Classroom on the poor side of Berkeley (who knew there was such a thing?) consisted of a one-acre landscaped garden complete with greenhouse, rainwater irrigation system, chicken coop, and meeting pavilion, alongside a fully equipped teaching kitchen. Linda raised all the seed money herself, but the school had to hire not only a head chef, a garden manager, and a team of "ecoliteracy specialists" (furnished by Americorps) but a full-time development professional to keep the whole operation solvent. Hey, it takes a village, right?

Linda, meanwhile, had her sights set on the rest of the country: L.A., D.C., New York. A single fundraising dinner (her contribution to the menu was a dandelion salad dressed in vinaigrette) had apparently brought in enough private donations to recreate the Living Classroom, meeting pavilion and all, at the local elementary school in Gravesend. Elliot and I suspected that our comparative advantage lay in counterprogramming, pitching ourselves as a more cost-effective, academic-oriented alternative to Linda's high-minded herbaphilia, which, however admirable, let's face it, tended to exasperate everyone who encountered it. Nonetheless, Brad and Kenesha at Prometheus were keen for us to score a face-to-face with Linda's Brooklyn team so we could "harvest lessons." I had a funny feeling that by "harvest lessons" they meant "gather intel," The Living Classroom being one of the only high-profile nonprofits operating in the city that wasn't part of the Prometheus portfolio.

That was fine by me. The only problem was we couldn't get anyone to talk to us. The principal was too busy, naturally, and didn't seem much more clued in than Mr. Jenner at Begin to Win. She couldn't tell us if The Living Classroom had hired a local site coordinator yet. The number listed on the website went straight to a generic voicemail recording, and our messages were never answered.

Then, on a Wednesday night, while I was busy making dinner—my chore exclusively since I'd stopped working a regular schedule—I got a call from Elliot.

"John says Linda Light is at Rita's. We've got to get over there."

Tricia didn't seem thrilled to take over the Greek salad—I'd only got through the cucumbers and peppers, leaving her to get teary over the onions.

"The egg coddler? You really think she's going to be helpful?"

"You never know. She's new to New York. Maybe we can help each other."

My supportive wife made her whatever-you-say face. "I'm watching *Breaking Bad* without you."

Linda was already drunk when we got there. And not tipsy either, except in the literal sense that it appeared she might topple over. It was hard to reconcile her public persona with the red-faced hellraiser sitting cross-legged on top of the bar, shouting along to "Barracuda" on the sound system, pounding puttanesca-style pizza with one hand while pouring hundred-dollar wine into the open mouths of John and Francisco lying on the floor beneath her. For a while, we just gawked from a distance, Elliot trying to discreetly take video with his phone.

Eventually, John somehow noticed us from his spot on the floor. He waved us over and introduced us to Linda as "my political guys," a designation that would have given me greater pause if he'd been upright and wearing a shirt. Linda bowed her head, a regal gesture of acknowledgement that threatened to send her ass over tit. Then she reached out, laid her hand on my arm, and fixed us with a bleary eye.

"Stick with this guy," she said, aiming her chin down at John. "He's the real deal. I mean a true-blue fucking man-the-barricades revolutionary. That's what this country needs, right? Right?"

We agreed, and she saluted us with her wine bottle. "See, that's why I love Brooklyn. In Berkeley, everyone's got soil under their nails, but sometimes you need a little dirt!"

* * *

I figured our work was done; we could now tell Prometheus we'd had an actual meeting of the minds with Linda Light. Elliot decided to stick around and see how the night unfolded. When I called his cell the next day around 11:00, he answered with a low moan.

"Where are you? We were supposed to go over the marketing plan."

"I'm in bed, like all decent folk."

"Is Linda there?"

"Wait, let me check."

I waited. It seemed Elliot was actually making sure he hadn't dragged a wasted Linda Light into his marriage bed.

"I wonder if she ever made it out of Rita's. That woman is an animal. A grass-fed, free-range animal."

"So you enjoyed yourself?"

"You know that copper spoon? It's not just for eggs."

"As much as I'd love to be regaled with the details..."

"Marketing plan. No problem. Give me twenty minutes."

I could hear Elliot thumping around his apartment. A cast-off toy squawked as he trundled over it.

"Actually, that's why I called," I said. "I have to cancel. I got a letter about my unemployment."

"Shit, I have to get moving on that."

"Yeah, well, they're making me go to the Career Center for some kind of workshop."

Elliot yawned. "You're going to make something of yourself, I just know it."

It took me a second to realize he'd hung up.

The Career Center thing was a major pain in the ass. The state of New York was enlightened enough not to drug-test unemployment recipients, but it did randomly spot-check to make sure they were really looking for work. That meant showing up at your assigned center, presenting your resume and a list of employers you'd contacted, and sitting through a lecture on career planning, interview techniques, blah, blah, blah. Of course, I hadn't contacted a single employer, nor had I bothered to update my resume—not since the last time I'd gotten fed up with Vivienne, anyway—but I knew the pencil-pushers at the labor department looked kindly on entrepreneurs; I figured I could do a passable John Cardini impression if it came to that.

The nearest center was in the Fulton Mall downtown, Brooklyn's very own bazaar, rife with Rocawear and prepaid cell phones, irregular nurses' uniforms, and lightly used Beanie Babies. Like the rest of the borough, in a few years, it would look a lot more like

Manhattan. The Gap, Armani Exchange, and Starbucks were all on their way. The center itself was beige in the way only a New York City government office can be beige, but it was clean and quiet, not as obviously hellish as the DMV. I was directed by the woman at the front desk to a classroom that was really just an open space marked off by a different shade of carpeting. She didn't ask to see my resume or a list of contacts.

Most of the chairs were already taken, so I had to sit close to the front. Giving my classmates the once-over, I was struck by the variety. There was a white guy who looked like his entire wardrobe came from the stores just outside the center—XXL T-shirt and jeans, knock-off Tims—sitting next to an older black guy in a suit, checking his two phones. There were two Middle Eastern women, one chewing gum and staring at the ceiling and one with a notebook in her lap and pen at the ready. It hadn't crossed my mind until that moment there might be people taking this class by choice, but it was open to anyone with free time in the middle of the day.

This, I thought, was what "the worst economic crisis since the Great Depression" looked like up-close. Here were the real victims of the big Wall Street gangbang: the lady with the chewed-up nails and anxious eyes, the chubby dude in the NYU hoodie looking bewildered by his presence here. Seeing them brought home how much was riding on the farm. Without it, I'd be just another drop in the bucket marked "unemployed." But if Elliot and I could make it work, before long we'd be the ones doing the hiring.

Our instructor, Mr. Clark had a whole look going: dreadlocks, hoop earring, bow tie, vest. For the first minute or two of the class, he conducted a silent inspection, prowling the rows of seats, sometimes pausing in front of someone and extending his hand for a shake. The NYU grad stared at the offered hand as if it were a foreign word he had to translate. The white guy in Fulton finery reached up for a soul-shake from a nearly horizontal slouch. Mr. Clark returned to the front of our notional classroom and cleared his throat.

"First impressions are the only impressions when you're trying to land that dream job. Lack of eye contact, a weak handshake, casual attire or attitude. Any one of those is enough to disqualify you."

He paused to glance at the sloucher, who gave no indication he got the message. Mr. Clark was undeterred.

"I'm going to give it to you straight, people. This economy is brutal. You're competing with thousands of jobseekers just like you. Employers have their pick. So when you show up late for an interview or you fail to ask relevant questions about the position or you try to negotiate salary before an offer is made—that's game over. And you're back here with me, saying, 'Mr. Clark, I don't know what happened. I thought I had it.'"

"Let's start with the resume. How many of you have a resume down on paper?"

About half of us raised our hands. Mr. Clark turned to me. I guess my whole this-doesn't-apply-to-me vibe wasn't getting across.

"May I?" he asked. I took my stale resume out of the manila folder I'd brought along and handed it to him. He held it primly at the edges, as if it might be my only copy, and read aloud, trying to impart some flair.

"Director of Policy and Intergovernmental Affairs. Nice. Now it says here you 'briefed' a member of the City Council on issues affecting her constituents. What does it mean to brief someone?"

In practice, it mostly meant telling her what the people she liked thought about a given topic, and more importantly, what the people she hated thought. But that didn't seem like the right answer. I told Mr. Clark I presented the councilwoman with background research and made recommendations about positions she could take. He listened intently, modeling proper eye contact.

"So you researched and you recommended. Good. Would it be fair to say you *orchestrated* your office's response to the issues?"

"Well..."

"Would it be fair to say to you *led* these high-level strategy sessions?"

"I guess..."

Mr. Clark handed back my resume with a flourish. "Action verbs, people. The stronger and more active, the better. You didn't make copies at your last job, you mastered office technology to facilitate the smooth exchange of vital information. You didn't flip burgers, you ran the grilling station to ensure timely delivery and consistent quality. Now let's talk about the interview process."

He pressed a couple of my classmates into service to run through some mock scenarios. Once it was clear he was through with me, I zoned out for the duration, contemplating how I could spice up the farm's nascent mission statement with a few juicy action verbs: innovate, collaborate, germinate.

The second hour of the workshop turned out to be a self-directed session in the center's computer lab. I realized no one was going to be scrutinizing my paperwork. While the others bulked up their resumes and cruised the job boards, I checked email and political gossip. Mr. Clark was making the rounds, offering words of encouragement and advice—or rather *facilitating the job search process to ensure maximum productivity*—but he steered clear of me until the allotted time was up and I was heading for the door.

"Hope you don't mind me using you as an example back there," he said.

I told him I didn't. He lingered at my side.

"So you're in politics, then."

"Well, I was…"

"Come on, now. You're not going to have any trouble finding something. Between you and me, most of the people I work with, they're never going to have 'director' on their resume. 'Policy'? That's not even a word in their lexicon."

It seemed like Mr. Clark put a lot of stock in vocabulary. I considered telling him I was exiting the political arena voluntarily, but I decided to just smile politely instead. It felt like there was a right and wrong way to respond to this guy, and saying I was trying to break into farming definitely seemed like the wrong way.

"I've actually been planning to make a move into politics myself," Mr. Clark said.

Ah. I tried to fix an expression of cordial but mild interest on my face. Not sure if I succeeded, but it hardly mattered. Mr. Clark didn't need much encouragement.

"I've been a member of the Community Free Democrats for a couple of years now. My wife is telling people all the time, 'Bernard was out at that club of his again last night,' and they all think I'm partying! Anyway, maybe you and I could meet for coffee at some point, pick each other's brains. That's what it's all about, right? Building that network?"

I said my own job search was keeping me pretty busy, but the center had my contact information on file now, so he should feel free to get in touch if he needed anything. I told him he would go far in politics, and I meant it. An enthusiastic young man who could command a room and reel off sentences by the yard? He was going to be fine. We both were.

The Professionals

It was time to put our team together, caper movie style.

Of course, it started with a friend of Elliot's, a landscape architect who'd been involved in designing the most high-profile new park in memory. The High Line was a stretch of elevated freight rail, unused for decades, on the West Side of Manhattan. A neighborhood group led by a magazine writer and a consultant, with backing from the Bloomberg administration and Chelsea bigwigs like Diane von Furstenberg, were in the process of transforming it into one-and-a-half miles of grass, plants, and art installations. The first leg had opened the previous summer, and it was pretty sexy, like a MOMA annex dropped in a meadow—a meadow that just happened to be 30 feet off the ground. It was the beau ideal of Bloomberg's New York, free to one and all but with a sleek, exclusive feel. It almost pissed me off how much I admired it.

Needless to say, Elliot's friend was too busy to donate her services to our little project, but she knew a landscape designer named Seth Greenberg from architecture school and thought he was just what we were looking for. He'd recently started a company called Green 'Burgs—"I know, I know, but my mom likes it" was one of the first things he said to us—devoted to bringing "high-quality design and sustainable practices" to places that typically couldn't afford them: schools, senior centers, prisons. That was the idea, anyway. I couldn't tell if he'd had an opportunity to work his magic in any of those places yet. We promised to be just the high-profile client he needed to boost his visibility, which I suppose was why he was so excited to be working with us even though we weren't in a position to pay him anything close to the going commercial rate.

The Green 'Burgs offices were in a repurposed factory in Gowanus, an industrial no-man's land that realtors were strenuously trying to turn into a real place. Gowanus sat right between my neighborhood and Carroll Gardens where Elliot lived, yet I didn't even know the area had a name till a few months earlier. Why those vested with christening power chose to identify it with the Gowanus Canal—a festering toxic slurry, breeding ground for gonorrhea, last resting place of nautical wreckage (and the rare, improbable houseboat)—was a mystery to me. Maybe they figured it would provide just the right note of squalor to compete with Bushwick, but if so, they were underestimating the canal's power to offend the senses. On mild days, it was blanketed with an opaque, milky scum. When temperatures rose, it stank. It had even killed a baby minke whale; coined "Sludgie" by the blogs, he got stuck between the canal's banks and was presumably poisoned by the remnants of coal and petroleum that used to be processed there. Back in 2005, Whole Foods had bought up a huge swath of empty land for its first Brooklyn store, only to find out that the ground was contaminated and required years of heavy-duty environmental clean-up. It was difficult for me to picture a restaurant like Rita's or a bar like The Customs House moving in and turning the place into a hipster, and eventually yuppie, paradise.

Shows what I know. The reason Seth decided to base Green 'Burgs in Gowanus—aside from the cheap rent and the fact that it was exactly the kind of urban wasteland he hoped to revive—was that the factory (the landlords were calling it an "entrepreneurial incubator") was steps away from a new condo development that claimed to be "the most energy efficient and environmentally sustainable residential project in Brooklyn." More meaningful to space-starved sophisticates, the apartments were duplexes with private entrances and backyards—an impossibly precious luxury in the neighborhoods on either side of the canal. In Gowanus, the asking price was a comparatively reasonable $1 million. Who cared if those floor-to-ceiling windows looked out on a channel of iridescent muck, if July barbecues were pervaded by a foul effluvium? In New York, real estate is a force more inexorable than nature. The developers were heavily invested in the premise that Gowanus would be cleansed and their building would be the anchor of a thriving waterfront community. They were promising to throw Seth some work down the line.

As it was, there was something vaguely exciting about rambling through Gowanus in search of Green 'Burgs HQ. For years, I'd lived within walking distance, yet I'd always assumed the area was pretty much abandoned. Tricia worked with a shelter that was trying to get a handle on the feral cat population, but that was about all I knew. In the course of our wanderings, though, Elliot and I came across an art-gallery-cum-performance-space (full, at the time, of dense, apocalyptic line drawings); a bakery with tin ceilings, plank floors, and a crew of hot-yet-hospitable bakers (and hence our new regular meeting spot); a shop that sold only terrariums (the sign said, "imagine your world and let us create it for you"); a Zen meditation center. It was a self-contained little society of enterprising pioneers, Brooklyn's own Deadwood.

To the extent that Gowanus had a center, the incubator was it. Green 'Burgs' next-door neighbor was a respected indie hip-hop label. Upstairs was a start-up devoted to cutting-edge sneaker design (they published a slick zine for sneaker freaks out of the same space). Nobody was entirely sure what was going on the top floor, but Seth insinuated it was porn-related. Maybe one day, when we were managing a network of rooftop farms across the borough, Elliot and I would have our headquarters in this hive of industrious cool.

With Seth around, at least we wouldn't be the only bourgeois white boys. Earnest and enthusiastic, he was the kind of slightly doughy Jewish guy whose idea of being his own boss is wearing a Patrick Ewing jersey (over a T-shirt, of course) to the office. But that was fine by me. As far as I was concerned, the Rita's gang was giving us more street cred than we knew what to do with. Seth was just what we needed, an agreeable achiever out to do well by doing good (his words), a team player with the jersey to prove it. He was eager to take the brief we'd given him—to design a teaching farm as picture-perfect and state-of-the-art as the Living Classroom at a tenth of the cost—and run with it. In our first meeting, he was already sketching us pictures of bird feeders, a woven bamboo fence with pea shoots, a hoop house that could function as a winter classroom.

The first step was to make sure the Begin to Win roof was structurally sound and could handle the weight of the farm and all those half-pint farmers. That's where Twitchy came in. A Mormon recently relocated from Salt Lake, Twitchy was a structural engineer but for some reason looked like a collage of '50s style: rockabilly pompadour, Buddy Holly hornrims, black skinny jeans, cowboy boots. Seth found him on some engineering message board. We called him Twitchy because he seemed to be in a constant, low-pitched struggle to master his nerves. The steel toe of his boot was always tapping, his head always darting as if he'd just caught sight of something shiny out of the corner of his eye. In combination with the pompadour, it gave him a birdlike quality.

He'd come from Utah to work for one of the big architecture firms, where for six months he'd done nothing but check blueprints for measurement errors. Suffice to say, he didn't need to be convinced to donate his services pro bono. He even took a sick day to meet us and check out the roof.

He'd asked us to bring the blueprints so he could come up with a game plan. If they were sufficiently detailed they might be enough to satisfy the insurance company. I was embarrassed the issue of insurance hadn't crossed my mind until then, doubly embarrassed there was a problem with the blueprints. Edgar the maintenance chief hadn't been able to track them down.

"They weren't in the drawer where they're supposed to be," he told us when we called for an update. I thought about the stacks of paper forming a kind of bureaucratic Stonehenge on and around Principal Jenner's desk—what were the chances of finding them there? Elliot enlisted a drinking buddy at the Department of

Buildings to see if he could locate the copy on file with the city, but said buddy didn't sound optimistic.

The lack of blueprints had set Twitchy off on a foot-tapping, head-jerking jag. "Right. Okay. Let me think. We'll have to do a stress test."

We said that sounded good to us and asked him what was involved.

"Well, normally you'd just use a bunch of weights, pile them up gradually so you can measure the stress on the beams. But we're not going to be able to get the weights all the way up here without a crane. Darn it!"

It was hard to figure how a guy could get so worked up without any caffeine in his system. Maybe it was characteristic of the trade. Makes sense that roof tester wouldn't be the mellowest of professions.

Twitchy went still for a moment. "I got it. We'll do a pool test. You get a bunch of kiddie pools and a hose, fill them up one by one. It's the same as the weights but without the transport problem."

Elliot was having a little trouble taking him seriously. "I get it. You just keep filling up pools till the roof collapses."

The mere suggestion seemed to horrify him. "Of course not."

He muttered something about putting tension sensors on the load-bearing beams in order to gauge the strain. I wanted to suggest we put a tension sensor on him but decided to let it go. Instead I asked whether he'd done a pool test before.

"I saw some kids do it in school. Didn't look too hard."

I gave the others a chance to say something, but if they had any misgivings, they were keeping them to themselves.

"I'm fine with waiting for the blueprints," Twitchy said. "I can analyze blueprints in my sleep."

I didn't doubt it. It actually sounded like he might be more comfortable waiting for the blueprints, but John, who had insisted on joining us, was shaking his head.

"No. We've got to move. I'm renegotiating with my suppliers based on this. I've got other restaurants that are interested in joining up. We can't miss the growing season."

That's how we ended up back on the roof the following day with a half dozen kiddie pools from a nearby Home Depot, Twitchy manning the hose while Edgar looked on, scratching behind his ear like he was witnessing an act of such bewildering stupidity he had no frame of reference for it. Seth was taking pictures with his phone; he maintained a slide show of his projects on the Green 'Burgs website. Elliot had rolled up his pants and was sitting with his feet in one of the pools, a beer at his side. John was surveying the scene with his hands on his hips, looking for all the world like he was supervising the rest of us. As for me, I was determined to take an interest in every aspect of the project, so I mostly just hovered over Twitchy's shoulder, asking questions about what was, in fact, a stupendously tedious procedure.

After a while, Edgar said, "I've got work to do," leaving the "unlike some people" implied, and took off. That prompted John to check his watch and say he had to get back to the restaurant. As soon as he was gone, Seth pulled me aside.

"Is he serious about renegotiating with his suppliers and all that?"

I said he was, though the question must have been rhetorical.

Anyone who'd spent any time at all with John had to know he was always serious.

"You guys realize this farm is never going to yield enough to supply a restaurant, right?"

I couldn't speak for Elliot, but I realized no such thing. I stared dully at Seth and waited for him to fill in the blanks.

"With this amount of square footage, even if you completely rocked the growing season, which never happens your first year, it just doesn't add up. I mean, maybe if you covered every inch in lettuce seed, you'd end up with enough for it to pay off. But we're envisioning more diversity, right? And then there's all the space you're giving up for the hoop house, the welcome circle—all the features that make it a great space for the kids. I mean, the kids are the priority, right?"

An image appeared before my eyes: elementary school children shuffling among tightly packed rows with baskets hanging from their spindly necks, picking lettuce for the boss man. I pinched the bridge of my nose to make it go away.

"This is all for the kids," I told him. "Don't worry about John. Just keep doing what you're doing."

It felt good to say. I tried not to think about the fact that John had put the kiddie pools—and all of Seth's up-front expenses—on his credit card.

* * *

Elliot didn't seem especially concerned about Seth's assessment when I recapped it for him at Flake, our bakery in Gowanus, the next day.

"You handled Seth the right way," he said, reading my unease as self-doubt. "He doesn't need to worry about John, and neither do we."

"You sure about that?"

"John's a big boy. If we don't produce enough to supply the restaurant, he won't be any worse off than he was before. And we'll still have a kick-ass program for Prometheus to bankroll."

I searched for flaws in Elliot's logic, couldn't find any, and took that as permission to let it go. I'd done my due diligence, and now there was other business to attend to. We were meeting Marnie to go over the marketing plan.

Marnie was Vivienne's director of communications back at the council. We tried telling Vivienne we didn't need Marnie's help, but she insisted. "Image is everything, boys. Leave it to a professional." Marnie must have been subjected to a similar arm-twisting session; she was the first person we'd roped into this project who didn't seem especially thrilled to give of her time. She stepped warily into Flake in her punishing red-and-black heels like she was stepping over a body.

"So this is how you do business these days? It's like the set of a zombie movie out there."

She slung her red leather tote bag over the back of her chair but left her sunglasses on, so making eye contact with the girl behind the counter was a challenge. I had to restrain myself from yanking her arm down when she raised two French-manicured fingers in a beckoning gesture. We'd only just begun to establish ourselves as regulars at Flake, and I didn't want to jeopardize our standing with the staff.

"You order up at the counter," Elliot said.

Somehow I could tell Marnie was rolling her eyes behind her shades. "Of course you do."

As soon as she settled in with a latte and a granola parfait, she started checking messages on her phone. "Sorry. Running your own shop is 24-7. But you must know that."

Marnie had started her career as a spin doctor for the pharmaceutical industry: *Sure, there have been isolated reports of change in eye color and suicidal ideation, but what we know for sure is that Humilify has provided relief to millions of Americans suffering from the pain and stigma of restless spleen syndrome*. That kind of thing. She'd always hoped Vivienne would run for mayor, giving her a wider stage for her sledgehammer rhetoric ("Look, it's not rocket science. Every child deserves a school with a working water fountain. Period."). That ship had sailed, of course, so now she was busy launching her own consulting firm called Marnie. That's "Marnie." with a period at the end of it.

Her plan, we suspected, was to lure potential clients by dangling the prospect of Vivienne as an endorser or spokeswoman. Which is why Vivienne could still force her to schlep from Tribeca to Gowanus to talk to us pro bono, the last thing she would ever do of her own free will.

"So tell me why anyone should care about your little garden," she said, mixing her parfait with a disturbing intensity.

"It's a farm," Elliot and I answered as one.

"What's the difference?"

I still wasn't one-hundred-percent sure of the answer, but I'd at least learned to anticipate the question. "A garden's for enjoyment, a farm's for work."

Marnie smirked. "Then how did you guys end up with one?"

We gave her the whole song and dance: model curriculum, cost-efficient design, supply chain, sustainability. She looked bored, and having delivered this litany at least half a dozen times now, I was beginning to share the sentiment. Maybe we needed her help after all.

"Frankly, I don't see a *there* there," she said, dipping into her bottomless bag of professional cant. "Maybe if you were rolling this out in twenty schools. Or you had the mayor standing with you. Whatever. You've certainly got Viv all hot and bothered."

"I don't know what she told you," Elliot said, "but we're not looking for a big marketing campaign."

"That's good because I've got real paying clients to deal with. What're you calling this thing?"

"You mean the farm?"

"That, too, but I'm talking about your company, nonprofit, whatever it is. You may not need a campaign, but you still need basic branding: a name, a tagline, a logo. Or are you planning to submit reports to funders with your names in the upper right-hand corner like you're in kindergarten?"

She had us there. Up till now, nobody had asked us for a name, so we hadn't given it any thought.

"We've been kicking some ideas around," I said. "We need something that puts us in the same conversation as Living Classroom—like the Planted Playground or Nature's Laboratory."

"How about getting kids in there somehow?" Elliot said. "Children's Harvest?"

"Kind of sounds like we're harvesting children for their organs."

Marnie pressed her palm into her forehead, like she was trying to force what she was hearing back out of her brain. "You don't want people to think you're copying your bigger, better-funded competitor, okay? What's your edge? What sets you apart?"

"We're cheaper," Elliot said.

"No. When you're talking about schools, cheaper isn't better. Where have you been?"

The conversation stalled. I felt like I had to break the silence. "Ours is on the roof."

Marnie looked up from her phone. "That's actually good. Kids on a roof. It's visual."

Elliot was tearing pieces off his napkin and working them into pellets between his fingers, like he was stockpiling for a literal spitball session. "Roof Runts?"

Marnie turned to me. "Is he serious?"

"We need to get the idea of the farm in there," I said. "Green, organic, sustainable, leafy, earthy…

"I've got it!" Marnie clapped her hands. The girl behind the counter shot us a dirty look, thinking it was another attempt to summon her. I tried to apologize with my eyes.

"Raise the Roof," Marnie said. It sounded like she wanted to add a "period" to the end.

She sat back and waited for the gush of appreciation. Elliot rooted through the scruff under his collar, his go-to stalling tactic. I let my head list from side to side, swaying between opposing thoughts.

Marnie crossed her arms. "What?"

"It's good," I started. "It's just kind of..."

"Patronizing?" Elliot finished the thought. "If we were starting a reading program, would you call it Word to Your Mother?"

"Don't be an idiot," Marnie said. "'Raise the Roof' is fun. 'Raise' is an inspiring word. It's got that Up with People vibe. And it works on two levels because you're raising vegetables."

"'Raise vegetables' doesn't sound right," I said. "You must be thinking of cattle."

"Will, I assure you I am not thinking of cattle."

Elliot wanted to keep fighting, but when Marnie demanded alternatives, we couldn't think of any. Raise the Roof was already growing on me anyway. We moved on to the tagline, Marnie now fully in charge.

"There's two ways to do this. There's the six-word description, this is who we are and what we do. Something like, 'Rooftop farms for kids and communities.' Kind of dull, but it gets the point across."

We nodded. Not bad.

"Then there's the 'Eat. Pray. Love.' approach, three words only. You could do nouns— Kids. Crops. Classes. But I prefer verbs— Plant. Teach. Grow."

She traced the words in the air, making a dot between each for the silent period.

Elliot shook his head. "No 'Eat. Pray. Love.' or I'm going to gag, puke...Will, what's one word for 'lose all self-respect'? 'Die inside' with a hyphen?"

"I think the descriptive approach works better for us," I said. "It's kind of a complicated idea to get into three words."

Marnie lowered her glasses, the better to look down her nose. "Yeah, real complicated. Why don't you call it The Will and Elliot Early Retirement Plan, backed by Viv?"

Elliot gave her the finger. "You should talk. You've probably already sold her endorsement in the next election. Or maybe she can be the first female spokesman for boner pills..."

"Actually, if you must know, I'm getting a chair at Baruch named after her. How's that?"

"I don't know. Is it a nice chair? Does it recline?"

"An endowed chair in public policy and urban affairs. Anyway, what've you got? A pile of dirt on a roof in a place nobody's heard of? Maybe you can call it Viv's Pile."

"Tommy Brutti's probably going to want us to put his name on it," I said. "Or Martin Gollick, since he's giving the most."

Marnie's face froze. "You didn't tell me you got Tommy Brutti and Martin Gollick on board."

"We have trouble keeping track of all our donors," Elliot said. "You know how it is."

If she was chastened, she didn't show it. As always, Marnie was all forward momentum.

"This changes things. With names like that, you're going to want to do an announcement and some kind of event, a party, a ribbon-cutting ceremony..."

"Is there even time?" I said. "We've got to be up and running by May."

"You're going to need to start sending out invitations within the next week or two if you expect anybody with any juice to show up."

Elliot scowled, a rare look for him. "You're cordially invited to our pile of dirt in a place nobody's heard of?"

"Just let me handle it," Marnie said, already working her phone with both thumbs.

"So you can invite everyone on your hit list of potential clients?"

"My hit list is all the people you want talking about Raise the Roof. Come on, you know Viv is going to agree with me."

There was no doubt about that. In Vivienne's world, there was no good deed that didn't warrant a party. And the more I thought about it, the better I liked the idea of a formal kick-off to announce our presence in the Triangle and on the urban farming scene. To salvage Elliot's pride, I insisted on a sober tagline: "School-based agriculture for urban communities." Marnie sketched out a logo concept on a napkin, a grid pattern with interspersed blocks of green representing a network of rooftop farms. I had to admit, it was good. She later turned it over to the graphic designer on her team who preserved the rough quality of the sketch, giving the finished logo the rustic look of a woodblock print.

Marnie was exultant on the phone when she sent us the mock-up of our stationary and website banner.

"Congratulations," she said. "You're a brand."

Till the Revolution Comes

We had a name, a tagline, and a logo. We had an anchor donor with bottomless pockets, a matching grant from a famous name, and a planning grant from the city's most powerful foundation. We would soon have a logic model, a curriculum, and a website.

The logic model was proving to be a major undertaking. Brad at Prometheus had sent me the "toolkit" he mentioned in our meeting, but it turned out to be just a piece of software on the Prometheus website that allowed you to arrange a series of color-coded bubbles under the headings "Inputs," "Outputs," and "Outcomes" and draw arrows between them: "advice from curriculum development experts" (input) leads to "standards-based science and art lessons" (output) leads to "increased test scores" (outcome). Tricia called it wonk Sudoku.

After a couple of days, my dreams were haunted by bubbles and arrows. I decided I needed a few examples of A+ logic models I could crib from. Brad said it wasn't the foundation's place to "prescribe the process" and suggested I hit up our "peers in the field" directly.

Our peers in the field weren't much help, though. Living Classroom was as unresponsive to my calls as ever; Duncan at In It Together was solicitous and unexpectedly guarded at the same time. "Dude, I've been there. Fucking logic model, right? I sweated blood over ours. That's the thing. You put in all that time and effort, and you start to get proprietary about it. Not that I ever even look at the fucking thing, but you don't want anyone else looking at it either. Kind of like the Colonel's secret recipe." Wasn't this the guy who told us, "You help the people who need your help"?

Elliot, meanwhile, was busy hammering out Raise the Roof's curriculum, our bid for innovator status. He cc'd me on epic email threads with his former academic advisors and their colleagues, who seemed more than willing to lend their expertise, especially once they heard that Prometheus and Martin Gollick were involved. I tried to keep up with the discussion, like I was auditing a particularly abstruse seminar, but most of the details whizzed over my head. Before long I was just skimming, content in the knowledge that we had our very own brain trust, and it was deep in cogitation, hashing out the appropriate "dosage" of farm time for each age group (one hour three times a week or three hours once a week?); shuffling the sequence of activities so they would "facilitate project-based learning"; debating which benefits to aim for, "intrinsic" (fresh air, exposure to the wonderful world of salad fixings) or "instrumental" (an up-close lesson in photosynthesis). I was confident we'd have the most pedagogically sophisticated vegetable patch around.

The website was Marnie's doing, or more likely a flunky at "Marnie."'s doing. Either way, it was pretty slick. There was a flash animation version of our logo on the welcome page, the green blocks on the grid filling in one by one. There was a meet the team section with bios of me, Elliot, Seth, even Kat, who was identified as Raise the Roof's "administrative director and chief gardener." I had no idea where that came from. The news section already had one post, a "sneak peek" of Seth's design for the site. The blog so far consisted only of photos of Rita's and Begin to Win. It was up to me and Elliot to keep it fresh.

"Just be conversational," Marnie said. "'Great meeting with Tommy Brutti today...Heirloom tomatoes or green beans: tell us what you think...So psyched for spring!' That kind of shit. Lots of pictures." I swore I'd try to take it seriously.

Everything was going so swimmingly, I was almost excited when I found we had a problem to solve.

"Arthur and Barbara don't want it on the roof anymore."

Vivienne was calling from Palm Beach; an esteemed designer of ladies' evening wear was weekending there with his children, and they needed a fourth for tennis.

"What?"

"They say the community won't get anything out of it if it's on the roof."

"Just tell them that's what the green market is for."

"Don't try to be reasonable. What they really want is for it to be at eye level so anyone passing by can see what a wonderful thing they're doing for the children."

"No one ever passes by."

"Well, that's not what they think. And it's their roof."

"We did tests. The architect has been planning for that space."

"If he's any kind of architect he knows that plans change.

Changing plans is more or less his job."

"We're called Raise the Roof." The hinge of my jaw was starting to throb. "We have a website. We ordered business cards."

I could hear the thwack of racket on ball. Was she playing while she was talking?

"That's a good name. You should keep it."

"It won't make sense."

"Coca-Cola doesn't have cocaine in it anymore, but they kept the name because it's catchy. Speaking of, would you be a dear and fetch me a Coke on ice?"

That last part couldn't be addressed to me, but it sure sounded like it was. I could feel the zest for problem-solving dribble out of me. I tried to will it back.

"All right, fine. No roof. Do they have any suggestions of where else we can put a half-acre farm?"

"Actually, they do. They want you to put it in Peter's Place."

"Who's Peter?"

"How should I know? Peter's Place is what they call that dreary little playground with the handball court. Hello? Still there?"

I'd gone silent because I was genuinely befuddled by the suggestion. "I don't get it. They want us to uproot the playground? That's supposed to make the community happy?"

"You don't need to uproot anything. They say there's a ring of grass around the blacktop. You can plant your vegetables in that."

"Viv, the school used to be a drug factory. The ground is probably full of chemicals."

"Even better." *Thwack!* "Nothing brings a community together like a nice environmental cleanup."

I was starting to wonder if the thwacking sound was coming from inside my own head. "Arthur and Barbara know the playground doesn't belong to them, right? It's Parks Department property."

But nothing was going to throw Vivienne off her game. I realized she wasn't even breathing hard.

"Well, that's not an issue," she said. "We'll just talk to Jack."

* * *

That's how the whole team—me, Elliot, John, Seth, Twitchy, and Kat—wound up in Peter's Place with Jack, a Parks lifer Vivienne knew from her days with the Central Park Conservancy. Jack was the city's bureaucracy made flesh, not that there was much flesh to him, mostly just yellowing skin and rickety bone. He looked like a civics teacher circa 1962: flattop, short-sleeve button down—with a pocket protector no less!—orthopedic shoes. He seemed content to contemplate the smoke from his cigarette while the rest of us sized up our predicament.

John's temper was as close to the surface as I'd ever seen it. "No. Not enough space, not enough control. It's got to be the roof."

Twitchy picked up a square plastic wrapper, then quickly threw it away, wiping his hand on his pants. "If you're looking for my recommendation, I say do it here. From a child safety perspective, it's the best bet."

I was getting the impression he wasn't a hundred percent confident in his jerry-rigged stress test.

"Not if the ground's contaminated with Pfizer's backwash," Elliot said.

Jack spoke in a papery rasp without looking any of us in the eye. “We tested the soil years ago when the playground was first built. Came back clean, believe it or not.”

I asked Seth what he thought.

“Less space, no way around it. Funky shape, too. We'd have to completely rework the design. But this is supposed to be about serving the community, right?”

John took a step closer to him, carefully parceling out his aggression. “You know the community's not paying you, right?”

Before I knew it, I had wedged myself between the two of them. “It's the Schlossers' school, remember? And they want it here.”

John eyed me like he was thinking about removing me from his path. “I'll talk to them. We made a connection.”

“No way. We've got to speak with one voice.”

Kat had drifted over to the gate to talk to a woman in an army surplus coat walking a bedraggled black lab. She made her way back to the group, unaware of the pissing contest she was interrupting.

“She wanted to know what we were doing. She said it sounded like a good idea, but only if there's a dog run. This is where everyone brings their dogs to poop.”

Twitchy winced. “I noticed.”

Jack's cigarette had disappeared between his thumb and index finger, but he seemed reluctant to dispose of the butt. “Look, gentlemen,”—either Kat was exempt from what he had to say or he'd granted her honorary gentleman status—“I think I can make this easier for you. We're not going to be able to let you use the swale.”

My head snapped back. “When we talked on the phone, you said it wouldn't be a problem.”

"I didn't think it would be. But I hadn't been out this way since—I'm ballparking here—the late '80s. I'd never seen those."

At first, I couldn't figure out what he was pointing at. "You mean the trees?"

There were three of them, scraggly pines with sallow bark. One of them was barely taller than Twitchy. A second was drooping morbidly, nearly bent double.

"Not much to look at, I know," Jack said. "But the mayor's got his million tree initiative. The Million Tree March, I like to call it."

He waited, without much hope, it seemed, for the laugh he desired.

"Every tree in this city is counted toward that goal, gentlemen, and Parks is under strict orders not to remove a single one of them."

The whole group was momentarily united in its stupefaction.

"You've got to be kidding," I said.

"You realize they actually make the neighborhood more depressing," Elliot said.

"I can put in something a hundred times nicer," Seth said.

"Fucking government," John said.

Jack placed the cigarette butt in his pocket protector. Far be it from him to litter in the presence of three of Bloomberg's million trees.

"I should have said from the beginning, Parks would like to see this happen," he said. "And if it's going to happen, we'd like it to be as accessible to the community as possible."

I made a point of not looking at John.

"To be completely honest, we forgot that Peter's Place existed,"

Jack said. "Don't even ask me who Peter is because I have no idea. I feel a personal responsibility to spruce things up a little here."

"But the trees..." Twitchy said.

Jack held up a hand, appealing for patience. "If I may, I have an alternative suggestion."

He looked off into the distance, and we waited, until we realized we were supposed to follow his gaze, that his suggestion lay on the other side of the chain link fence, behind the swale.

I ventured a guess since no one else was volunteering. "The handball court?"

"You've been out here how many times?" Jack asked. "A dozen?"

That was a bit of an overestimate, but we nodded anyway.

"And have you seen a single person playing handball in this court?"

I was under the impression you needed more than a single person to play, but I grasped his point. I couldn't claim to have paid any attention to the court specifically, but I couldn't recall anyone using it either.

"And do you know why that is?" Jack was enjoying himself now. "Because there's another handball court six blocks away from here. A much better one. No cracks, no graffiti, no condom wrappers lying around. Gentlemen, it is the official judgment of the Parks Department that this court is abandoned and in need of revitalization. We'd like Raise the Roof farms—cute name, by the way—to take responsibility for that."

With that, he drew a fresh cigarette from his pocket protector and lit up with a disposable Bic. It was clear that he would just silently savor his smoke until we came up with a response.

Seth was the first to speak. "This is a new one for me. Are you sure it's cool for us to take over a public amenity?"

Jack answered with an equivocal tilt of the head. "We'll go to the community board for approval, of course. That's a given. But look at what's here now. Hard to argue your garden wouldn't be an improvement."

"It's a farm." Elliot beat me to it.

Jack raised his hand, begging our pardon. He was able to wring many meanings from the same basic gesture and always be understood. "Terrific. And a farm needs space. The court will give you just as much square footage as the roof."

"What about the wall?" Twitchy asked, probably anxious he'd have to figure out how to get rid of it.

Seth ambled over to the fence, heeding the call of destiny. "The wall is the best thing about the space. It gives it history, authenticity. Picture a ten-foot trellis covered with hanging vines, beans, peas, tomatoes."

Elliot joined him, stepping over the offering left by the black lab. "The kids could paint a mural on the other side. For some reason, I'm seeing Johnny Appleseed with Jay-Z's face."

Kat was snapping pictures with her phone. "What about rainwater collection? You could put cisterns on top of the building next door and run a pipe down to the court. Landlords get an abatement for that. I read about it for one of my classes. And that way, you'll still have something on a roof, so the name won't sound so wack."

I wasn't sure if I wanted to kiss her or Elliot for hiring her. The rapt looks on Elliot and Seth's faces suggested they were feeling the same.

John was keeping his own counsel. Elliot gave him a tentative thumbs-up and raised his eyebrows to make it a question.

"This community board thing," John said. "Any way around that?"

Jack inspected the ash accruing at the end of his cigarette. "Let's put it this way. The decision ultimately rests with us, and the decision is made. But we're more comfortable moving forward with projects that have the community's seal of approval."

All eyes, except Jack's, were on John.

"I don't want to fall down the rabbit hole," he said.

"Nothing to worry about. I'll be there to help you grease the skids. And aren't these two"—Jack waved in the direction of me and Elliot—"Vivienne's protégés? They must know their way around a community board."

I locked eyes with John. "Trust us. We know how to handle this."

His nod was almost imperceptible, but somehow Jack picked up on it with his back turned.

"Right, then. I'll see about getting you on the agenda for the next meeting. In the meantime, we'll set you up with a community garden license. My colleague Winston will take care of that. You may need a school garden license, too. Winston will know. Once you're licensed, we can supply you with soil, tools, whatever we've got lying around really. You'll be part of the family."

Maybe that should've made us think twice, especially Elliot and me, who knew firsthand that, as families go, city government is more Borgia than Cleaver. But really, what was there to think about? The Schlossers, Twitchy, that tree-hugger Bloomberg, even John—it looked like everyone was going to get what they wanted.

* * *

Winston from GreenThumb—the city's community garden program—was a reedy young black guy with sleepy eyes, a goatee, and a houndstooth newsie cap.

"So you guys want to join the movement, eh?" That was his opening line when he met us at the handball court later that week.

"You know it," I said, though I wasn't exactly clear on what he was talking about.

"Cool. I like to make sure people know their history before they sign up. It's a lot to live up to."

We agreed maybe a bit too eagerly. Winston sized us up. "You know, this shit is personal to me. My moms was a Green Guerilla back in the day, throwing seed bombs over the fence in Bed-Stuy."

Lucky for us, it wasn't hard to get him going on the subject, and soon enough we were fully up to speed on the Green Guerilla movement. Apparently, during the fiscal crisis of the '70s, when the city was a patchwork of vacant lots and bombed-out buildings, neighborhood activists would pack balloons with tomato seeds, fertilizer, and water and then chuck them over barbed wire, rogue acts of beautification. Liz Christy, the founder of the Green Guerillas and a friend of Winston's mom, took over a lot on the Bowery in 1974 and eventually convinced the powers that be to lease it to her for a $1 a month: the city's first official community garden. GreenThumb came along a few years later. The Guerillas were still around, too, only now they were more into plant giveaways than seed bombings. I wondered what they'd make of our plans for the handball court, the welcome circle, and the woven bamboo fence. So much for the days of pelting the concrete with dirt and seeds till something sprouted.

Winston clearly longed for that grimy, anarchic era. A lot of city kids I knew who came of age in the Giuliani years felt like they'd missed out on all that crazy, rip-it-up-and-start-again energy. Most pined for Television, Spoonie Gee, and Basquiat. For Winston, it was Liz Christy and the Guerillas. Elliot said something flattering about him carrying on his mother's legacy, and a faraway look came over him.

"Yeah, it's deep. Really, though, I don't believe in change from within the system. I'm just doing this till the revolution comes."

Fair enough. Winston inspected the handball court and made some desultory checkmarks on his clipboard. "This would be a great spot for growing weed. You'd probably need armed guards, though."

I could tell Elliot wanted to follow up on that suggestion, but the window of opportunity closed quickly.

"What are you guys planning to do for water?" he asked.

It was an issue we hadn't really thought through clearly since the big change in plans. I mentioned Kat's rainwater collection idea.

Winston smoothed his goatee. "Cool, cool. But it's not going to be enough to get by on." He flipped through the papers on his clipboard. "My records say there's a pipe somewhere under the playground. They probably thought about putting in a fountain at some point. I'm telling you straight-up, though, Parks would have to tear up the whole place to find it. I don't want that shit and neither do you."

We nodded. No way was I telling the community board we were going to have to destroy the neighborhood's only playground to water our radicchio.

Winston peered through the chain link at something on the other side of the street. "There's a fire hydrant over there. Problem is, you have to call the firehouse every time you need water. If they're good dudes and you bring them some beers every now and then, they may come when you call. Then again, they may not."

We told him that sounded less than ideal.

"Some gardens have permission to open the hydrant themselves, but it looks like they put a custodian lock on this one. Too many block parties in the summer. What do they expect? It's not like there's a pool anywhere in walking distance. But that's the man for you."

"Can't they just give us a key to the lock?" I asked.

"You need a magnetic wrench to get it off."

"So can they give us a magnetic wrench, then?"

Winston shoulders rose so slightly I could hardly tell he was laughing at me. "They've probably only got the one. They're custom made to fit the lock. Cost a few thousand each."

"A few thousand?"

"If I were you, I'd make friends with whoever owns this place"—he nodded towards the building next door—"and if you can't make friends with them, make friends with someone who lives there and knows where they keep the hose."

"Guerilla style," I said.

Winston didn't answer. Whether it was a you-didn't-hear-it-from-me silence or a how-dare-these-white-boys-appropriate-my-mother's-legacy silence was hard to say.

* * *

Before Winston could issue us a license, we needed to collect signatures from the farm's ten charter members. We tried to explain that this wasn't to be a traditional community garden, that the primary users would be the Begin to Win students and teachers, but he didn't seem particularly interested. Dude was a revolutionary in waiting, but when it came to the execution of his GreenThumb duties, rules were rules. Not that the signatures represented a major hurdle; really, we could have just rounded up Seth, Twitchy, Kat, Edgar, and the teachers Elliot had gotten to know at the school and called it day. (Something told me John would be cagey about signing an official document, however benign.)

But why pass up an opportunity to introduce ourselves to the neighborhood? We decided that we'd canvass the building next door first, since we needed to figure out the situation with the hose anyway. Buzzing various apartments didn't get us anywhere. Either everyone was at work or the intercom was broken. Peering into the narrow, unlit vestibule, it was hard to escape the impression that the place wasn't kept up too well. The linoleum was dingy and peeling. The garbage cans around back were uncovered.

I'd be lying if I said I was expecting the first tenant we encountered to be a willowy white girl with waist-length hair pushing a vintage Schwinn, a rolled up canvas balanced atop the basket. She was a Pratt graduate named Sasha, and she was psyched about the farm.

"Not much going on to make this feel like a real community," she said. As our chat went on, she mentioned that she was also a part-time art teacher at Begin to Win.

"Didn't you hear about us from Principal Jenner or the teachers on the farm committee?" Elliot asked.

Sasha shrugged. "They don't tell us anything. Honestly, it's kind of a shit show over there. I try to just keep my head down."

Sasha was soon joined by Xander, a cartoonist she knew from Pratt. Xander had a bleach blonde crew cut and a skateboard with a Keith Haring design. We seemed to have stumbled on a den of slumming artists. Xander said he spent most of his time at a studio space he shared with some of the other residents, but he was happy to help out whenever he was around. "I'm all for it. About time someone did something about that situation." I wouldn't have said the state of the handball court was so bad it constituted a "situation," but then again, I didn't live next to it. Sasha and Xander both signed on to be members of the farm and said they'd spread the word. Neither had any insight into the whereabouts of the hose.

Around lunchtime, a black SUV rolled up, and out of it stepped a young Hasid in shirtsleeves, a black fedora fighting the jack-in-the-box trajectory of his ginger curls. "There's our landlord," Elliot whispered as he crossed the street towards us. He was smiling, but he didn't extend his hand as he approached.

"You fellas were here yesterday, looking around." Apparently, we'd already succeeded in establishing our presence in the neighborhood. "You with the city?"

We explained what we were up to. As he listened, he tugged absently at one of his sidelocks.

"A garden, huh? That's good. Because this"—he waved at the handball court—"this is a problem for me."

He didn't say why it was a problem, and we didn't ask. Maybe his "problem" was the same as Xander's "situation." Whatever the case, it was promising for us.

"Will you be installing a gate in the fence," the landlord asked. I hadn't noticed till then that the entrance to the court was just a gap in the chain link. "Believe me, you need one around here. Razor wire and cameras, too, if you want to protect your investment."

We agreed a gate was a must but let the other suggestions lie.

"And what would you think of a second gate connecting my courtyard to your garden?"

By "courtyard," he could only mean the back alley with the uncovered garbage cans, separated from the handball court by another length of chain link, which was indeed topped with razor wire. I was starting to see why he was so interested in our little project. Elliot told him the farm—he made sure to emphasize the word—would be full of children from the school most of the time and therefore off-limits to other visitors. The landlord didn't seem particularly fazed.

"So evenings and weekends, then. We'll just put up a sign with the hours and tell them not to eat the kiddies' asparagus."

"It's an intriguing idea," I said, measuring the words. But not a very good one, I added silently.

The landlord laid one hand on my shoulder and the other on Elliot's. "Sure it is. You get your water supply—and water isn't cheap these days, believe me—plus whatever you want to do up on the roof. Sounds kooky, but what do I know? I'm no farmer." He gave the word "farmer" a little extra tickle. "And I get the only property in the neighborhood with garden access for every tenant."

"The main thing you'll be getting is a major tax abatement," I said.

The landlord nodded. "The tax abatement *and* garden access. Everybody wins."

"By law, we can only grant access to people who sign up to become members." I was pretty sure what I was saying wasn't true, but I didn't want to give in just yet. "At the very least, you'll have the only building in the neighborhood with garden views."

The landlord pursed his lips. "You just put in the gate, and we'll work out the details. You've met them, my tenants? They're good kids. They get a little crazy, some of them, with the piercings and the tattoos, but they're all from solid families. Everyone who knows me knows: I only rent to good people."

That this was code was lost on none of us. I had the urge to walk away from the deal, but instead I grit my teeth and shook the landlord's hand. We'd have to revise Seth's assignment: give the farm enough wow-factor to make it a model for schools across the nation but not so much that it would give the landlord an excuse to jack up the rent on our new artist friends. Was that even possible?

"Please tell me this is going to be worth it," I said to Elliot as we parted ways with the landlord.

He tousled my hair like I was his youthful ward. "Pizza time, kemosabe."

Shovel Ready

There was a notable new addition to the decor at Rita's: scattered across the communal tables was a herd of ceramic piggy banks, painted gold with Chinese characters on the side, probably bought in bulk at Pearl River Mart. A handwritten label stuck on our piggy's flank said, "Don't be such a tightwad. Help us build a kickass farm and bring REAL FOOD to the people!" I had questions, naturally—Did Elliot know? How much money had John raised? Where was the money? Was anybody keeping the books?—and I was in the mood for a principled confrontation to make up for our vaguely grubby negotiation with the landlord. John, however, was nowhere to be found. Instead, we got Greta, Tommy Brutti consigliere by day, rock-and-roll pizza slinger by night, only it was mid-afternoon and here she was in stonewash jeans and a muscle shirt so faded I couldn't make out the band logo. Hard to tell if she was on the clock, and if so, for whom.

"I'm supposed to be meeting with John, but he's too busy running shit," she said. "That's cool, though. I needed to talk to you guys anyway. Tommy's not happy."

This came as a surprise. On TV, Tommy always seemed happy, aggressively so.

"He wants to know what happened with the roof. He was *very* excited about the roof."

We explained the situation: the thought of sequestering the farm high above the ground where average folk couldn't reach made the Schlossers' big hearts hurt. Fortunately, the handball court was turning out to be an exciting prospect; our partnership with Parks was adding another level of innovation and collaboration to the whole shebang. It was an impressive spin—at least I thought it was. Greta seemed unmoved.

"Reclaimed space, that was one of your major selling points."

"The handball court is reclaimed space," I said. "It's abandoned."

"It's *a* reclaimed space. But how many abandoned handball courts could there be? We were talking about every school in the city having a rooftop farm. 'Fuck the supply chain.' Tommy loved that."

I wanted to remind her that those were John's words, not ours, but it didn't seem like it would be helpful. I said once the pilot was up and running there was nothing to prevent us from replicating the model on rooftops.

"So maybe get back to us when you're ready to take that step. Because that's really Tommy's interest here."

"I thought his interest was helping kids."

It was out before I could stop myself. Greta, to her credit, didn't rise to the bait. Instead, her expression softened, and she adopted a gentler tone.

"Look, I'm sorry it has to be this way. It sucks. Normally, I'd try to fix this, but between you and me, he's really pissed he didn't hear it directly from you. He's used to having a say."

It hadn't occurred to me to ask how he'd found out. I was about to, but Elliot stepped in, offering to apologize directly to Tommy if it would help.

Greta shook her head. "It won't. Just this morning he was saying, 'Their name is Raise the motherfucking Roof, for Christ's sake.' He thinks you tried to mislead him."

I was starting to babble about how technically the name was still valid because of the rainwater cisterns, but she cut me off.

"Look at it from his perspectives. The foundation's brand new. This was going to be his first big project. But if he's not all in, he's not going to dip a toe. The man's just not a toe-dipper."

I was no longer entirely sure what she was talking about, but it hardly mattered. I asked her if Tommy could at least keep his decision quiet for now; I didn't want the other funders, least of all Prometheus, to find out we'd lost our matching grant. She assured us he'd forget we ever existed by tomorrow.

"Now, let's get wasted, so we can go back to being friends."

Elliot was game, as always, but between the landlord's garden access, Tommy Brutti's reclaimed space, and those golden piggies with their cartoon eyes, I just wasn't in the mood. Some of us, I said, had a community board meeting to prep for.

* * *

Community Board 3 met in a low-ceilinged office space above the

Applebee's on Fulton Street, a far cry from the auditorium where Vivienne faced the most active of her well-heeled constituents. The room was jammed with concerned citizens, standing room only, with board members seated behind three long folding tables arranged in a horseshoe. The only white people were Seth, Elliot, and me. There was one bodybuilder type who was paler than us, but I was pretty sure he was albino.

Fortunately, our delegation had come with an ambassador: Winston was stepping in for Jack, who wouldn't be joining us, after all. We didn't find out until we arrived at the meeting, and Winston had no explanation for us, but we were so relieved to have him in our corner, we weren't even put out. He was wearing a Comandante Biggie T-shirt: the Notorious B.I.G. with epaulettes and a Che cap.

Tonight was the Parks, Recreation, Arts & Culture committee's show, and we were the second item on the agenda. The first was a review of various applications for block parties and street festivals, and it was hard to follow. What I gathered was this: Apparently, there can only be a certain number of block parties in a given district on a given day, and now that spring was upon us, the competition was fierce. Certain upstart blocks had dared to apply for the same day as other blocks with longer-running, better-established parties. A woman with speckled skin and reddish hair suggested with a vaguely Caribbean lilt that the upstarts had no respect for history. Her counterpart on Team Upstart wasn't hearing that. A more energetic woman, her copious beaded braids danced when she spoke.

"This ain't about what someone was doing thirty years ago, Bernice. This is about the young people. We're always saying there's nothing positive for the young people to do. How are we supposed to get them off the corner with the same tired old booths selling hair oil and tube socks?"

That earned a few titters of recognition. Bernice wanted to respond, but the upstart was prepared to filibuster. "Poetry slam, African dance, basketball tournament. That's what we're proposing."

Entertaining stuff. You didn't get this kind of turf war in Vivienne's district, where a spring party was more likely to involve a ballroom than a bounce house, and "the young people" included anyone not collecting social security. The chair of the committee, on the other hand, seemed less than enthralled. Portly with a silent movie villain's pencil mustache and sweat beading on his bald pate, he interrupted to ask the upstart if she'd actually talked to any teens to gauge their enthusiasm for poetry slams and African dance.

"No disrespect, Suzette, but these young people today, they may not be any more interested in poetry than they are in tube socks."

There were some sighs and tsks from the assembly. These kids today…

"You tell 'em Jay-Z is a poet, they'll come."

Old guard Bernice made a face like she'd caught a whiff of something funky. "Might as well have a crack-dealing contest."

The chairman didn't seem convinced by either side. He moved to postpone the vote so the committee could review the applications more carefully. He was seconded by the maybe-albino, and the combatants withdrew grumbling to their corners.

Our turn. Winston gave us the signal, and we shuffled up through the crowd to face the committee. We waited while the chairman blotted his glistening brow with a hanky, to little effect.

He eyed the hanky as if it might be defective before giving up altogether and making the introductions.

"A lot of you know Winston. He's always coming around bugging us for one thing or another."

A chorus of chuckles, and a good-sport smile from Winston.

"He's here tonight with these gentlemen from"—he consulted his notes—"Raise the Roof Farms to talk about a new program they're doing with the Parks Department."

Winston half turned so he could address both the committee and the audience. He spoke just as softly as he did in one-on-one conversation; several of the older folks had to lean in to hear. "Thanks to all of you for having us here tonight. As the chairman said, you all know me. Bed-Stuy has some of the oldest and most progressive gardens in the city. I know it seems like I'm always hanging around, but really I'm just trying to keep up with y'all."

"No harm in trying, son," someone shouted. All around us, I could see shoulders loosening and faces opening. Whatever Jack's contribution might have been, we couldn't have asked for a better representative than Winston.

"I want to take a second to recognize Miss Lorraine, who's joining us tonight. Miss Lorraine has been gardening over on Lafayette for, what, thirty years?"

All eyes turned to a small, plump-faced, turtlenecked woman, her silver hair pulled back in an unforgiving bun. "Forty," she said, her voice as taut as her 'do.

"Forty years," Winston marveled, shaking his head. "And I know some of you have been a part of this movement for nearly as long. These men here are the next generation of community gardeners, and they're looking to you for inspiration and guidance. I'll let them explain their vision and then give you a chance to share your wisdom with them."

I was up first. We'd agreed to start with my food desert bit, but it didn't seem to be making much of an impression on the good people of CB3. Should have led with the kids. I decided to cut it short and turn the floor over to Elliot, but if he managed to win them over, they didn't show it. Seth wrapped up with a presentation of the latest schematics, and he certainly gave it the old college try. He was honored to add to the community's rich tradition of green activism, humbled by the responsibility, excited to take counsel from Miss Lorraine and her apostles. Whether the feeling was mutual was hard to tell; Miss Lorraine's face didn't move once during the presentation. It's possible the torque of her bun limited her range of expression.

Throughout our presentation, the chairman squinted at us as if we were specks in the distance.

"I didn't hear you mention where this Peter's Place is at. Can't say I'm familiar."

We told him the cross streets, which got a blank look. So we referenced the Broadway Triangle; that didn't seem to do the trick either. Finally, we name-checked the hospital and the projects, and the chairman nodded impatiently.

"Now we're getting somewhere. And you say this is Peter's Place? Anybody know a Peter lives down in Marcy Houses?"

I started to explain that no one could remember the exact origins of the name, but he cut me off. "That was a joke, son."

I could feel the heat on my ears and neck.

"You know, this area you're talking about is more Williamsburg than Bed-Stuy. Have you got the folks in District 1 with you?"

I said that, since the proposed site was actually in District 3, we thought it important to come here first and consult the community board with jurisdiction. The reasonableness of this explanation didn't seem to move the chairman.

"I understand, but there's jurisdiction and then there's what we call facts on the ground. You follow?"

I didn't. Were we talking about a little urban renewal project in Brooklyn or negotiating peace between the Israelis and Palestinians?

A hand shot up. It belonged to Suzette, the upstart. She didn't wait for the chairman to recognize her. "I have to say, I'm disturbed by what I'm hearing. The young people in this community—*our* young people—they need support, they need programs, they need positive outlets. So why are we talking about sending our precious resources to Williamsburg?"

There were murmurs of agreement from the crowd, a sleeper stirred by an upsetting dream. Winston's eyes were hooded. I knew a bureaucrat feigning contemplation when I saw one.

"We're actually not talking about sending resources outside the district," I said. "The farm is going to be inside your district."

Suzette bowed up, her hands on her hips. "Not unless we say it is."

The tendon in my jaw was so tight, I was afraid it might snap. "That's why we're here." I left out the "obviously."

Elliot took the wheel and tried to steer us away from the ditch. He pointed out that we weren't asking for any community resources. The beauty of the project was that we'd already raised outside funding and would be investing it in the community.

"In *Williamsburg*," Suzette said.

Seth's turn. Maybe he could honor and humble our way out of this shit show.

"What I'm hearing is that the folks in this room don't feel a sense of connection with the folks in the Triangle," he said. "Part of what we're trying to do at Green 'Burgs is help make those connections. That's why I'm so excited about this project. It's a chance to build a bridge between communities. And since the school we're partnering with is a charter, kids and families from neighborhoods across the city are going to benefit."

My stomach dropped. Elliot stared straight ahead, a mutineer about to walk the plank. I really thought Seth had it there for a second with his sense of connection and his bridge between communities; I could see on his face that he did, too. Poor bastard didn't even realize he'd said the magic word.

I swear Suzette's eyes lit up. "So all these resources you're talking about, they're not even going to a public school?"

Seth started to answer, then stopped. He was in over his head. Elliot pointed out that charter schools are technically public and mentioned the District 75 school co-located with Begin to Win. But it all came out sounding like a sigh.

Suzette cut him off. "A charter is a charter. Maybe you don't know the history—"

We did, but there was no stopping her. "We're tired of outsiders taking over our school buildings, skimming from our school budgets."

"Tell 'em, sister." This from Old Guard Bernice. The block party wars were apparently on hold. To us she said, "You three better go back to the people who sent you and let them know Bed-Stuy still stands up for community schools."

"Nobody *sent* us," I said.

Bernice didn't seem convinced. "Mm-hmm."

The chairman coughed and shuffled his papers. He may not have been sympathetic to us, but he didn't seem eager for a disquisition on charter schools either. "I'd like to hear what Miss Lorraine has to say. Miss Lorraine?"

Miss Lorraine stood slowly; Winston roused himself to give her a hand. She brushed him off, stoking the air of dignity about her. When all eyes had shifted her way, she said, her voice clear, if a little shaky, "I have a question for these young men."

"Go right ahead," the chairman said. We waited.

"You want to put your garden in a handball court?"

"An *abandoned* handball court," I said.

"Then why are you calling yourself Raise the Roof?"

There was laughter all around us, led by the chairman's high-pitched giggle, and even though we were the butt of the joke, we laughed along with everyone else because it seemed to release some of the tension that had been building in the room. The only one who wasn't laughing, or even smiling, was Miss Lorraine. Here was our chance for redemption, and I seized it. I told her it was an excellent question and explained that, while our original intention had been to build on the roof of the school, we wanted to ensure that the entire community, not just the students of Begin to Win, could participate. By that point, we'd grown attached to the name.

"It's catchy," the chairman said. "I'll give you that."

I probably should have just quit while I was ahead, but now that the fight or flight instinct was ebbing, I was starting to think clearly again, and I finally knew what to say. I could practically see the words dangling in front of me.

"Actually, the main reason we're keeping the name is that we still plan to put farms on rooftops...*and* in schoolyards and vacant lots, wherever people will have us. I may not have been clear about this before."

Bernice knit her brow. "You weren't."

"I apologize for that. The project we presented to you is a pilot. We're partnering with a charter school in an isolated location so we can work out all the kinks, make the model as strong as it can be, and then spread it to Bed-Stuy and Brownsville and Flatbush. If we can get it right in the Triangle, that means a bigger, better program for your kids in the future."

Suzette shook her head, rattling her beads. "We hear what you're saying, and we've heard it all before. Our young people can't wait anymore. The future is *now.*"

The chairman made a placating gesture, like he was patting her shoulder from across the room. "How long before you can start working with one of the public schools in Bed-Stuy?"

"If we can get the pilot off the ground in time for the growing season, we'll be back here again before the end of the year."

"That a promise?"

I paused to collect myself. Elliot and Seth were watching me along with everyone else. I hoped I was only the one who could hear my shallow breathing.

"That's a promise."

The chairman turned to Winston. "And you're prepared to back that up?"

I could barely endure the suspense as Winston languidly emerged from the depths of himself.

"Right now, Parks' commitment is to the project in the Triangle," he said. "But you all know what can happen when you speak with one voice."

A righteous hum rippled through the crowd.

"So I recommend you accommodate these gentlemen and then hold them accountable."

"You can count on that," Suzette said. "Accommodation is one thing. You want our blessing? It's going to take a lot more than what we heard tonight."

Bernice nodded. "Around here, we go by deeds, not words."

The chairman nodded, too, liking the sound of that. Being an elected official, though, he wasn't through covering his ass. Or, as those of us in the biz like to call it, consensus-building.

"Miss Lorraine?"

Miss Lorraine was still standing, wobbling ever so slightly. "When I first started with the Green Guerrillas, we didn't do so much talking. For heaven's sake, it's just a fucking garden."

* * *

The meeting ended in anti-climax. Since we didn't really need the board's approval, there was nothing for them to vote on. Instead, the chairman just thanked everyone for their input and advised us to discuss our plans with Community Board 1 in Williamsburg and keep both boards up to speed on our progress. Then he called it a night.

In the Green 'Burgs van on the way back to our own corner of Brooklyn, my head was swimming, my armpits clammy. We'd gotten out alive, but I felt hollowed out. Seth wasn't thrilled either, especially with his own contribution.

"Sorry, guys. I thought charter schools were popular in black neighborhoods."

Elliot shrugged. "Nice to know there's at least one community board that isn't stacked with ringers."

"I promise to leave the politics to you from now on," Seth said. "So if you don't mind, I'm going to sit out the meeting with CB1."

"No more meetings." The voice I heard didn't sound like me, but I was past caring. Maybe this was the new me talking.

"I hear you," Seth said. "But the man was clear. He expects us to do our due diligence."

"Fuck that."

We drove on in silence for a minute or two. Seth kept his eyes on the road. Elliot was riding shotgun. I was in the back, so I couldn't see their reactions.

"Just so I understand," Seth said, "you don't think it's a good idea for us to talk to the people who have a real stake in the Triangle?"

At age thirty, I somehow found myself with my very own Jewish mother.

"The Triangle isn't in District 1! It's in District 3!" I said. "What just happened, that kangaroo court—that was our due diligence! Is it our problem they don't know what the fuck is going on in their own district?"

Seth lifted his hands off the wheel like he was placating a madman. "Hey, I'm with you. I just want to make sure we've got the community on our side."

"What community? Seriously, we've been out there a dozen times now. Have you seen any community? All I've seen is a tenement full of hipsters, and they love us already."

"Hipsters do love themselves a farm," Elliot said.

"We've got the neighbors. We've got the school. We've got the city, which owns the land. What are we waiting for? You heard Miss Lorraine. Let's build the fucking thing already!"

We stopped at a red, and Seth twisted around to face me. "I'm just the hired help. So you tell me. Is that really how you want to play this?"

Funny how life is: Watching Vivienne bumble through press conferences and town halls over the years, I was quick to wince at every botched talking point and missed opportunity. Now, flattened by my trip through the CB3 ringer, I understood with blazing clarity what I'd never bothered to consider before: Vivienne may not have been the most golden-tongued or sure-footed pol, but she was willing to stand up in public and make herself a target. Her peers in government were amoral apparatchiks, her constituents bottomless pits of grievance; the press jumped at the slightest chance to depict her as a ditzy dowager. And yet for some reason—call it noblesse oblige or just a stubborn streak—she kept showing up and taking their shit. Elliot and I did our best to prep her, but once she hit that podium, she was on her own. Only now could I fully appreciate how tough she had to be.

But that didn't mean I wanted to follow in her footsteps. For some goofy reason, I'd been under the impression that getting out of politics meant, you know, getting out of politics. Instead, this project had been nothing but politics so far, all fast talk and compromises. We'd been at it for less than two months, and we'd already bent our principles by working with a charter school; given in to the Schlossers' self-serving whims, losing our grant from Tommy Brutti in the process; struck a distasteful deal with the landlord next door; and pandered to Suzette and Bernice, promising them a farm of their own. The way I saw it, enough was enough. If we didn't cut out the horse-trading and get some dirt under our nails, I might as well slink back to the world of rumpled suits, manila folders, and lunch buses.

"Look," I said, "we've done everything that's been asked of us. But if we miss the growing season, we have to give Martin Gollick his money back, and all of it was for nothing. There'll be plenty of time to make friends once we have plants in the ground and people can see we're for real."

Seth turned to Elliot. "Is that the consensus of the team?"

Elliot drummed his fingers on the armrest. "One of the reasons we got into this was to be our own bosses, right? So why do I feel like I've got a hundred bosses all of a sudden?" The drumming stopped. "I'm with Will. We don't work for the chairman of CB3."

"So if my guys show up on Monday morning, you'll be ready for them?"

Elliot caught my eye. I nodded. "Shovel ready, brother. That's us," he said.

Our confab was interrupted by a staccato honk. We looked up, and lo and behold, there it was: the green light.

Vegetable Unity

The truck arrived at 7:30 Monday morning, bearing a ton of gravel. Actually, it was closer to twenty tons. The plan was to cover the handball court in a layer of gravel and then top that off with soil. The point of the gravel, apparently, was to allow water to drain. I wasn't sure where it came from, only that it was relatively cheap: $200 for the truckload. I tried to imagine what it was like to make a living hauling huge amounts of tiny rocks from place to place. How did one break into that business? And what was the motivation? Was there a hidden appeal to it, or was the money better than the retail price suggested? Maybe the gravel business was a family legacy, like owning a restaurant or palm reading. "I've got gravel in my blood"—doesn't that sound like something a gravel supplier might say? I wanted to take a good look at the truck driver, but he never got out of the cab. He just backed the truck up to the opening in the chain link fence and tipped the bed back, letting the gravel fall out in a giant heap. The racket caused a few of our next-door neighbors to poke their heads out of their windows, their statement hairdos pillow-flattened. A cloud of rock dust settled on our clothes and skin.

Seth's "guys" were a band—an actual band called Ambrose Fierce. Their front man, Vic, said their biggest gig to date was opening for Ryan Adams, so I had them pegged for one of those Americana-type acts, moonshine stills and black lung. Not that they looked the part exactly. Vic had a shaved head, an assiduously manicured beard, and round specs—a professorial skinhead. Ash was a tawny beanpole with lank black hair that fell to his shoulders, pockmarked cheeks, and a peach fuzz mustache. Craig arrived by skateboard; it was hard to believe a single plank of wood could support his bulk, which was rendered even heftier by the bolts in his ear, the studded leather wristband, and the most serious-looking wallet chain I'd ever seen. Roman must have been the drummer; he was utterly nondescript, just your average Brooklyn dude in Converse and jeans. He happened to be wearing a Creedence T-shirt that first day, and whenever I thought about the guys after that, I always pictured him with a face like John Fogerty's, but that was probably my mind playing tricks.

Sizing them up and then sizing up the gravel pile in front of us, I admit I had my doubts. Craig looked like he'd tossed some rocks around in his day (possibly under the auspices of the justice system), and Vic had the arms of a man used to lugging around his own amp, but I was pretty confident I could bear-hug Ash off the ground. As for Roman, his build was part and parcel of the overall impression he made—there wasn't much to him.

Seth showed up at eight to drop off the shovels and wheelbarrows. He had a meeting with a prospective client—an assisted living facility in Jersey—so he wouldn't be joining our little work crew. He didn't seem too broken up about it, and neither was I. Just helping Vic unload the wheelbarrows from the back of the van had left him damp and panting.

We each took a shovel. I wasn't familiar with the optimal procedure for spreading gravel over a handball court, so I hung back to watch the band, figuring I'd follow their lead. There didn't turn out to be much technique involved. The four of them—along with Elliot, who dove right in without a moment's hesitation—just started flinging gravel into the wheelbarrows. When one of the barrows was full, Ash or Roman would wheel it over to the other side of the handball wall and dump the contents. I was genuinely surprised they didn't have a more sophisticated game plan. It seemed to me it would take weeks to get the job done like this. I thought about saying something, but who wants to tell a bunch of indie rockers shoveling gravel in the sun that they're doing it wrong? Besides, this was the chance I'd been waiting for.

As a kid, I never spent much time skipping stones or digging up worms. I needed to stick close to the living room to confirm that Charles was still in charge. Part of the initial appeal of the farm had been the promise of shedding my old softness once and for all. The time had finally come to get out of my head, roll up my sleeves, and do some real work.

One catch: gravel is heavy. I attacked the pile with brio, but I could barely lift a shovelful. Worse, I was the only one who seemed to be having this problem. Elliot was just as much of a sedentary, Rita's-fed creature as me, but he had the advantage of size. He would have found himself on the low end of the seesaw with any of our crew except the hulking Craig. And there he was, throwing gravel over his shoulder like there was a treasure chest buried underneath. Even scraggy Ash was unfazed; he'd wrapped his T-shirt around his head, and now his ribs showed with every heave of the shovel, yet he didn't seem to break a sweat. Meanwhile my T-shirt—a piece of Vivienne campaign swag, which I had no intention of removing—was already heavy with my own spent fluids, and I felt a tremor in my knees every time I tried to pry my shovel out of the pile and maneuver it over to the nearest wheelbarrow. By my count, I was adding one shovel-load for every five of Elliot's. I reminded myself that every little bit brought us closer to our goal. Still, I hoped the others were too intent on their own labor to notice.

That hope was in vain. After about an hour, I caught Vic watching me with a look that could have been forbearance or pity or concern but was most likely a combination of the three.

"We need someone to spread out the gravel on the other side," he said, "make sure it's all in one even layer."

I wanted to say, "Nah, I'm good," and tough it out with the others. But by that point a sharp pain had flared up under my shoulder blade, and it forced me to be honest with myself.

"I'm on it." I said, ignoring how parched my throat felt.

Compared to shoveling gravel, spreading gravel was a relatively cushy gig but not without its trials. For one thing, it was tedious, not quite strenuous enough to distract from the total lack of stimulation. The best I could do was commit to making the most perfectly even layer Vic had ever seen, painstakingly inspecting my handiwork for any one piece of gravel stubbornly lying atop another and then pressing it down with the back of my shovel.

Then there was the cloud of grit that hung in the air as Elliot and the band continued to hack away at the pile and dump new loads of gravel on my side of the wall. It formed a grainy crust on my skin, which was only getting sweatier as the sun rose. It was also doing a number on my shoes, a pair of pricey trainers. When I peeked around the wall, I noticed that all the members of Ambrose Fierce had on work boots (professional attire for both construction workers and rock bands, conveniently enough). Elliot was in the same tortured boat shoes he always wore.

When noon came and Vic passed out Gatorades from the corner store, I accepted the neon blue Glacier Freeze as my due and guzzled those cold electrolytes with the same gusto as my comrades. My contribution may have been less noticeable than theirs, but my thirst was no less real.

It took us three days to cover the court with gravel. On the second day, Sasha the art teacher and her cartoonist friend Xander came down to help. On the third, Kat showed up, even though we'd told her we'd let her know when we needed her. She came in her idea of workwear: hiking shorts, white T-shirt, suspenders.

"Sorry to interrupt your manly bonding, but I was going crazy at Vivienne's place."

I said there wasn't much for her to do at the moment, but she just took my shovel from me and got to work, spreading gravel far more efficiently than I had managed. To keep my dignity intact, I volunteered for a Gatorade run. By the time I came back, the work was all but done, and Ash and Kat were playing handball, trying to anyway, with a sun-bleached tennis ball they'd found. Kat whooped as she took a slap at the ball. My first reaction was an adolescent pang of missing out, but I reminded myself that Elliot and I were in charge here. Probably best not to be seen slacking.

A trio of guys had been watching us from across the street most of the morning. They looked to be Latino and in their late teens or early twenties, and though they were dressed head-to-toe in basketball gear—jerseys, loose-fitting shorts, hightops—they didn't give off an athletic vibe. They must have been waiting to approach us and saw Ash and Kat's goofing off as their opening. Elliot and I met them at the fence.

"What're you doing to the handball court?" the baby-faced one in the Sprewell jersey asked.

Elliot blotted his forehead with the hem of his T-shirt. "We're turning it into a farm."

The way the three of them looked at each other, he might as well have said we were building a UFO landing strip.

"A farm? Like with chickens and cows?"

"A vegetable farm."

"Vegetables?" This apparently didn't sound any more reasonable than chickens and cows.

"You gonna have tomatoes?" asked the one with the Oakley jersey and the tribal tattoo on his calf.

Elliot said we would.

"I hate tomatoes."

The third musketeer was wearing an Oakley jersey, too, but it was from Oak's pre-Knicks stint in Chicago. Clearly, this was the free spirit of the group.

"Yo, who's this for, anyway?"

Elliot pointed to the school and gave him the Cliff Notes.

"You mean that retard school? Man, retards don't even like vegetables! Everyone knows that."

I was about to challenge him, but then doubt snuck in. There couldn't possibly be any truth in this bit of folk wisdom, could there? Edgar said it was mostly the "special kids" who came to help him with his garden, but maybe he wasn't dealing with the ones on the far end of the spectrum. I'd have to Google it when I got home.

"So no more handball?" Baby Sprewell asked.

"Not here."

"But when you're done growing the vegetables, you're gonna put it back the way it was?"

How he could see that as a realistic possibility after watching us move twenty tons of gravel was beyond me. Our hope, Elliot told him, was that the farm would be a permanent addition to the neighborhood.

"Damn, son. Do you know how many girls I felt up in this handball court?"

I hadn't realized we were dealing with a romantic.

"You know there's another court six blocks from here, right?" Elliot asked.

The tattooed Oakley scowled. "We can't go over there, man. That's Borinquen Plaza guys that play over there. We're Tompkins Houses."

This tidbit would have been helpful to know when Jack first told us about the other handball court. I guess he wasn't up on the territorial claims of the local residents. He'd said himself he hadn't been out to the Triangle in decades.

"Well, I hope you'll give us a chance," Elliot said. "We think this is going to be a good thing—especially for the kids."

The free spirit shook his head. "It's all about the kids, right? Whatever, man."

He and the other Oakley walked back to their post on the other side of the street. Sprewell lingered.

"Hey," he said in a low voice, "you guys hiring?"

We told him to check back in a week or two.

* * *

Next came the soil. Winston had arranged a donation from the Bronx Zoo. Or maybe it was Jack with Winston acting as his agent. We could never be sure when Jack was taking a personal interest in our fate. In any case, the soil arrived in the back of a Parks Department truck. Like Natty Bumppo, Seth let a handful of it run through his fingers and declared it would do the job. As we got to work with our shovels, we uncovered a few miscellaneous bone fragments. "I think we found Jimmy Hoffa," Vic said. Winston later told us remains sometimes found their way into the mix with the rhino and elephant dung, but it was nothing to worry about. I was inclined to take his word for it and never think about it again.

Elliot, on the other hand, was tickled. "Now, that's what I call terroir!"

It was a relief to switch from gravel to soil, but my place in the pecking order didn't change much. While the rest of the guys shoveled and carted, my job was to tamp down the dirt with a rake and pick out any debris. As the soil bed took shape, Kat planted sets of stakes at either end and stretched a length of twine between each set, setting up the rows. Then I drew the edge of a hoe down the middle of each row to create the furrow. It was satisfying work; I was literally making my mark. I didn't even mind much when I noticed Kat trailing me, straightening out and tidying up my impressionistic furrows. Teamwork and all.

We'd been in construction mode for about a week when we got a visit. The delegation was led by Miss Marcella, the head of the teachers' committee that had been working with Elliot on the curriculum. She was joined by Sasha, who had volunteered for the committee after meeting us; our old buddy Edgar; and Sal, a teacher from the District 75 school. Miss Marcella was an imposing figure, her burly arms crossed, shrewd eyes cast in shadow by her enormous straw hat. But it was Sal who first commanded my attention. Specifically, I couldn't tear my eyes away from the gold Playboy bunny medallion that nested in the graying chest hair sprouting from his discolored tank top. His acute stoop gave the impression that the medallion had some heft to it. This guy was a teacher? A teacher of kids with special needs?

"Where's the rest of the committee?" I asked.

Miss Marcella's cheeks puffed up with stifled amusement. "It's final exams week. You're not dragging them out here to look at a pile of dirt."

"I understand. But there'll be time between the end of exams and summer break, right? Because we'd love to have some kids take part in the first planting. Think of it as a dress rehearsal before everyone comes back in the fall."

Miss Marcella yawned. "That's why we're here, isn't it?"

Sal scratched his chest hair. The glint of the sun off his medallion made me squint. "Personally, I don't know why I'm here.

As usual, we weren't consulted until the last minute. Our kids were not taken into account."

Miss Marcella wasn't having it. "When it was going to be on the roof, you complained. So they moved it off the roof, and you're still complaining. It gets old, you know?"

"I bet they only did that because the Schlossers' lawyers told them to. Wouldn't want Daddy Warbucks to get caught with his ass out."

Vivienne had convinced me the Schlossers wanted the farm on the ground so their benevolence would be visible to passersby. It hadn't occurred to me the real issue was liability, but what Sal was saying had a plausible ring.

"You're not happy unless you can take over the whole thing," Miss Marcella said. "Isn't that what happened last time?"

Elliot and I exchanged a glance. Last time?

Sal sucked his teeth. "See, the way I remember it, you decided you couldn't fit any outdoor time into your busy testing schedule, so you left it for Edgar to take care of. And he didn't want to see all that work go to waste, so he came to us."

Edgar had become intensely interested in a stray piece of gravel by his toe.

Miss Marcella's chin quivered. "I don't have the luxury of ignoring test scores."

Did she mean to suggest that teaching mentally disabled students was a luxury? I wanted to believe she didn't, but it sure sounded that way.

"Come on, guys." Sasha said. I suspected she typically reserved that tone of voice for first graders. "We're all on the same side, right?"

For a moment, it looked like Sal and Miss Marcella might actually be on the same side after all, united by their contempt for Sasha. Time for a full-bore Elliot charm offensive—a kamikaze mission, most likely.

"Sasha's right. Let's forget about last time. Will and I weren't here to help last time."

There was no audible scoffing, so Elliot pressed on. "Why don't we plan to have kids from both schools out for a planting next week and see how it goes? We can do separate shifts or one mixed group, give the kids a chance to get to know each other."

"Separate," Sal and Miss Marcella said as one.

Elliot turned up his palms in submission. "Fine. Whatever makes sense. Miss Marcella, your group can plant from seeds. We'll do Unit 1: The Life of a Vegetable. Sasha, maybe you can get them started on a mural or a banner."

"I'm seeing Diego Rivera. Instead of Proletarian Unity, Vegetable Unity—all the carrots and beets and pea shoots joining hands."

"Sounds fruity." Sal's lip curled; he seemed to think there was a pun in there somewhere.

Elliot wasn't about to be sidetracked. "Sal, your group can bring over the seedlings from Edgar's garden, and we'll replant them."

"Hold on. You think you're taking our plants?"

"No one's taking your plants. We just think it makes sense to put everything in one place. That way our gardener can do all the watering, and the burden isn't on Edgar anymore."

Edgar looked up, his forehead creased. "But I can still help out, right?"

"Everybody's welcome."

Sal shook his finger at Miss Marcella. "I don't want them eating our squash. Our kids get very attached to things."

Miss Marcella snorted. I could tell what that snort meant: Retards don't even like vegetables. Or maybe I was the jerk for thinking that's what she was thinking.

"For fuck's sake," I said. That got everyone's attention. "You can have your own special section of the farm. No one will touch your squash. We'll put up a sign and everything. Better yet, let the kids make it."

Segregating the disabled students probably wouldn't be considered a best practice for a model school farm. But the sun was beating on my head like it was a tom-tom, and I had rows to hoe. If we had to make another concession, at least it was a small one.

Sal turned his head and spit. "That works."

I shifted my attention to Miss Marcella. "Work for you?"

"Whatever."

Peace in our time. I couldn't wait for the teachers to leave so I could get back to the zen of tilling. But when I took a closer look, I saw that Kat had finished it all: the entire court was striped with evenly spaced, perfectly straight furrows, and she was taking a victory lap on Ash's shoulders, her lips blue with Gatorade. I left them to their fun and went looking for Vic so we could go over the game plan for tomorrow.

* * *

With the gravel and soil laid and the furrows in place, we turned to assembling and installing the structures in Seth's plan: the tool shed, the hoop house, a gate with a lock to go into the gap in the fence. Putting in a second gate where there was no gap, as we'd promised the landlord next door, was an engineering headache best left for another day. Meanwhile, Kat was researching the cheapest way to rig a rainwater collection system; her eyes lit up when she found a pile of castoff PVC pipe behind the school and Edgar said we could have it. A few rubber garbage cans from Home Depot, and we'd be set. "We're going to Rube Goldberg the shit out of this bad boy!" were her exact words.

Seth, for his part, was feverishly reworking his schematics, trying to make room for the welcome circle he'd envisioned when the plan was to build on the roof. The problem was the damn handball wall smack in the middle of the court, which made it impossible to fit a big enough circle anywhere in the space. Only, Seth wasn't willing to admit defeat just yet. Instead, he was erasing inches from the garden rows, changing the angle of the hoop house, hoping a solution would present itself. The poor guy desperately wanted this first foray into educational agriculture to be picturesque enough for the splash page of the Green 'Burgs website.

While all this was going on, I was hauling and sanding plywood, hammering nails (until Vic grew impatient with my aim), driving stakes for the hoop house—basically any task that required no skill, expertise, or even intuition. It had become standard practice that I was the one to pick up Gatorade and sandwiches. My transformation into a man of the soil wasn't yet complete, but I was satisfied that I wasn't dishonoring my clan.

One afternoon a scrawny black boy, probably seven or eight, in flip-flops, camo shorts, and an undershirt wandered through the fence (we were still working on the gate). He stared at us for a good ten minutes before asking "What the fuck you doing?" of no one in particular.

Big Craig, busy cutting sheets of plastic to cover the hoop house, was the first to turn his head. "We're building a farm. No cussing on the farm."

"Where are all the animals, then?"

"No animals. Vegetables."

"Is that your skateboard?"

"Yeah."

"Can I ride it?"

"Come help us out for an hour. Then you can ride it."

"What do I have to do?"

"I don't know, go sand plywood or something."

"Is it hard?"

Craig pointed at me, sucking my bloodied knuckle. "If he can do it, you can."

The boy—we later learned his name was Daryl—did exactly what Craig said. He dropped into a squat beside me, watched what I was doing for a minute or two, then picked up a spare piece of sandpaper and got to work. His technique—putting his bony shoulder into it like he was scrubbing a dish—was no worse than mine, but he was a lot faster. He dropped his sandpaper almost exactly an hour later, uncanny since he didn't have a watch or phone to check. Craig came over for an inspection, pointed out a few rough patches he'd missed (I was glad he didn't take a close look at my handiwork), and waited while he finished up, giving him the occasional pointer, even taking over the sandpaper to show him the proper push-pull motion, "real light and easy." Then he took a smoke break to watch Daryl skate around the school parking lot. The kid's ambitions exceeded his abilities, to put it mildly. He could barely stay upright for more than a few seconds, yet he insisted on attempting a series of spastic ollies and kickflips. With each flailing wipeout, he would bounce back up and try again, while Craig shook his head and chuckled to himself. After about a half-hour, he waved Daryl back to the worksite.

"Break time's over, little man. Come back tomorrow and I'll show you how to make your own board."

"Like I got nothing better to do?"

But of course he came back, wearing the same clothes as the day before. He helped the Ambrose Fierce guys fit the pipes for the hoop house frame, then sanded and painted the skateboard deck Craig had cut for him. The design was inspired by the *Saw* movies: a vaguely Fauvist depiction of the creep in the mask surrounded by various instruments of torture and corresponding severed limbs. Craig lured him back the next day with the promise of wheels, and this time he brought a couple of friends, both a head taller than him and probably a year or two older. At this point, we had to start making up tasks for them. Seth had them break down about a third of the garden rows and rebuild them on a diagonal to see if he could squeeze in the welcome circle that way (no dice). Elliot got them to sort the equipment he'd picked up at a GreenThumb give-away in Queens.

The two older boys (I never caught their names) didn't talk

much, except when they were in the vicinity of Kat, who put them to work jerry-rigging her rainwater cisterns. That assignment, punching holes in garbage cans and jamming in the pipes, was the occasion for much vulgarity. Ash grumbled about the lack of respect, but Kat kept her cool. "I can tell by the results neither of you has done *that* before," she said.

Daryl, on the other hand, stuck close to Craig. Watching the runt tag along with the gentle giant, I was a little jealous. The most any of the kids had said to me was, "I wanted the purple one," when I came back from a Gatorade run. At the same time, I was proud. The bonding, the life lessons—it was exactly what I'd hoped for when we'd started. And if I had to experience it all at a slight remove, at least I could draw a quiet satisfaction knowing I was the one (one of the ones, anyway) who'd set it all in motion.

I think we were all a bit pleased with ourselves. I'm sure every agrarian utopian movement in history had the same feeling early in its run when everything seemed like it was coming together and you believed you might actually pull it off. Which may explain why we were caught so completely off guard by the young man who came charging through the fence a couple of days before the first planting. He was Latino, apparently an acquaintance of the trio we'd met the other day; I'd noticed him talking to them on the other side of the street moments earlier. But he wasn't another baller. His hair was short and neat, scissor-cut, not shaved. He was wearing a white-button down, chinos, and sneakers. And unlike his impassive friends, his face was hard with rage. We could hear him screaming before we could make out the words.

"Where's your permit?"

"Huh?"

Vic, Elliot, and I walked up to meet him at the gate. Seth was in Jersey again, but otherwise we had a full house.

"I said, 'Where's your permit?'"

"Can we help you?" Elliot asked.

"I asked you twice already, man."

Elliot held out his hand. "I'm Elliot. This is Will and Vic. Do you live around here?"

"Yeah, I fucking live here. Do you? Do any of you? Because I sure as fuck never saw you before." The guy didn't even look at Elliot's hand, let alone take it.

"We've been out here every day for the last few weeks, working on this farm for the community. We met your friends over there already."

"Yeah, those fools told me what you're doing. They don't know enough to ask to see a permit. But the party's over because you're dealing with an educated motherfucker now."

"Well, then, I'm sure you'll understand," I said. "This land is owned by the Parks Department. The Parks Department gave us a license for a community garden here. We don't need a building permit."

Our inquisitor was shaking his head so hard, I started to wonder if he was having some kind of attack. "Nah, nah, nah. See, you think you're talking to some thug. But I already told you, I know what's up. My pops is the councilman for this district."

"Your father is Hector Contreras?"

"That's right. So you can forget your weak bullshit. If I don't see a permit in ten seconds, I'm calling the DOB, the cops, *and* my dad."

I almost felt bad for him. The guy's special claim to authority was that his dad was a backbench councilman. To be fair, every bench was a backbench in the toothless council of the Bloomberg years, but Contreras wasn't even connected enough at DOB (the very DOB his son was threatening to sic on us) to help John when Rita's had a permitting issue. The fact was we were covered. We didn't need DOB's permission to build on Parks' property. But try telling that to the crown prince of the Broadway Triangle.

"You know," Elliot said, "we used to work for Vivienne Huxley."

"Man, I have no fucking clue who that is. Now let me see your permit, and don't even try pulling some weak-ass community garden license on me."

A fleck of spit landed on Vic's glasses. He took them off carefully and wiped the lens on his shirt. "Listen, he already told you we don't need a permit. And there are kids here, so maybe you ought to calm down and clean up your language."

Hector Contreras's son took a step toward him. "Who the fuck do you think you are? These kids hear worse every goddamn day. See, this isn't Park Slope. This isn't DUMBO. This is Brooklyn, motherfucker. And you don't come in here and tear our shit up without permission."

Vic took a step of his own. They were practically nose to nose now, and I noticed he'd put his glasses in his pocket. "Well, I live in Kensington, but what's the difference? No matter what, I don't work for you."

The other members of Ambrose Fierce had quietly formed a line behind him. Craig had slipped his studded wristband over his knuckles. Ash was carrying a shovel over his shoulder. Out of the corner of my eye, I saw the three ballers slowly crossing the street toward us. Kat was hustling Daryl and his friends off the court, pulling on the neck of Daryl's shirt when he dawdled.

"Hold up. I wanna see this shit!"

The Contreras kid reached into the pocket of his chinos. To this day, it fills me with shame that I flinched. Did I think the son of a city councilman was prowling the streets with a switchblade? What he actually took out was an iPhone. He snapped a picture of the menacing indie band arrayed against him and then stepped around them to document the state of the handball court. Elliot's shoulders slumped with relief. Vic calmly put his glasses back on. Craig actually looked a little disappointed. Me? I was taking deep breaths, hoping my heart wouldn't break my ribcage.

He backed out through the opening in the fence, still holding up his phone. "Yeah, I've got you now. This ain't over. Believe that."

Craig blew him a kiss. Vic watched him brush past the three ballers and disappear around the corner.

"Let's put up that gate," he said.

Kids Are People

That Friday, the students came. It had been quiet since our run-in with the Contreras scion, and other than the welcome circle and Kat's rainwater collection rig, all systems were go. Still, I was nervous. What if we had more trouble while the kids were on-site? One of the perks of working with GreenThumb was that it settled the insurance issue. As a licensed community garden on city-owned property, we weren't required to have our own liability insurance. Nonetheless, a brawl in the presence of two dozen children would probably be bad for business.

That was just the first item on my list of worries: What if it rained? What if the Begin to Win group and the special ed group overlapped and a turf war ensued? Most importantly, what if they hated it? Conscripting Daryl and his friends as unpaid labor was one thing. This was school. If the kids weren't willing to get their hands dirty, if they were bored by any activity that didn't involve glowing screens, all our work would be for nothing. And Craig couldn't bribe them all with custom skateboards.

Miss Marcella's third-grade class was up first. There were fifteen of them, their faces as bright as their little outfits. Had Miss Marcella warned them they'd be getting dirty? Had we told her to warn them? Too late now. As for the teachers, Sasha had really gotten into the spirit of the occasion: She was wearing overalls, her hippie hair tied back with a bandana. Miss Marcella, on the other hand, was making no concessions: long sleeves, long skirt.

The Raise the Roof delegation was bigger than it needed to be. The band had more or less finished their work, but they'd asked if they could stick around to see the fruits of their labor. It looked a tad shady, these scruffy characters lurking by the tool shed as the children filed in. Miss Marcella narrowed her gaze as she passed them but said nothing. Craig, who'd been leaning against the side of the shed, straightened up and stuck his hands behind his back.

Seth was there, too, an expensive camera slung around his neck. That was more than Miss Marcella could let pass.

"No one said anything about pictures. You need signed permission from the parents."

We'd assumed Begin to Win had the parents sign a photo release form at registration. After all, they had their own brochures to fill.

"The copier was broken, so we skipped it this year."

We promised not to use any photos that showed the kids' faces.

Kat was in her element. Come to think of it, Kat never seemed to be out of her element. But the children brought out a sunnier side of her. She smiled and greeted them as they stepped through our brand-new gate, bending over to hand them each a seed taped to a square of colored construction paper—green for cucumbers, red for radishes, orange for carrots, and so on. Her idea. Ash had contributed a one-of-a-kind doodle to each piece of construction paper: a cucumber with shades and a goatee (signifying "cool as a…"), a carrot with a diamond chain (get it?).

After a brief confab with Elliot, Miss Marcella clapped her hands. The kids, who'd been squirming, fanning themselves with their construction paper, shooting ray beams at each other, immediately clapped in response. I couldn't see Craig from where I was standing, but I pictured him clapping, too.

"Students, this is your new garden. Mr. Elliot and his friends made this all for you."

Ridiculous as it sounds, I got the impression she was trying to claim the farm for Begin to Win before Sal's group showed up.

"Now I want you to listen closely"—she made a show of tugging her ear—"so you'll know what to do. This is a chance for you to show your values. Can you tell Mr. Elliot what the Begin to Win values are?"

"Respect! Preparation! Excellence! Spirit!" the children shouted in rough unison.

"All yours," Miss Marcella said, stepping aside for Elliot.

I'd always found it hard to picture Elliot as a kindergarten teacher; he seemed too sedate to handle a bunch of pants-wetters tweaking on pixie sticks. What I'd failed to take into account was that kids were people, and people were Elliot's thing. It didn't matter that their personalities were still amoebic. Elliot could vibe with anyone.

He crouched so he could look them in the eye. "How many of you like eating your vegetables?"

A few hands went up, but they were the exception.

"And how many of you know where vegetables come from?"

"They come from the store!" shouted a boy with an old man's hairline.

"No, stupid!" said a girl in a bedazzled top. "They come from the ground."

"And where do you think the store is, *stupid?* On the ground!"

"Respect each other!" Miss Marcella glared at them. "No respect, no achieve-bucks." She brandished what looked like a stack of Monopoly money.

Elliot forged ahead with a beginner's guide to photosynthesis and a game of name that plant. It was disconcerting how many of the students were stumped as he flipped through a set of Ash's drawings. Since we started drumming up support for the farm, I'd figured out how to talk a good game about food deserts, but in my mind, the concept had remained abstract. Here, though, was the proof: if these kids were to be believed, half of them had never even seen a cucumber, let alone tasted one. Elliot asked one of the initiated, a girl with scabby elbows and drugstore glasses, to describe the experience.

"They're kind of cold and wet. Like, slimy almost?"

"Are they crunchy?" Elliot asked.

The girl looked down at her hands. "I don't know." Had she overplayed her credentials as a cucumber connoisseur? It was enough to break your heart.

"They are when you grow them yourself," Elliot said. "And that's what we're going to do." He wiggled his eyebrows, the Willy Wonka of greens.

That was the cue to split into groups. "If you've got a red sheet, you're with me," Elliot said. "If you've got an orange sheet, you're with Miss Kat."

Kat waved her arms over her head like she was stranded on a desert island.

"And if you've got a green sheet, you're with Mr. Will."

I gave an ironic little salute. As they gathered around, I adopted a businesslike demeanor, no pleasantries, no mugging, just the facts. Trying to beat Elliot and Kat in a popularity contest was a fool's errand. My goal was more modest: to show my charges, without screwing up, what Kat had shown me the day before. With slow and steady movements, slightly exaggerated for their benefit, I built a mound in the dirt, made a well in the mound with my thumb, placed a seed in the well, and covered it with a thin layer of soil, patting down the soil so it was compact. They went about copying me with almost ritualistic solemnity, a few getting carried away with one step or another. One boy had a look of bliss on his face as he corkscrewed his thumb into the mound he'd made (paging Dr. Freud!). Then again, he might have had a lazy eye. A girl with a missing eyetooth insisted everyone drop what they were doing when she thought she'd lost her seed. After I rescued it from the sole of her shoe, she made a big show of cosseting it, smoothing the dirt over it like she was brushing a pony's tail.

Mostly, they were proud of their handiwork and eager for my seal of approval. For reasons I can't entirely explain (stick around, Dr. Freud), I was tight with my praise, doling out a "Not bad" or "Getting there" when a "Great job!" or "Awesome!" would probably have been more developmentally appropriate. I even told one boy he needed to start over because his well was too close to his neighbor's. Part of it, I think, was that I didn't want mine to be the remedial group. If Kat had to fix my rows later, I would carry the shame with me for all my remaining days.

Amazingly enough, the kids responded well to my style. They seemed motivated by the idea that this was a job to be taken seriously. The girl with the missing tooth, for instance, had apparently overheard me critiquing her classmate; she asked for a ruler so she could make sure there was enough space between all the seeds. I thought that might be taking things too far, but the others seemed to like the idea of an official inspection. Maybe it was a side effect of being tested all the time. Happily, I was saved by the bell: Sasha came by just then with popsicle sticks and felt-tip pens. Each plant would be marked with the name of its caretaker, who would observe its progress over the coming months and, when the time came, feast on its ripened goodness.

Farming done for the day, it was time for art. Wasn't that just how Marx envisioned it?

Clapping for the kids' attention, Sasha told them to turn over their construction paper and, with the pens she'd given them, draw pictures of their own. The theme was what your seed will look like once it grows. Interpretations varied. Some tried to copy Ash's friendly cartoon veggies. Others had a field day with scale, scrawling carrots as tall as buildings. Still others depicted family scenes: mom, dad, and siblings sitting down to a single cucumber. My favorite was an expressionist take on Elliot's photosynthesis lesson: a bulbous pepper gobbling up jagged sunrays and breathing out swirling gusts of oxygen. The saddest came from a mousy girl who turned in an accurate representation of the seed she'd been handed, nothing more. Whether she'd been conditioned to keep her expectations low or just lacked imagination, I couldn't say.

Sasha collected all the drawings and, with Ash's help, began taping them to the handball wall, while Seth snapped away like a paparazzo. She informed the kids that their big art project for the summer would be turning the drawings into a single mural for the whole neighborhood to enjoy. That seemed to go over well, though a few suddenly had second thoughts about their contributions. Kat told the group she'd be tending to their plants all summer; anyone who wanted to help her water and weed should bring a note from their parents. Before we knew it, Miss Marcella was checking her watch, the children were filing out, and we were waving goodbye, our first class in the books. The finicky girl stopped on her way out to ask for my assurance that no one would move or otherwise mess with her seed in her absence. I promised.

Class dismissed, the Raise the Roof team indulged in the satisfaction of a job well done. Ash and Kat pored over the pictures taped to the wall like they were at a Chelsea gallery. Seth was glued to his viewfinder, clicking through the precious moments he'd captured, grumbling, "So many adorable faces, and no permission slips." I was inspecting my seedbed for any irregularities, when Elliot sidled up.

"So?" His eyebrows hadn't gotten the message that the children were gone.

And I guess I was stuck in tough love mode because all I said was, "Not bad."

"Yeah, if by not bad you mean totally fucking awesome."

Daryl and his silent partners showed up at their usual time. They were none too pleased when they saw how much they'd missed.

"You gonna let those kids mess up our wall with all that trash?"

"It'll look better once we get it all plotted onto a grid," Ash said. "I promise."

"Whatever, man, I just work here."

They were even more aggrieved when we told them they had to leave before the special ed class arrived.

"So it's like that, huh? Y'all forgetting your roots?"

Kat told them to come back tomorrow. The rainwater collection system still had a ways to go.

"We'll see. We could be busy tomorrow."

They skated off on the boards Craig had made them.

Sal's class came in the afternoon. It was a much smaller group: eight students in all, with five adults—including Edgar and Sal—attending to them. There was a range of ages; the oldest seemed to be a teenager, the youngest about the same age as Miss Marcella's third-graders. Their conditions varied, too. Several weren't noticeably disabled, maybe just a bit less attentive and slower of speech than the Begin to Win students. Others showed signs of autism or palsy. The teen was the most severe case. The entire right side of his face and body sagged; his mouth was open and his upper lip pulled back from his teeth in a permanent grimace; his left hand was upturned, the fingers crooked and splayed. Watching them slowly shuffle through the gate, bearing their tomatillos, chilies, and herbs in plastic pots, I had to smile like a Nickelodeon host just to keep it together. I tried to buck myself up by reciting the Begin to Win values—Respect! Preparation! Excellence! Spirit!—under my breath.

Elliot led them to the section of the farm we'd set aside for their plants. A moment of awkward hesitation followed, as the students milled around; one of them tugged on Edgar's sleeve, while another pressed her face against the chain link fence. I noticed the three ballers—Oakley, Oakley, and Spre—keeping an eye on us from across the street.

Sal's Playboy medallion was concealed by a velour track jacket. He appeared to be waiting for us to make the next move.

"Do you want to say something or should I?" Elliot asked him.

Sal cracked his neck with what seemed to me exaggerated indolence. "Doesn't make a difference."

Elliot went for it. "Hey, guys. Welcome to the farm. We're so glad you could be here today. Are you excited to plant some vegetables with us?"

No response, aside from a sort of wordless mumble from a girl with a hearing aid, and she didn't even make eye contact. Sal shook his head, as if to say, "What an amateur."

Now it was Sal's turn. "Listen up, kids. These guys are trying to start a garden, but they don't have any plants. So they asked us if they could borrow our plants. What do you say?"

He didn't get much more of a reaction than Elliot, just some redoubled mumbling and a couple of head bobs, but it seemed to meet his satisfaction.

"Let's get to it."

There was no primer on photosynthesis, no construction paper or popsicle sticks. We didn't try to teach them proper planting technique. What happened was this: each of us—Edgar, Sal, the other teachers, Elliot, Kat, and me—squatted beside one of the students and helped them remove their plant from its pot and transfer it to the ground. I was paired with the mumbling girl. My job was first to dig a hole that could accommodate her chili plant, which she held close to her chest like a doll. It was a beautiful plant, the first buds already coming in a glossy red. The girl was reluctant to give it up. I asked her if she wanted to place it in the hole herself, but I couldn't understand her answer or even tell for sure if she was answering me. We seemed to have reached an impasse, until Sal came over and, putting his arm over her shoulder, gently talked her through it. She set the pot down between us, and together, we burrowed in with our fingers and carefully extracted the plant. My instinct was to quickly get it into the waiting hole, but Sal stopped me with a look. Leaning in close to her ear, he continued to quietly encourage her. Her inchoate commentary grew more excited, her blazing blue eyes wider, as she lowered the plant into the ground herself. All that was left for me to do was top off the hole with soil. I didn't realize until we were done that I'd been holding my breath.

That experience alone was enough for me, enough to justify the sore back and bruised ego I'd picked up over the last few weeks, the groveling at various feet—Gollick's, Greta's, the battleaxes of CB3—not to mention the chintzy economies at home, canceling the cable, asking Tricia not to run the AC, even though our fourth-floor apartment was stuffy as a motherfucker. Finally, here was the proof it was all worth it. But it was nothing compared to what happened next.

The girl began to stroke the chili plant like it was a pet. Again, my gut reaction was wrong: I was nervous she might damage it or get a burn from the capsaicin in the chili buds. This time, though, I didn't need a look from Sal to keep me from ruining the moment. I held myself in check, letting the situation unfold of its own accord.

And what unfolded was a blissed-out communion so mesmerizing it was a while before I realized I was as absorbed in watching the girl as she was in petting the plant. Subconsciously, I must have wanted us all to be connected because I actually caught myself reaching out to pat her head. I glanced at Sal to check whether he'd noticed; the way he looked at me, thin lips ratcheted into a shape resembling a smile, gave me the sense he knew what I was thinking and it was all right.

"Touch is the thing for her," he said. "It's the thing for a lot of these kids. We're gonna need the jaws of life to get her back to class."

"Sorry about that," I said.

"Hey, we'd be doing this with or without you, or did you forget already?"

"Right. I guess I should be saying thanks for including us."

"Don't mention it." Sal punched my shoulder, a little harder than he needed to. "These kids love to help the less fortunate."

When everyone had finished, we found ourselves surrounded by a heady jumble of colors and scents. We'd brought the farm—a piece of it, anyway—to life. Now the entire neighborhood, from the three ballers to the artists next door, could see for themselves we were for real. The word was out: a calabaza grows in Brooklyn.

As Sal had anticipated, the goodbyes took longer than they had for Miss Marcella's class. My girl with the hearing aid whimpered when he told her it was time to leave. He promised she could come back to visit her chilies next week, but that didn't console her. Then he said they had to go because it was time for Zumba, and that did the trick. She slowly drew her hand back from the plant and held it out so Sal could help her to her feet. Even then, she didn't take her eyes off it until they were halfway across the parking lot that separated the farm from the school.

Once they'd gone inside, I stood for a while, as reluctant as she was to let the moment go. Eventually, I found Elliot over by the shed consulting with Kat on next week's watering schedule.

"Now *that*," I said, "was totally fucking awesome."

* * *

That evening, Seth sent us a link to a gallery of the photos he'd taken. I sat with Tricia on the couch, the laptop between us, and narrated as she clicked through the record of my day. It was hard to get a true sense from the pictures; ever-diligent, Seth had weeded out any that showed the children's faces. I went on at length about the ones I got to spend time with, especially the chili whisperer. Tricia lingered over every photo. When we got to the end, she slipped an arm around my waist.

"Wow, you guys rocked it."

"We did, didn't we? We actually made it happen."

"You sound surprised."

"Relieved maybe. I know this was only the beginning. We haven't even made it to Marnie's ribbon-cutting. But what we did today…that's my life now."

Tricia laid her head against my chest. She'd recently gotten her hair cut short, and the sight of her bare neck was a novelty. I brushed it with my fingertips.

"You know," she said, "it's cool to see how much you like being with the kids."

"Who knew, right?"

"Especially since I'm pregnant."

I couldn't see her face because it was still buried in my chest. I took her by the shoulders and tried to wriggle out from under her.

"Are you serious?"

Tricia was quiet.

"I don't understand. How could this happen?"

"About a month ago I switched to a different pill. In retrospect, there was a week we should've used back-up."

"Aren't you a doctor?"

"I spay my patients! I'm not giving them Seasonique!"

"Why did you switch in the first place?"

Tricia barely opened her mouth to answer. "I was trying to save money."

"Oh, well, I hope you kept your receipt!"

"Stay with me here, buddy. I'm just as freaked out as you are."

My eyes started roving around our apartment—the uneven wood floors, perfect for upending a wobbly toddler; the exposed heat pipe; the kitchen window that didn't lock. And had it always been so small? The previous tenant had used the closet as a second bedroom, so maybe we could make it work…

"We're going to need a bigger place," I said.

"We might."

"Jesus. We can't even afford cable right now."

"But once Gollick's check comes in, you'll have enough to start paying yourself, right?"

I was slow to answer. "We should have enough."

"Should?"

"I mean, that's the idea, but there are a lot of factors involved."

"Factors?"

For starters, we owed Seth for materials and labor. We also had to get Kat on the payroll. She'd been on loan from Vivienne up to this point, but we needed her to officially take charge of all the plants that were now in our care. Summer had come early, and it was shaping up to be a scorcher; one day without watering would be enough to wipe out our crop. Elliot and I could pick up a few shifts a week, but we needed to focus on curriculum development, grant-writing, big-picture stuff.

Like coming up with an out-years budget. Gollick had warned us we needed a sustainability plan, and Prometheus wasn't likely to give us another dime without one. So whatever was left after paying Seth and Kat, we'd have to think about rolling at least a portion of it over to next year. Of course, next year we wouldn't have construction costs to worry about—unless we decided we were ready to replicate the program at another school. Come to think of it, hadn't I promised the good people of Bed-Stuy something to that effect?

Tricia had been inching backwards as I talked. Now she was perched on the arm of the couch. "Do I need to be worried?"

I tried to reassure her. In theory, there would be enough to do it all—pay our bills, staff up, set aside something for next year, *and* compensate ourselves for our considerable troubles. After all, we'd asked Gollick for way more than we thought we needed.

"When was the last time you heard from him?"

The truth was we hadn't had any contact with Gollick since our meeting. Vivienne said he was incommunicado on his annual pilgrimage to Israel. It was his time to reflect on his faith, to recharge his spiritual batteries after another year of pillaging the global markets; disturbing him to ask whether the check was in the mail would be considered, at best, bad manners, at worst, sacrilege.

Tricia got up and started pacing. "Okay, now I am worried."

"Sorry, but this was not part of the plan!"

"I hate to be the one to break it to you, but the plan has changed."

"We just had our best day out there. Do you want me to quit now and go back to the council? Get a job at Marnie period?"

"That's not what I'm saying. But like it or not, you're going to be a dad soon. I need you to think about that."

I touched her arm before she could do a full lap around the living room. It took a moment for me to find the words.

"I don't want to be just a dad. I want to be a dad our kid can look up to."

"Will…"

"Just think, all those little Jaspers and Fionas in this neighborhood, what do they have to say when Career Day comes around? 'My daddy's a portfolio manager.' 'My daddy's an efficiency expert for McKinsey.' Our kid is going to be the only one who can say, 'My daddy's a farmer.'"

That got a smile out of her—a small one. "The Park Slope Hillbillies."

"What do you say, Ma?"

"You still think it can work? For us?"

This time, the answer came quicker. "I promise you, I've got this."

I hugged her and sent a silent prayer to the Holy Land.

No Peas

The next morning, it was my turn to water the plants. The G train was all but deserted. I was still buzzing from Tricia's news, seeing the world in all its strangeness and potency. The spectacle of a guy in fingerless gloves and some kind of ill-fitting jumpsuit doing a line of coke off one of the orange plastic seats had a kind of exotic glow to it. I could already hear myself telling Tricia about it later, a tale of life on the Brooklyn frontier.

I arrived to find the farm destroyed. The gate had been knocked off its hinges. The seed beds were disheveled. Worst of all, the plants from Edgar's garden had been ripped from their beds. I started frantically searching for the chili plant, the one the girl with the hearing aid had poured herself into. I found it lying on its side, trampled. Most of the drawings the Begin to Win group had put up on the handball wall had been torn down, too. One had been left in place, albeit in modified form: a giant marauding carrot reimagined as a drooling monster cock. On the wall itself, the vandal had spray-painted a leaf with a red strikethrough sign over it, the equivalent of the no-smoking symbol, only the message here seemed to be no gardening. The weirdest touch was the ratty sofa that had somehow been maneuvered on top of the remains of the hoop house. There was something demented about its exposed spring, like a clownless jack-in-the-box.

I eventually noticed the three ballers eyeing me from their usual post on the other side of the street. I knew it was a bad idea to come charging at them in a rage without Ambrose Fierce to back me up, but the thought was like the analysis of a sports commentator, a mere observation with no power to affect the action. In any case, they didn't seem too concerned. If any of them blinked, I missed it.

I pointed back at the carnage. "Did you do this?"

Chicago Oakley—they were wearing the same jerseys as the other day—made a *pssh* sound with his lips. "Just because we're brown, you accuse us of doing something like that? Yo, that's some racist shit."

New York Oakley shook his head. "Man, how you gonna bring people together, if you go around pointing fingers? It's sad."

I could feel the arm I was pointing with start to shake. "I'm calling the cops." Another stupid move, but I'd hit my limits as a diplomat.

Chicago Oakley held a finger phone to his ear and put on his best white-boy whine. "Hello, 911? I'd like to report a serious crime. Someone pissed on my vegetables! Yes, it's an emergency!"

"It's a herbicide!" New York Oakley chipped in.

"What's that? Ten break-ins? Three murders? Well, were they white? No? Then what are you waiting for?"

All the air went out of me in a single sigh. "You really pissed on them?"

"They told you, we didn't do that shit," Sprewell said. He seemed to be the only one who was genuinely nervous about possible repercussions.

"Was it Contreras? You can tell me. I'm not going to call the cops."

"Look, we don't know who did it," New York Oakley said. "Could be anybody, the way you're pissing folks off, coming in here with no permits, taking shit over."

"We tried to explain the permit thing to him."

"Is that what you and all your boys were doing, coming at him with shovels and shit? Explaining?"

There was nowhere left for this little powwow to go. I turned to face the wreckage.

Sprewell followed me halfway across the street. "Hey," he whispered. "You hiring for the clean-up? Let me give you my number."

I said I knew where to find him. I wasn't sure if I was threatening or humoring him.

* * *

Vivienne was livid when we told her what had happened.

"We can't have this. Marnie invited a hundred people to the ribbon-cutting ceremony. Martin even said he might come back early to attend. And we need to impress him so he'll help us out with Baruch."

I'd forgotten about Marnie's quest to get a chair named after Vivienne. From the beginning, she'd seen the farm as a Trojan horse, and clearly she'd gotten Vivienne thinking along the same lines.

"I'm calling Hector," Vivienne said. "He needs to get his kid on a leash."

Elliot told her that was a bad idea, but she'd made up her mind.

"You can't let people push you around, Elliot. It's like you don't even remember my anti-bullying campaign."

I was with Vivienne on this one. Surely, an ambitious pol like Hector Contreras wouldn't want word to get out that his son was a rageaholic who wantonly destroyed city property and peed on a disabled child's chili peppers. Maybe he could broker a ceasefire.

"See, boys, this is why you always ask for more than you need. At least we know we can afford to rebuild."

We should have enough. That's what I'd told Tricia. I'd used up twenty-three of my twenty-six weeks of unemployment. Unless Obama and the Democrats rammed another extension through Congress, things were about to get hairy.

Where Vivienne was outraged, Seth was distraught.

"The hoop house, too? This is so fucked up. I've never been a part of anything so fucked up."

His concern turned out to be mostly for himself. "I'm supposed to speak at a conference next week. 'From the Barn to the Block: Urban Agriculture in the 21st Century.' What the fuck am I going to say now?"

I suggested that he could have an inspirational triumph-over-adversity story to share—if he pulled himself together and helped us rebuild.

"But what if they just fuck it up again?"

We told him to let us worry about that.

"Are my guys going to be safe out there?"

As long as Vic doesn't throw the first punch, I thought. We assured him it would be fine.

Like a hardy weed, Seth rallied. Ambrose Fierce was back at work the following Monday, and with some help from Sasha and Xander, they were able to resurrect the tool shed in a matter of hours. We decided to scrap the hoop house for the time being; we wouldn't really need a covered growing space until colder weather arrived anyway. The downside was there would be no place for the kids to take shelter from the rain, but that was the least of our worries.

Vic made it his personal mission to reinforce the gate with heavy-duty steel hasps and bolts. There was a debate about topping it with barbed wire—hadn't the next-door landlord warned us we'd need it? Still rattled, I was all for it, but Elliot put his foot down.

"This is a farm for kids, not a supermax facility," he said.

"The school's for kids, too, and they have barbed wire!"

"We might as well get a Doberman."

Big Craig screwed up his face. "How would you keep the dog away from the plants?"

In the end, I saw that Elliot was right. Deep down, I knew there was no way even the most imposing gate was going to stop another ransacking anyway. Elliot was holding out hope the vandals had gotten it out of their system, a one-time protest. My own pipe dream was that Vivienne would fix this for us. In the meantime, all we could do was keep our eyes open and our fingers crossed.

"Your funeral," Vic said.

In any case, our biggest concern security-wise wasn't for the farm itself. It was for Kat. Seth had a greenhouse full of plants in an abandoned lot near the Green 'Burgs office, and he'd offered to clean himself out in order to restock the farm. (It was too late in the season to start from scratch with seeds.) That meant we'd need Kat out there watering at least three days a week. And on most days, there was virtually no foot traffic on the surrounding streets. For all intents and purposes, she'd be in a cage by herself. I was hoping Elliot would tell me I was paranoid, but he took the danger seriously. Seriously enough to raise the issue with Kat.

"Are you guys telling me to come at my own risk? Because I'm pretty sure that's against OSHA guidelines."

I threw out some half-cocked suggestions: Xander and his neighbors could act as lookouts. Begin to Win must have security guards; we could work out some arrangement with them. Elliot, true to form, proposed a more personable tack.

The next day, the three of us went out to the farm together. Seth met us there, and while he and Kat sorted through the new plants, Elliot and I headed across the street to parlay with the three ballers. They were fixed to their usual spot, but there was something different this time. It took me a moment to pick up on it: they weren't wearing their jerseys. Instead, they had on identical white T-shirts with the same symbol that had been spray-painted on the handball wall: a green leaf in a red strikethrough circle. They raised their chins to acknowledge us as we approached.

I didn't return the greeting. "Where'd you get those?"

The one with the tribal tattoo shrugged. "Everyone's wearing them."

"It's the new fashion statement in the 'hood," the free spirit said.

For Elliot's plan to work, we'd have to ignore the provocation. "We never asked you your names," he said.

They hesitated—maybe they thought we intended to sic the cops on them—but in the end civility carried the day. That's how we came to be formally introduced to Nelson (New York Oakley), Felix (Chicago Oakley), and Dante (Sprewell). We told them our names, and then we all shook hands. As shows of respect go, it wasn't the warmest, but it was something.

Elliot raised his thumb over his shoulder in the direction of the farm. "See our friend back there? She takes care of all the plants. But now she's scared to come out here by herself."

"Yeah? And why is that?" Felix asked.

"Because of what happened," I said.

Felix flung his arms in the air, as if we'd pulled a fast one on him. "Man, we already told you we had nothing to do with that."

"But you can understand why she'd feel unsafe," Elliot said.

"What is it with white girls? They see a little graffiti, some broken bottles, automatically they think they're getting jumped. You say good morning, they look at you like you took your dick out."

"So you're saying she has nothing to worry about?" Elliot asked. "This is your block, you're out here every day, so if you tell us it's safe for her to be here, we'll take you at your word."

Felix looked to his associates for confirmation. They straightened up, a united front. "You go tell your girl she's got nothing to worry about."

"I can tell her you personally vouch for her safety?"

Dante cupped a hand over his mouth, a pantomime of confidentiality. "Yo, if you need security, just put us on the payroll. We'll have this place on lockdown."

Felix raised a hand like he was going to cuff him. "You ever heard of extortion, dummy?" To us he said, "We'll make sure she's safe. For as long as you can keep this mess up and running, anyway."

"Fair enough."

We all shook hands again, our respective grips firmer this time. Elliot invited them to come back to the farm with us so they could meet Kat, but they demurred.

"No offense," Felix said, "but we don't want nobody to see us associating with you people."

Fair enough.

* * *

Walking back to the farm, we saw Kat, Ash, and Craig huddled around a gangly kid. As we got closer, I recognized him as one of Daryl's older friends. By the time we made it to the gate, he'd scooted off on his DIY skateboard. Kat and the guys were still standing there, heads hanging.

"What now?" I asked.

Kat looked up, teary-eyed. "Daryl got beat up. He was on his way here the other day, and some other kids jumped him."

"Because he was helping us?"

She glared at me like I'd lost my mind. "No. They were just picking on him because…I don't know why. Because kids are assholes, I guess."

I was upset, of course, and angry, but mixed in there was a whisper of relief we weren't responsible.

"He's at home recovering," Kat said. "I tried to get an address, but his friend didn't know. Or he didn't want to tell me, maybe. He says Daryl's grandmother—I guess she's his guardian—probably won't let him come out here anymore."

I noticed that Big Craig was staring at nothing, chewing on his lip.

"Is he all right?" For some reason, I asked Kat even though Craig was standing right there.

"I'm out," he said quietly.

"You're out?"

"I can't be here anymore. Otherwise, I'm going to go find the kids who did this."

"OK, Craig's out." I turned to Ash. "Can you make sure he doesn't go vigilante on his way home?"

That earned me more dirty looks. Craig was the only one who didn't seem to take offense.

"Job's almost done anyway. Tell Vic I'll settle up with him next time. And if you do see Daryl, tell that little fucker…tell him…"

He couldn't finish the thought. Kat did her best to wrap him up in a hug, and Ash patted his head like he was an overgrown child. And that was the last we saw of Big Craig. He made walking away look simple.

***

The hoodoo wasn't all bad all the time. Before long, Kat was on speaking terms with the three ballers, though the speaking consisted mostly of "'Sup?" and "Later." Even after the band finished their quickie rebuild, Ash joined her most days, unless Seth had lined up another job. They got plenty of help from Xander and some of the Triangle's other foremost artists in residence. We'd decided to keep the grubby sofa that had crushed the hoop house as a totem of our resolve. At any given time, there was usually at least one mixed media sculptor lolling on it in a heat-induced daze.

More encouraging was the visit from an older black gentleman named Henry. He lived on the opposite side of Peter's Place in one of the houses built by Pfizer in the '80s. I happened to be there the day he came, wearing matching khakis like he was on safari, bearing a potted basil plant.

"My place is nice and all, but they didn't leave much room for a garden."

Kat found a place of honor for his basil—space wasn't an issue since the break-in. He said there was plenty more where that came from, so she offered to sign him up as a member. Henry was reluctant.

"I don't need to sign a piece of paper to come out here and water my own plants, do I?"

It occurred to me I hadn't spoken to a single person from his side of the block. Looking now at the tidy row houses, I realized we'd neglected a potential trove of allies.

"Did you work for Pfizer?" I asked him.

"I did, till they left town in '04. Won't hear a word against them either. They stayed longer than they had to. Built those houses, gave space to that school, put in cameras on the corners. Ask anybody. The neighborhood was better off then."

"We're trying to bring it back." I could feel Kat cringing, and I didn't blame her, but I was beyond shame. I desperately wanted this man on our side.

"You with the city?" he asked.

I explained the nature of the relationship to him.

"Well, you tell them what we really need around here is some cops. What happened to that boy the other day? It's a damn shame."

"You know Daryl?" Kat asked.

"I know his grandmamma. Good people."

I was about to tell him how much Daryl had meant to us all, but he had other matters on his mind.

"And how about someone to look after the playground? Condoms, needles, trash can overflowing, people letting their dogs crap everywhere. It's a mess."

I promised to pass on his concerns the next time I spoke to our contacts at the Parks Department.

"Well, I appreciate that, son," Henry said.

"We're trying to do our part. We just wish some of your neighbors were more welcoming." I tipped my head toward the other side of the street.

Henry's lip curled under his neat gray mustache. "Those project spics? Son, what do you expect?"

* * *

Okay, so the hoodoo was pretty consistently dismal. Henry may not have been the cuddliest fellow, but other than the local artists' colony, he was all we had. It was becoming clear that getting another group of students out to the farm would be tough.

Sal, no surprise, was pissed at us. Never has the term "spitting mad" been so apt.

"I knew you dipshits were trouble. It's my fault for trying to be a good guy."

We took our medicine, waiting for him to wear himself out, then meekly pleaded for a second chance.

"Uh-uh. No way. Believe me, nothing would make me happier than to dump my class on you and your fellow jerk-offs for a couple of hours, see how you do, but unlike you, I've got scruples. And if those kids find out their precious plants are dead, they're going to freak. That my poor, soft heart can't take."

I pointed out that we'd replanted their section of the farm, and in another week or two it would be looking as lush as before. Sal cocked his ear as if he'd misheard me.

"Are you saying that, because of their impairments, they won't be able to tell the difference?"

"No!"

"No? Because it sounds like you're suggesting we try to deceive a bunch of handicapped children, use their disabilities to our advantage."

We assured him we'd figure out a way to make it right.

Sal was already walking away. "Here's an idea: Build a time machine, travel back to before you decided to make a difference, and go fuck yourself."

I'll say this for Sal, he made his position clear. Begin to Win was harder to pin down. Miss Marcella always seemed to be busy when Elliot went to see her. Principal Jenner pretended not to see us and started walking faster when we tried to waylay him on his way into work one morning.

"Oh, they're definitely ducking you," Sasha told us when she came by to lend a hand. "I think they're freaked out by the opposition from the community."

"For fuck's sake," I said. "It's one guy!"

"I don't know. That's a lot of signs for one guy to put up."

"Signs?"

"Don't you guys ever walk around the neighborhood?"

The honest answer was not really. I always made a beeline from the subway to the farm and only left to hit the bodega for Gatorade and sandwiches. Elliot didn't seem to know what Sasha was talking about either.

She took us around the corner past a check cashing place and a barbershop offering "Dominican style" unisex cuts in flaking candy-colored paint. Halfway up the block, taped to a street lamp, was a piece of poster board, professionally printed by the look of it, with the same anti-farm logo we'd seen on the handball wall and the ballers' shirts. Beneath the logo was a block of all-caps text: "GARDENING WITHOUT A PERMIT = GENTRIFARMING. STOP THE UNLAWFUL TAKE-OVER OF OUR PUBLIC SPACE." "OUR" was underlined. In smaller type, there was an email address: "saveourcourt@yahoo.com."

"I have to admit," Sasha said, "'gentrifarming' is good."

Elliot leaned in like he was contemplating a piece of conceptual art. "'No justice, no peas' would have been better."

For the first time in who knows how long, I took a good look at my partner. His hair and beard had grown snarled, anarchic. I had no idea what a "Dominican style" cut was, but I was thinking it might be an improvement. He'd taken on the burnt umber hue of someone who lives outdoors, and I was starting to wonder about his grasp of our situation.

I reached out to rip the sign down, but Sasha caught my hand.

"You can't do that."

"She's right," Elliot said. "Trying to out-vandalize this guy is not the way to go."

Funny, just as I was having doubts about his state of mind, he was having doubts about mine. When he suggested I take the rest of the day off, I didn't even try to argue.

I didn't get much of a reprieve, though. Before I'd even made it back to my apartment, my cell was ringing. It was Marnie. I figured I'd better answer; I'd promised Elliot he wouldn't have to deal with her anymore.

Marnie didn't waste time on pleasantries. "We have a problem."

"What do you mean 'we,' white man?"

"What?"

Maybe I was starting to lose it.

"Nothing. What's the problem, Marnie?"

"Have you seen the *Times* today?"

I hadn't, but I happened to be standing in front of a stack of papers on display outside the organic grocer that used to be a regular grocer. I scanned the front page.

"You're right. That gridlock in Congress is a bitch."

"The Metro section, numb nuts."

There it was above the fold, accompanied by a photograph of a sprawling rooftop covered in rows of soil. Standing among the rows were John Cardini and several others I recognized as members of the Rita's crew, in various stages of planting, hoeing, and watering. Behind them, in the near distance, an archetypal New York City water tower and the American flag; in the far distance, the spires of Lower Manhattan. The headline was, "For One Brooklyn

Restaurant, Farm to Table is Just a Few Blocks."

"I've got to call you back," I said.

The story was written by a real estate reporter with name recognition. It started by setting the scene ("Bushwick, Brooklyn is as far from pastoral as it gets…"), then morphed into a typical dubious trend piece ("A new breed of urban farm, more ambitious than the familiar community garden, is appearing in cities across the country."), before hitting the colorful highlights of Rita's rise to glory (John's quasi-military background, the brick oven from Sicily, the wacky pizza names), of which *Times* readers apparently could not get enough. I was four graphs in before I got to the facts I needed: The rooftop in question belonged to an old industrial building owned by a big-time developer. He delivered a bland quote about energy efficiency and sustainability. The reporter mentioned the tax abatement he'd be getting, but reading between the lines, I suspected there was more to the arrangement. My guess was that the farm was the first step toward converting the place into a green condo like the one in Gowanus.

The farm itself was 40,000 square feet, more than four times the size of ours. Only about 25,000 square feet would be cultivated in time for harvest this fall, and the produce—mostly tomatoes, eggplants, peppers, herbs, and leafy greens—would go straight to Rita's kitchen with plans to sell to other restaurants next year. In his quotes, John was clear that this was a for-profit venture, and he was confident it would operate in the black. The seed money to start the project had come in large part from donations made by Rita's patrons. "These are people who care about Brooklyn and care about where their food comes from" he said. "They want local, and they're willing to pay for it—so that's what we're giving them." In my mind's eye, I saw those gold piggy banks from Chinatown loafing on the tables at Rita's. They winked at me.

But the best was yet to come. The donations from Rita's patrons were matched dollar-for-dollar by none other than Tommy Brutti. He was excited that the first grant from his new foundation would help fellow restaurateurs set New York City on a course toward a truly local food system.

"This isn't the same old philanthropy," Brutti said. "We're not sticking a few sorry tomato plants in a schoolyard, hanging up a sign with my name on it, and calling it a day. This is social entrepreneurship, and I expect that others will see this as a worthy investment."

Reading on, I learned money wasn't the only thing Brutti was contributing to the endeavor. The article named Greta as the farm's manager and gave her a graph of her own to expound on the farm's outreach to the community. Tours and volunteer opportunities were already available upon request, and a full-scale education program with workshops on earth science and nutrition would be up and running in time for the new school year. The article also credited Greta with coming up with the name: Crop Top Farm. I could just picture the merchandising opportunities John had lined up.

There was more—a perfunctory tip of the cap to Duncan Donner and In It Together, a wide-eyed account of how the soil was hoisted up to the roof by crane—but I couldn't bring myself to keep reading. I could barely direct my fingers to dial Elliot's number.

"And here I was thinking you don't know how to relax," Elliot said.

Following Marnie's example, I skipped the banter. Elliot was quiet for the six minutes or so it took me to read him the story.

"Fuck," was all he said when I was done.

"Yeah."

"Is that the *Times?*"

"Yeah."

"It sounds like the *Times.*"

"It's the *Times.*"

"Fuck."

I waited for him to collect himself.

"I'm in Rita's at least once a week. Nobody said a word."

"Must have slipped their minds."

"Now that I think about it, Greta's been asking me a lot of questions about the curriculum. How it's going, who we're working with…"

"She clearly feels invested in our success."

"Okay," Elliot said. "I'm going to Rita's."

"I'll meet you there."

There was a long pause. "Don't bother. I'm right around the corner. Anyway, John's not the kind of guy you gang up on."

At that point, the idea of never again setting foot in John Cardini's lair sounded pretty good to me. I wished Elliot luck and scheduled a debrief at Flake in the morning.

I was still staring at the *Times* piece, and just as I hung up, my eye was drawn to a detail in the background of the photo: behind John and the others, a series of wooden posts stood against the parapet, each with vines spiraling down its length. The vines were mostly leaf, but if you looked closely, you could see they were studded with nubs of pale red.

"Motherfucker." Fucking *fraise de bois.*

Lone Ranger

A Park Slope mommy's club had annexed Flake, so we took our business outside. We sat on the curb while Elliot nursed his coffee, the waft from his cup strong enough to cut through the curdled sea smell of the canal and make my mouth water. Flake did a $4 pour-over using Stumptown beans roasted in Red Hook. Despite a gnawing headache, I'd decided I couldn't afford a $4 coffee of my own.

Elliot recapped his showdown with John. "He said it wasn't personal."

"Don't tell me he used the words…"

Elliot nodded. "'It's just business.'"

"So he didn't even say sorry?"

"He said he'd been upfront about his interests. When he saw the way things were going, he had no choice."

"He could have chosen not to poach our biggest donors."

"Well, Tommy Brutti was his connection to start with, so I can't really blame him there."

I told him about the *fraise de bois*.

"That didn't come up," Elliot said.

"I'm sure he's fucking over so many people, it's hard to keep track."

Elliot had nothing to say to that, so I kept going.

"What I don't get is why he snuck around behind our backs. Why not come to us and say, 'Hey, this isn't working for me. Let's figure it out'?"

Elliot took a slow slug of coffee, then wiped his mouth with his sleeve. He swirled what was left in the cup like he could read our fortune in it. I could tell he was stalling.

"Spit it out."

He took a measured breath. "John felt like he wasn't clicking with certain members of the team. He thought it was best if he did his own thing."

"'Certain members' meaning me?"

Elliot left the answer unsaid.

"So this is my fault now? Because I didn't kiss his ass like everyone else? My bad. I didn't realize mercenaries were so sensitive."

"Don't be too hard on yourself. He didn't like Seth either."

I knew he was trying to lighten the mood, but somehow that just made me pissier. "I bet you still meet his approval, though. Right, Miss Congeniality? How did you two leave it, anyway? No harm, no foul? Free Psycho Kale'ers for life?"

"Actually, he offered me a job."

If I hadn't been too poor to buy myself a coffee, I'd have done a spit-take. "What?"

"He wants me to run the education program at Crop Top. Got the money set aside and everything."

I felt a rush in my gut and armpits. There was absolutely no way I was capable of running the farm without Elliot.

"What did you say?"

"I told him we'd come too far. I couldn't abandon my partner."

"That's noble and everything," I said. "But if you want to take the job, I'm not going to stand in your way."

"It's not just you. Part of the reason we got into this in the first place was so we could be our own bosses, right? Besides, I really think we're over the hump now."

"You do? Because I feel like we might be under the hump."

Elliot ticked off our accomplishments on his calloused fingers. "We got the thing built. Then we got it rebuilt. We hosted our first group of kids, and they ate it up. We've got a bulletproof logic model, and our curriculum is the shit. If we can just make it to the start of the school year, we can get the parents on our side, and this Contreras bullshit will all blow over. Then it's harvest time, and by winter we'll have solid outcomes we can take to Prometheus."

Listening to him, I could just about believe it. "So you don't think John fucked us?"

"Only if you buy the idea that we're in competition."

I could see where he was going. "They're for-profit. We're not-for-profit."

"Exactly. They're a large-scale agricultural operation with a sideline in education. We're all education all the time."

"Tommy Brutti doesn't want to stick a few tomato plants in a schoolyard. Well, we do."

Elliot tipped an invisible cap in my direction. "Now you're talking."

"We're not setting up on some random rooftop and telling schools to come to us. We're customizing solutions for each school we work with."

"Customizing solutions? Nice."

I'd picked it up from Seth's website and held onto it for the right occasion. But just when I was getting warmed up, the *Times* photo snapped into my mind.

"What about the *fraise de bois?*"

"Fuck the *fraise de bois!*" Elliot said. "If Gollick wants to throw a little money at Crop Top, what's it to us? He's got enough for everyone. And we still have something John doesn't, something way better than *fraise de bois.*"

"Viv."

Right on cue, Elliot's phone buzzed. Sure enough, it was Vivienne. Elliot put her on speaker.

"We were just talking about you."

Her voice came out trebly, small. "Boys, we have a problem."

The door of Flake creaked open and a tyke with cereal-commercial-blonde locks toddled past us into the street, perhaps drawn by the sparkle of broken glass. A shriek of "Liam!" followed him, but for a long, unsettled moment that was it. The boy looked at me, and I could see the doubt in his elfin eyes. Maybe mommy wasn't coming to the rescue.

* * *

The problem of the hour was this: Gollick's office had sent a check. That sounded like good news—manna from heaven, even—until

Vivienne revealed the dollar amount: $5,000.

"A first installment?" My voice had breached the line between hope and desperation.

"That's what I thought," Vivienne said. "Then I saw the note in the memo section. 'Good luck with your endeavor.' He didn't even write it himself, the weasel. Must have dictated it from the Temple Mount."

"Maybe it's not what it sounds like."

"Trust me, it's what it sounds like."

Elliot and I looked at each other. I'm sure my face was just as slack and empty as his. We'd already spent twenty times the amount of Gollick's donation on construction and reconstruction. Kat would be expecting her first month's wages within a matter of days.

"I tried getting in touch with him," Vivienne said, "but his cell doesn't work over there. How convenient, right? I swear, I have half a mind to send that check back."

"No!" Elliot was just a split second behind me.

"I have other friends, you know. We'll just turn the ribbon-cutting ceremony into a fundraiser. Some wine and cheese—no, make that crudités from the garden—some kids singing 'Old MacDonald,' we'll be flush in a matter of hours."

I didn't have the heart to tell her the ribbon-cutting ceremony was a dead end. Crudité? Even if our first planting hadn't been desecrated, we'd be lucky to scare up a few wan stalks of celery before the fall. Wine was a non-starter; it would take half of Gollick's contribution to keep Vivienne's crowd well-lubed. Hell, we couldn't even book the singing kids, not with everyone at the two schools either avoiding us or openly rooting for us to fail.

Even if we could pull it off, my guess was that Marnie's enthusiasm for planning a big to-do was on the wane. Why, I could hear her asking, would anyone important want to wallow in some sad pile of dirt, when they'd just read about a far more impressive farm in *The New York Times?* Crop Top was four times the size of Raise the Roof; John was already a recognized visionary and media darling; he had the support of Tommy Brutti, an icon renowned the world over for his passion and integrity. Any potential donor showing up at our gate would recognize immediately that Crop Top was bound to be more influential, more successful, just plain better than we'd ever be. How we were going to raise the money we needed to settle our accounts was more than I could contemplate; my pressing concern was getting our hands on the money we did have. That brought on a queasy realization: we never got around to forming a 501c3.

"Who did Gollick make the check out to?" I asked.

There was a staticky rustle on the other end, Vivienne sighing. "I was getting to that. It's made out to 'Farm Project, care of the Begin to Win Foundation.'"

Made sense. Begin to Win was the only licensed nonprofit with a connection to the farm. Then why did I feel so uneasy? I was about to say something—what, I don't know—but Vivienne cut me off.

"I already talked to Arthur and Barbara. They're happy to handle the money for us, but they're going to charge a twenty-percent administrative fee."

"Twenty percent?" Elliot had been in a daze, but now his head snapped up just as mine was dropping to my chest. We must have looked like the world's most pathetic puppet show.

"They say they're incurring a lot of costs we didn't disclose.

Staff time, materials."

"What materials?"

"They said something about pens and popsicle sticks. Frankly, I think they're upset about that little incident the other day. They were hoping this would be a PR coup, and now they're being petty."

"This is extortion," I said. "Tell them, we can't give them more than ten percent."

"I know how you feel, kid, but you don't try to bargain with people like this. It won't fly. The sad fact is we need them more than they need us."

"But I'm having a baby!" It felt like the words were being ripped out of me. If we hadn't been in the middle of a forsaken industrial hinterland, I would've turned heads. Instead, there was only Elliot, blinking at me in confusion.

"Did I hear that right?" Vivienne said.

"Sorry," I said at a more socially acceptable volume. "Tricia's pregnant."

A jubilant yip came from Vivienne's end. "This is fantastic news! Children and work are life's greatest joys, I always say. Just don't ask me to rank them."

Last I heard, Vivienne wasn't on speaking terms with her daughter, a fragrance maker with her own boutique in the Village.

"Don't worry about a thing," she said. "The money is out there. It always is. And forget about Arthur and Barbara and their damn administrative fee. I'll write a check to cover it."

Better make it cash, I thought.

* * *

We needed to give Seth a heads-up on our little cash flow issue, and since Green 'Burgs was just a couple of blocks away, we figured we might as well get it over with. We came bearing a selection of fruit tarts from Flake, the money I'd saved by skipping coffee sacrificed to the cause. Seth seemed starved for company. He said it had been quiet around the incubator; the sneaker designers had already moved out, and the indie hip-hop moguls didn't give off an approachable vibe. We let him regale us with news of a commission to spruce up a traffic median in the Bronx. We humored him as he brainstormed about a partnership with the Flake ladies whereby Raise the Roof would become the official supplier of berries for their tarts. Then we dropped the bomb.

Sounds stupid, but I was startled by how abruptly Seth's mood shifted once we admitted we couldn't pay him. The guy had been so affable and obliging since we'd started working with him, I'd all but convinced myself he'd roll with the punches, commiserate on the lousy hand fate had dealt us, suggest a payment plan or some other practical accommodation. Not so much. Instead, he went through a time-lapse version of the five stages: denial ("This is not happening. Tell me this is not happening."), anger ("You motherfuckers! I should've known you'd fuck it all up!), bargaining ("How much cash *do* you have?"), depression ("This is going to ruin me."), and…well, we never quite got to acceptance. Instead, we circled back to anger and stayed there.

"When you said you weren't going to do any more community outreach—that's when I should've backed out. I knew right then you guys were trouble. But I needed a big win to get my name out there. And yeah, I needed the fucking money. Do you know how hard it is running your own business? Do you know how close to the fucking edge I am? I should've just called Green 'Burgs a nonprofit because then apparently I could do whatever the fuck I want."

He didn't seem close to calming down. His face was pink, and he was pacing with such velocity I thought he might literally bounce off the walls.

"You realize I saved your ass, right? I cleaned out my entire greenhouse so you'd have something to show for all your dicking around. You owe me five thousand just for the plants."

"I thought those plants were a donation," I said.

"The fuck they were!"

Elliot laid his hand on Seth's shoulder.

"You have to know we want to pay you," he said. "We're *going* to pay you. We just need some more time."

"And where does that leave me? Am I supposed to tell ConEd I need more time?"

"We may not have cash, but we still have connections. Buildings, Transportation, Environmental Protection...anybody with a say in city contracts, our ex-boss knows them."

Seth seemed to consider the offer and then physically shake it off, a dog with a fly in his ear. "No. The last thing I need is to get in any deeper with you guys. For all I know, my reputation is already shit by association. As a matter of fact, I'll make a deal with you: take my name off your website, never mention me to anyone in connection with this train wreck ever again. You leave here now, and we'll just pretend none of this ever happened."

I gave Elliot a quick look. Was Seth saying what I thought he was saying? It seemed improbable, but then, he may not have been in his right mind. In any case, we didn't press for clarification. We got the hell out of there before he had a change of heart.

Elliot had somehow managed to swipe one of the tarts, and he broke off a piece for me as we walked.

"You should've told him you were having a baby."

I scarfed the tart shard, my first morsel of food all day. An hour after purchase, it was still delicious. "My kid isn't even born, and I'm already a deadbeat."

"At least now you've got experience dealing with tantrums," Elliot said.

The concept of Papa Elliot had always been a mystery me. He certainly didn't look the part lately; in most jurisdictions, a beard like that would disqualify you from unmonitored contact with a minor. And yet I'd seen the rapport he had with Miss Marcella's third graders and how easy it came to him.

"I should've taken notes," I said.

"Wouldn't hold up in court. We're just going to have to hope Seth never comes to his senses."

"I meant the other day with the kids. Whatever magic power you have over them, I need some of it."

"The farm is actually good preparation for a kid. You're already exhausted, overwhelmed, and hemorrhaging money. All you need now is spit-up on your shirt."

"Jesus."

"You know what helps, in my experience? Drinking."

We set off in search of a bar—not a microbrewery or cocktail parlor but a real dive. It didn't take long to find our place, a nameless hole in the wall on Third Avenue: cheap wood paneling adorned with Christmas lights, a middle-aged woman with orange hair and fingernails tending to a couple of grim day-drinkers.

Elliot nodded in approval as our eyes adjusted to the gloom. "I figured out what our problem is. Too much daylight."

I tried to get into the spirit, but three-and-a-half IPAs were enough to make me dull and withdrawn, a brooder with no thoughts to dwell on. Elliot meanwhile was making friends with the bartender; she apparently lived in a houseboat on the canal, and Elliot let on that it was a lifestyle he was contemplating. I said goodbye without bothering to make a plan for tomorrow.

On my way home, I passed by the terrarium shop, and one of the wares on display in the window caught my heavy-lidded eye. Sitting on a stand that was either made from a tree stump, or cleverly designed to look like one, was a glass bulb, bigger than a snow globe but smaller than a fish bowl. Inside, a layer of gray stones was covered by a layer of soil, which in turn was topped by a miniature landscape of what looked like moss and ferns. In the midst of the greenery stood a plastic figure just slightly larger than my fingertip, a man in a black open-necked shirt and slacks, a gray sweater, or maybe it was a jacket, slung over his shoulder. Quite the little yuppie. His features were too tiny for me to tell what he was thinking. Was he pleased with himself for leaving the office and the condo behind? Or was he lost, desperate for a can of bug spray and a WiFi signal? Most importantly, did he realize he was trapped, sealed off from anyone who might have cared for him, all that indifferent nature closing in?

I was overcome by an urge to buy his freedom, extract him with a pair of tweezers, but the handwritten tag said $75, and I didn't have the cash.

Hang in there, brother, I thought as I dragged myself home.

* * *

"We have a problem."

Given my state of mind, it was entirely possible I'd begun to hear those words in my dreams. The evidence was mixed: a quick inspection revealed that I was in fact in bed; then again, I was sitting up and my eyes were open.

"Will?"

I traced the scratchy voice to its source: my cell phone, which I discovered pressed against my ear. I must have scooped it off my nightstand before I even woke up.

"Who is this?"

"Jack from Parks."

I happened to be wearing my watch (along with my clothes and shoes), so I checked it: a quarter to seven in the evening. Phase 2 of my intel-gathering operation was to listen for Tricia. It sounded like I had the apartment to myself. I dimly recalled her mentioning a yoga class—a lucky break. The last thing I needed was for her to come home from a long day of expressing glands and extracting swallowed string and find me sleeping one off.

"Are you with me, Will?"

"I'm with you. We have a problem. But, you know, we talked about it, and maybe it's not such a problem. John is doing his thing, we're doing ours. Fuck the *fraise de bois*."

There was a pause. "Okay. I don't know what you're talking about. What I'm talking about is Hector Contreras. I got a call today."

If Jack's voice was a cheese grater, my brain was a wedge of aged pecorino. I can't be this hungover, I thought.

"What the hell happened over there, Will? Didn't you go to the community board?"

I gather enough of my scattered wits to catch Jack up: the half-hearted approval of CB3, our decision (I was big enough to share the credit) not to meet with CB1, the discovery that the community was more attached to the handball court than he had led us to believe, the inane confrontation over permits, the rampage that followed. The silence on Jack's end was interrupted only by the occasional wheezy gasp, a response, I'm guessing, to the harshness of his preferred brand of cigarette, not the twists and turns in my account.

"And you're saying the kid who trashed the garden is Contreras' son?"

"What, he didn't mention that?"

"This is not good. You were supposed to reach out to the community, not stick your finger in their eye."

"I guess we overreached."

"You think this is a joke? Contreras is threatening to call a hearing. Maybe you can testify before the council about the misuse of Parks Department resources. Because I'm putting in for retirement."

"Don't worry. Viv is going to call him and straighten this out."

"Viv did call him. Suffice to say, he didn't appreciate her interest in the matter."

Score one for Elliot: letting Vivienne loose on Contreras had been a mistake. I curled into a ball, my knees touching my forehead. "What do you suggest we do?"

Jack didn't hesitate; apparently, the conversation up till this point had been nothing more than a preamble. "I wouldn't call this a suggestion so much as a kick in the ass. We're going to have a meeting this Friday. Outside at the site. I told Contreras to get the word out to his people. Anyone who's got a problem with the garden, this is their chance to get it off their chest."

"What if they all want us out?"

"Then you're out. We're not in the business of forcing amenities on communities that don't want them. So my advice to you is to make sure all your allies are there."

I tried to take a mental roll call of our allies; it was a short list.

"They really made T-shirts with the leaf crossed out?" Jack asked.

I told him they did. He chuckled—the same guy who'd scolded me for making light of our predicament. Maybe he was just coughing up phlegm.

"Congratulations, son. Gardens get vandalized every day. But in forty years, yours is the first to incite organized community opposition."

It was official. No matter what happened next, I'd accomplished something with my life.

* * *

Elliot didn't answer my first few calls. I imagined him and the other day-drinkers taking the party to the bartender's houseboat, a cellular dead zone. When he finally picked up, though, I could hear Sadie screaming in the background. Once I'd filled him in on my parley with Jack, there was a long pause, so long, if it hadn't been for the kiddie clamor, I would've thought we'd gotten disconnected.

"I can't do Friday," he said finally.

"You have to. The meeting's set. Jack's printing up flyers."

"It's Sadie's birthday. We have plans."

"The meeting isn't till six. Have your party in the afternoon."

Elliot's answer was muffled. I realized he was covering his mouth with his hand. "We have evening plans. We're going to a concert."

I was mulling this over when intuition struck. "The Pavement reunion?"

Elliot didn't answer.

"Your three-year-old's a big Pavement fan?"

"Well, she's going to be four at that point. But yeah, as a matter of fact, she is."

"Are you fucking with me?"

"'Shady Lane' is her jam. I have a playlist that's just 'Shady Lane' twenty times in a row, and whenever she's on the verge of a meltdown, I throw it on."

"I can't believe this."

"I'm more of a 'Summer Babe' guy myself, but hey, whatever works. You'll understand when you have yours."

Something about that last comment rubbed me wrong. It felt like Elliot was pulling rank, taking advantage of his status as a veteran dad. Which reminded me, Sadie had a mom, too.

"Why can't Cora take her to the concert?"

"Pavement is kind of our daddy-daughter thing."

"This isn't optional," I said, channeling my inner Jack. "Friday could be our last stand."

I was acutely aware that I used to be his boss. Used to be.

"It's just another meeting," he said. "You and I both know there's no anti-farm movement. It's one guy handing out free T-shirts."

"You really expect me to face this alone?"

"You said you didn't want to be the behind-the-scenes guy, remember?"

Had we been standing face to face just then, I would've kicked him in the shins.

"I'll make the rounds tomorrow," he said. "Line up our supporters."

"That should leave you a good ten, twelve hours to chill at Rita's."

As soon as the words had left my mouth, I wanted to reel them back in. Elliot had worked just as hard as me. Harder really, when you factored in curriculum development and gravel hauling. We both knew it. I wouldn't have blamed him for throwing it in my face.

He didn't. Instead, he said, "Look, if you really need me, I'll bail on the concert, tell Sadie I have to work." Those last words were barely audible.

I pressed the screen of my phone against my temple. All along, the dream for Elliot was to be his own man, free to follow his own funky drummer. I couldn't bring myself to take that away from him.

"I can handle it," I said.

"I know you can. You always do."

Tough to stay pissed at a guy like that. In fact, I wanted to live up to his confidence. Time to man up, kemosabe.

Power to You People

Elliot was wrong about the protest being a one-man show. It was the first time I'd seen anything resembling a crowd in Peter's Place. Hector Contreras' son was there all right, but he was joined by about a dozen others in anti-farm shirts, including Felix, Nelson, and Dante, the three ballers. Contreras the elder was nowhere to be seen, but the meeting wasn't devoid of political representation. Like the ghosts of officialdom past, the stalwarts of CB3 had come to haunt me: the chairman mopping the mugginess of the evening off his pate; the maybe-albino bodybuilder; Suzette the upstart, her braids swaying like a beaded curtain. They were conferring with a short woman, her soft features belied by a military-grade crew cut. An envoy, I figured, from the much-spoken-of, never-spoken-to CB1.

I immediately sought out the supporters Elliot had committed to rallying. No surprise, the pickings were slim. Sasha and Xander were there, along with some of their creatively pierced neighbors. They waved, and I longed to join them, but the optics wouldn't have been favorable. Henry, the former Pfizer employee, was standing with a couple of older black women in floral print dresses, probably fellow residents of the row houses. I caught his eye, but what I saw there looked nothing like an invitation.

The sight of Kat and Ash approaching was so comforting it took me a minute to notice what they were wearing: matching white T-shirts emblazoned with a crossed-out leaf. I headed them off before they could join the protesters.

"This is a joke, right?"

They looked at each other, then at me, Kat with an expression that split the difference between guilt and pity, Ash with something more like defiance.

"We've been getting to know the people around here," she said. "They feel ignored. No one's ever asked them what kind of improvements they want to see."

"You can't do this," I said.

Ash squared his shoulders. "Still a free country, last time I checked."

"I'm paying you, for fuck's sake! You work for me."

Kat frowned, a mother disappointed in her wayward son. "That's not what we heard."

"Seth told us nobody's getting paid," Ash said.

"Is that what this is? A shakedown? Because we've got money. Kat, there's enough to pay you through the season. As for you"—I glared at Ash—"we made a deal with Seth. If you've got a problem, you need to work it out with him."

"It's not about the money," Kat said. "It's about doing the right thing."

"You know how that movie ends? There's a riot."

"This doesn't have to be ugly," she said. "You and Elliot seem like okay guys. You've got good intentions. At least, I think you do. All we're saying is you need to open a dialogue with the community you're trying to serve."

I was afraid if I kept looking at her I'd start to twitch, so I turned my head. "Obviously, I can't have you taking care of the farm if you're siding with people who want to destroy it."

"No worries. I'm taking a job at Crop Top, Senior Gardener and Educator."

Perfect. "Good luck," I said. I'd need WD-40 to unclench my jaw.

They left me standing alone. I closed my eyes and tried to collect myself. When I opened them, there was a guy standing in front of me, his skin more freckle than not, red hair approaching afro proportions, eyes red-rimmed and watery like a mole's.

"You one of the organizers?" he asked me.

"Not exactly," I said.

"Oh, well, I'm from the *Post*. I got a call from Councilman Contreras, and it sounded like there might be a story here."

He held out his hand. It was weirdly cold, considering the weather, like he'd been icing it.

"So, you live around here?" he asked. I couldn't tell if it was a genuine question or a reporter's trap.

"I'm one of the farmers."

"Oh, great." He slipped his hand into the pocket of his cargo pants and pulled out a tape recorder. "So why don't you tell me what's going on here tonight?"

"Just trying to have a dialogue with the community we serve."

"Seems like a lot of folks are pretty upset about what you're doing."

"I wouldn't say that."

What was with "folks" all of a sudden, I wondered. Brad at Prometheus, Seth at the community board meeting, Obama, now this guy.

"Really?" the reporter said. "Because I'm hearing there's controversy over the use of the handball court."

You'd like that, wouldn't you, I thought, imagining the headline: TRIANGLE RESIDENTS GO BALLS TO THE WALL AGAINST PARKS BOONDOGGLE. They'd never been big fans of Vivienne at the *Post*, which suggested another possibility: PARK AVENUE VIV ON BROOKLYN BALLERS: LET THEM EAT SPROUTS!

"I wouldn't say that either."

"So what would you say?"

I was itching to give him a "no comment," but I knew that would be tantamount to an admission of guilt.

"I'd say give us a chance. We're trying to make a difference here. All we're asking for is a little understanding."

"So the problem, as you see it, is that folks here don't understand what you're trying to do?"

"No! I didn't say there was a problem. No problem, just dialogue."

I don't know if it was the pleading note in my voice or the utter lack of quotable material in what I'd said, but the reporter seemed to lose interest in pressing me. He said he'd follow up for comment after the meeting. With that to look forward to, I watched him burrow into the crowd.

Jack was the last one to show up, but there was no sign of hurry in his step. For all the world, he was just a man out for an evening stroll. He patted my shoulder as he walked by, but that was the extent of his solidarity. No pre-gaming, no sizing up the opposition. I had little choice but to tag along after him like a caddy. He zeroed in on the community board contingent, shaking hands with the chairman and company. I followed suit, but they didn't seem too enthused about getting reacquainted. All the while, Jack was scanning the faces of the protesters. At one point, he leaned in close to my ear and said, "Isn't the girl one of yours?" casting a glance in Kat's direction. I tried to convey the complexity of the situation with just the look on my face, but Jack's own expression—like he'd taken a sniff of expired milk—told me he'd already gauged the extent of my failure and moved on.

"Which one's Contreras?" he asked.

I didn't think it was a good idea to point, so, like a silent movie stooge, I directed Jack with my eyes. The Contreras kid was wearing the same uniform as when I'd last seen him—button-down and khakis—only this time he'd topped it off with an oversized anti-farm shirt, and he was wielding a clipboard. Watching him collect signatures, radiating a proud tenacity, I presumed this was a dry run for public life. The elder Contreras had lit the fire under Jack, but he was staying away so the son could have his moment and maybe lay the foundation of a political dynasty.

Jack didn't hesitate; gnarled hand stretched out in front of him, he cut a path straight to the Contreras kid, towing me in his wake. They shook as Jack introduced himself and thanked him for getting the word out. Then he pivoted neatly to the side so there was nothing between the kid and me.

"You two know each other, I think."

Contreras acknowledged me with an imperious nod. I nodded

back. Jack laid a hand on each of our shoulders like we were captains of opposing teams and he was the referee, laying the ground rules before the big game.

"Trust me, as long as everyone is calm and respectful, this is going to be a constructive conversation."

By this point, the rest of the assembled had gathered around us in a loose circle. With the deliberate nonchalance that was his habit (or more likely his preferred ploy), Jack removed a cigarette and a Bic from his pocket protector, lit up, and took a deep, serene drag while we all waited.

"All right." He spoke loudly enough for everyone to hear without making any apparent effort to project his voice. "What's the problem?"

Silence. I think everyone was expecting a bit more ceremony, some opening remarks— "On behalf of the Parks Department, I'd like to take the opportunity to recognize the esteemed representatives of Community Board 3…"—the usual. Eventually, after Jack made a show of checking his watch, it sunk in that the floor was open and the clock ticking. Contreras launched into a tirade about the illegal occupation of the handball court—he actually used those words—but Jack cut him off before he could build up a head of steam.

"Illegal? Illegal how?"

Contreras sputtered something about permits. Jack waved his hand for silence and, to my amazement, got it.

"Let me explain this so there's no misunderstanding. All of this"—he swept his arm to take in the playground, the parking lot, the handball court—"is owned by the Parks Department. Frankly, we haven't done enough over the years to put this land to good use.

That's on us."

Jack held his hand to his chest, mea culpa. "Now, based on our assessment, we determined that the handball court was underutilized, and so we issued a community garden license to this gentleman's organization. That gives them the legal right to be here."

Contreras couldn't contain himself any longer. "What about our rights? Why didn't anyone come to us?"

"We asked Raise the Roof to make a presentation to your community board," Jack said. "That's the process. And my understanding is there were no objections to the project."

The chairman of the community board cleared his throat. "We said at the time we weren't fully briefed on the situation in this particular neighborhood. Consequently, we recommended the gentlemen engage Community Board 1 before proceeding with the project."

Suzette stepped forward. "No disrespect, but we represent Bed-Stuy. We don't know the Broadway Triangle from Times Square. It could be a damn rhombus for all we care. We were promised services in *our* community."

Jack nodded as if this all made perfect sense and bore no further explanation. "Sounds like the process broke down," he said. "That can happen when a neighborhood falls on the dividing line between districts. But we're all here now, so let's figure this out. What I need to know is this: was the handball court being used regularly before the garden came in?"

The more vocal protesters confirmed that it was.

"What's wrong with the court up the street?"

Like a Shakespearean chorus, the three ballers stepped up

and recited the history of enmity between Tompkins Houses and Borinquen Plaza. Jack stared at the ground, hands folded behind his back, as if he were transcribing every word in some psychic ledger. When they were finished, he kept his head down, giving us all the impression he was reviewing the evidence assembled there.

Just when I thought he might have dozed off, Jack looked up. "All right, so our assessment that the court was underutilized was wrong. On behalf of the Parks Department, I take full responsibility for that."

This acknowledgement of accountability had a funny effect on the protesters: They seemed subdued, maybe even a little disappointed. It was up to Contreras to rekindle the fire.

"That's just talk," he said. "We want to see action."

Jack dipped his shoulders as if he were literally bowing to the pressure. "If the decision here tonight is that the handball court should be restored, we'll move the garden out first thing Monday morning."

A whoop went up from the crowd. Contreras looked dumbfounded — I could tell he'd never anticipated scoring such an easy victory. Now he must have been wondering whether this was as desirable an outcome as the press-worthy civil disobedience he'd envisioned. I was pretty stunned myself. Jack had warned me we might be out, but I'd expected at least a token effort to win over the naysayers. Now it was up to me.

"Wait a second," I said. "What if we each got half the court? Handball on one side of the wall, farm on the other?"

"I don't think safety regulations would allow it," Jack said.

So much for that. If there was a more persuasive plea to be

made on our behalf, it wasn't coming to me.

"I'm sorry," Sasha said, elbowing her way to the center of the circle. "This is bullshit."

I heard a high-pitched sound coming from the back of someone's throat, but I couldn't tell if it signaled indignation or mockery.

"Sure, they were using that handball court," she said to Jack. "They were using it to park their cars and blast music all night. Before Will and Elliot came, the ground was covered with broken bottles and used condoms."

From the outer edge of the circle, Dante said, "Don't forget the blunts, yo."

Felix punched him hard in the arm.

"You all should be ashamed," Sasha said. "We're trying to make this a better place for kids, and you're ruining it."

What she hoped to accomplish with that kind of talk I couldn't say, and I bet she couldn't either. What she got was Suzette, shoulders thrown back, raring for battle.

"Who's 'you all'? You think people of color don't care about kids?"

"Who said anything about people of color?"

"Look around you, child. This is a community of color."

"We live here, too," Sasha said, glancing behind her, perhaps to make sure her friends were still there.

"Maybe that's the problem," Suzette said.

"Mmm-hmm."

"Tell her."

Contreras looked anxious to resume the leadership role. "It's gentrification, plain and simple. You come in here, and right away you try to take over, turn our handball court into your backyard."

Sasha groaned. "Give me a break."

Now probably wasn't a good time to mention the garden access we'd promised her landlord in exchange for water.

She spotted Henry and pounced on him with her eyes. "Sir, I've seen you working in the garden. I'd like to hear what you have to say."

Henry rubbed his jaw as if he needed to warm it up before he could speak. "I don't care if it's a garden, a handball court, or a damn Ferris wheel. A child was beat up the other day. We've got rats everywhere because no one picks up the trash. And y'all talking about gentrification? Please."

He pointed at Jack. "This is the first time I can recall someone from the city coming out here. You're from the Parks Department, right? Okay, but where's Sanitation? Where's the NYPD?"

"We already got all these white people up in our shit," Felix said. "Now you want the cops, too? Man, you're crazy."

"Come over here and find out how crazy I am."

Jack flung out his hand like a traffic cop. "Okay, I think we've all said our piece. Let me see if I can sum up the main points."

He left his hand hanging in the air, index finger extended. "Number one: a majority of you want the handball court to be restored."

I could see that Sasha wanted to object, but there was no denying we were outnumbered. Jack raised a second finger. "Number two: there have been some incidents of disorderly conduct and vandalism associated with the handball court."

There were a few murmurs of dissent, but Jack ignored them, hoisting a third finger. "Number three: the city has been negligent in providing services to this area. How'd I do?"

No one saw anything to gain by answering one way or the other, so Jack pressed on. "If you bear with me, I think we can address all these problems tonight. First, I want to be clear that this is about more than just the handball court. We view this entire area—the court, the playground, the parking lot—as one piece of property, and our goal is to revitalize all of it."

A different kind of murmur fluttered through the crowd—not approving but receptive.

"A lot of things are going to have to happen in order to make that goal a reality, but we see tonight as the start of the process. You say no one's been out here, no one's listened to your concerns. Well, I'm here now, so tell me: if you could have any type of public amenity in this space, what would you want to see?"

For the third time, Jack had caught the protesters off guard. Naturally, the least inhibited of the group was the first to get into the spirit.

Dante raised his hand and spoke at the same time. "A football field!"

"A football field," Jack said evenly.

"We already play in the parking lot, but it's kind of hard with all the cars in the way."

"A regulation football field is 57,000 square feet, so we're short on space. How many of you play basketball?"

Naturally, the three ballers raised their hands, along with about a half dozen others.

"We can do a basketball court," Jack said. "What else?"

"A waterslide!" The suggestion came from a teenager in tear-away track pants and a bikini top. If Jack were to conjure a waterslide from thin air, she'd be ready.

"A water amenity is a major project, but it's possible," he said. "We've done some really creative shower sprays. Will, help me out. There's a pipe under the playground, correct?"

I nodded in wonder. Was this really how it worked? If they said they wanted a rec center, would he offer them a few picnic tables?

Suzette was next in line. "We're all about creating positive opportunities for the young people," she began. The chairman cast his eyes heavenward.

"What we need is a performance space with a stage and sound equipment so we can host poetry nights, a griot circle, give the young people a chance to express themselves and explore their heritage."

Lo and behold, the Triangle was in Bed-Stuy after all.

If Jack was on my wavelength, he didn't show it. "No reason you couldn't host performances here."

"What we need most is a dog run." It was the woman Kat had talked to back in the spring. Her black lab wasn't with her, but she was wearing the same army surplus coat.

"The damn dogs already have the run of this place," Henry said. "Just check your shoes."

"They have to go somewhere! If we had a dog run, no one would have to worry about their shoes."

"What about a skate park?" Kat said. "Daryl, the boy who was assaulted—he and his friends were learning to skate."

Jack hung his head, observing a personal moment of silence for Daryl. When he looked up again, it was back to business. "Okay, let's see what we've got so far. Basketball courts, some type of water amenity, a performance space, a dog run, a skate park. Anything else?"

The crowd was quiet. The question may well have sounded sarcastic to them. I myself expected Jack to deliver a lecture about budget constraints, staff resources, logistics, but that wasn't where he was going.

"Before we move ahead, we have to answer a couple of questions. First, is the handball court going to be part of the future of this site?"

Contreras waved his finger. Finally, something he could object to. "Uh-uh. You can't just promise us a bunch of stuff and take away what we already have. No handball court, no deal."

There were some low grumbles and sidelong looks. It seemed to me the protesters were hoping someone would break rank and say Contreras didn't speak for them; they'd gladly trade the handball court for basketball and a waterslide. Jack, on the other hand, accepted the kid's authority without question, raising his arms in surrender.

"Okay, the handball court stays. Had to ask. Next question: do you think we can find a little room for this man's garden, so the children who have plants growing here won't be disappointed? Maybe carve a little space out of the parking lot?"

"Won't it get in the way of the basketball court?" Felix asked.

Jack shut one eye and surveyed the lot. "We'll have to scale down a bit, take advantage of vertical space, maybe build more trellises. But there should be room for everybody. Will, would you be amenable to that?"

Suddenly, I was the center of attention. Jack was managing

the situation so briskly, it didn't seem real. Were we spit-balling or negotiating?

It felt like a minute before I found my voice. "We get our water from the building next door. I don't know if we can stretch a hose all the way out to the parking lot."

Jack dismissed my concern with a flick of the wrist. "Not a problem. Once we tap that pipe under the playground, that'll be your water source."

I wanted to ask when exactly we could expect that to happen, but that would've made me the turd on the waterslide. Instead I said, "We don't have enough money to rebuild again."

"This was a Parks mistake, so Parks will incur the cost. Any plants that don't survive the move, we'll replace."

I took a breath. I thought about saying I needed to consult my partner, but what was there to consult about, really? "We can work with whatever space is available. If the community's willing to share."

Jack faced Contreras.

"What do you say? Remember, we wouldn't even be here talking about revitalization if they hadn't taken the first step."

How's that for rhetorical jujitsu? In just a few words, Jack had recast us as neighborhood saviors. Judging by his expression, Contreras seemed reluctant to give ground, but he found himself with no credible reason to refuse.

"We get what we're promised, they can stay." He tried to put some weight behind the words, so everyone would appreciate that he was driving a hard bargain.

Jack wasn't done with him yet. "In that case, we're going to need your help keeping the garden *and* the handball court secure. Can I get your word on that? Because I can tell you Parks isn't going to invest heavily in an area that's a target for vandalism and loitering."

Contreras did something with his neck that could fairly be described as squirming. I could tell he didn't want to take responsibility for any criminal mischief, but now his authority depended on it.

"We'll get the word out," he muttered.

Jack flashed a set of faded dentures. "Isn't that terrific? We're making real progress here. I'd love it if you two could shake hands and seal the deal."

It's weird feeling like a marionette, at the end of another man's string. I figured Contreras must have been thinking along the same lines, but when he took my hand, the gesture wasn't perfunctory. He squeezed it hard and, looking me straight in the eye, said, "Nothing personal, man," with genuine emotion. Must have been contagious. An intense relief was spreading from my chest to the top of my head.

"Now, let's talk next steps," Jack said. "We've got a lot of work ahead of us. The first order of business is to form a steering committee that can oversee the planning and act as a liaison between the city and the community. The two of you will be on it, of course, plus a representative from Community Board 3, and Community Board 1, if they choose to participate."

I opened my mouth, but Jack wasn't finished. "It may take a year or two to put together a comprehensive plan, make sure all the relevant stakeholders get a chance to give their input, and steer it through the approval process. But I don't want anyone to worry. We're not going to wait to make changes. Like I said earlier, we'll be here Monday morning to move the garden and restore the handball court. We're also going to get the ball rolling on reclaiming the parking lot as public space, so when we do have an approved redevelopment plan, we can get started immediately."

I wasn't sure what reclaiming the parking lot involved—a flag maybe?—but the crowd liked the sound of it. Everyone was nodding furiously, trying to keep up with Jack's administrative zeal.

"And as a show of good faith—because I know how much this community's been through—we're going to do some beautification, too." He strode over to the fence surrounding the playground, spent a minute contemplating the sickly pines planted in the swale, then strode back.

"Those trees aren't looking too good," he said. "Let's replace them with something that'll give a little more shade, some visual appeal. Elms, maybe, or willows." He snapped his fingers. "How about a couple of fruit trees, say a cherry and a pear? I'm sure if Parks donated the trees, Will and his team would be more than happy to donate the labor."

Something in me broke at that moment. These were the same sad, ugly trees that four months ago Jack had declared sacred, untouchable. If he'd let us replace them, then we never would have ventured into the handball court of the damned in the first place.

"I think we've covered all the issues we came here to discuss," Jack said, readying a fresh victory cigarette. "Thank you all for making this such a productive meeting. Will, is there anything you'd like to add?"

I let my gaze wander from face to face: Contreras was strutting around now like all had gone according to plan, the three ballers slapping him on the back. Suzette was huddled with the chairman and the bodybuilder, sketching an edifice in the air, no doubt a stage for the poetry slams and griot circles to come. Sasha and Xander were standing behind them, nodding, trying to look like part of the solution. I imagined having to sit at a table with these people for the next two years, hashing out the devilish details of the grand revitalization, feeling the pressure to deliver on Jack's promises. Would balls hit from the handball court into the dog run be fair game for the dogs? Would it be feasible to use a rainwater collection system for the shower spray? How about a shower spray for the dog run?

Was this my penance for refusing to meet with CB1? I thought about Elliot at the Pavement concert, Sadie on his shoulders, singing along to "Shady Lane": "Freeze, don't move/You've been chosen as an extra in the movie adaptation/of the sequel to your life."

"I made a mistake," I said quietly.

Jack's forehead took on an extra crease. "Will?"

"I made a mistake," I said again, louder this time. "I thought I could do this for myself and help other people, too. But I was picturing people in general, not, you know, *you* people."

Suzette's mouth sprung open, but I held up my hand before she could protest.

"I didn't mean it like that. Actually, I don't know what I mean. I'm sorry."

Contreras stepped forward and threw his arm around my neck. "It's okay, man. The past is the past. We're putting it behind us. Everybody wins, right?"

In my numb state I didn't immediately recognize that this was our "cue music" moment. Jack, however, had no such trouble: time to get the hell off the stage. The meeting was adjourned. I stood where I was while the crowd broke into its constituent groups. Kat unlocked the farm gate for Henry so he could retrieve his basil plant before Jack's goons came to tear it out of the ground. Nelson and Dante went deep in the parking lot to receive an imaginary pass from Felix; they hadn't given up their football dream. I figured I'd better pay my respects to Jack, but when I looked around, I couldn't find him. Having made the Triangle safe for democracy, he'd slipped away without a word, not even leaving a cigarette butt in his wake.

Before I could do the same, the *Post* reporter descended on me, his tape recorder set to stun. "That was quite a meeting."

I peered at the recorder then back at his speckled face. "You said it."

"One more thing: this whole area's called Peter's Place, right? Who is Peter, anyway?"

No room for loose ends at the *Post*. "The steering committee will be taking suggestions for a new name," I said.

"That's an official announcement?"

I told him if he reached out to Parks they'd be happy to give him all the details. Then I said it was time for me to be heading home.

Astride the Hump

When I got off the subway in Park Slope, it was around eight-thirty. Fifth Avenue was full of people. True to the stereotype, there were yuppie couples with strollers and one more on the way, waiting in front of the gelateria and the crêpe place. But there were also knots of young, good-looking gadabouts smoking outside the many bars—the gay bar, the lesbian bar, the gastropub, the Irish dive, the wine bar, the craft beer emporium, the old timey cocktail club, the outpost of the cheesy Manhattan tourist destination where you could get a manicure with your Cosmo. On the other end of the spectrum were the graying couples in high-waisted jeans (not the stylish Williamsburg kind) and elaborate nylon sandals, retired school teachers and bookkeepers who'd bought their brownstones back when all of Brooklyn was still considered the dark continent. They were out reaping the return on their foresight, walking all manner of complacent dogs—from state-of-the-art doodles and poos to ineffable shagadelic mutts to fetish breeds like the gallant Spinone. No doubt many of these very dogs had submitted to Tricia's needle, understanding that even the cushiest life has its trials.

There were kids, too, of course, the younger ones tooling around on their silver razor scooters, the teens roaming in packs, looking for trouble, but not looking too hard. In a few years, one more would join their ranks, assuming we hadn't been priced out by then.

The majority of faces were white, but the ratio wasn't as lopsided as the Slope's reputation would suggest. I passed Latin American families, black couples, a South Asian bachelorette party, all out enjoying the evening. And what an evening. The sun was leaving a pinkish afterglow as it melted away. The heat had taken a hard-earned break. Unseen birds were making dulcet small talk in the trees. The trees! A phalanx of lush elms lined the sidewalk.

I was passing by the local playground and the Old Stone House. The Old Stone House was exactly that, an unimposing replica of an eighteenth century farmhouse where General William Alexander and the Maryland 400 had staged their last stand against the Redcoats and the Hessians in the Battle of Brooklyn. Later it became the clubhouse for the Brooklyn Superbas, the earliest, mysteriously named incarnation of the Dodgers. The rebuilt Stone House had been there, slumped at the far end of the modest playground, as long as I'd been around. But in the last couple of years, a group of concerned citizens had decided it was time for a renovation, and in true Park Slope fashion, they made it a blow-out. The Friends of the Old Stone House raised millions, and seeing the opportunity for a showcase, the Parks Department and the local pols flung themselves onto the bandwagon: $3 million from the council; half a million from the borough president; a quarter million from Bloomberg; another hundred large in state grants, courtesy of the local assemblywoman. Everyone donned tricorn hats for the ribbon-cutting.

The result was a lavish park-playground-museum complex. The farmhouse was turned into an educational and cultural center, its original retaining wall recreated using locally quarried granite. The playground was revamped with a battery of new equipment, the cutting edge (figuratively speaking, of course) in slides, swings, and jungle gyms with a special gated area for toddlers, adorned with cutouts of farm animals. I'd never noticed before, but the water features really were impressive: spray cannons on turrets, an old-fashioned water pump, even a channel of running water meant to suggest a colonial-era mill stream. The sleepy park surrounding the playground and the farmhouse was reimagined as a souped-up recreation complex: a skate park, a soccer pitch, two basketball courts, a dog run, café seating with chessboard tabletops, and—count 'em—eight handball courts, enough for Dante to feel up a different girl in a different court every night of the week and twice on Sunday.

What really caught my eye this particular evening, though, was the garden. It was slightly smaller than ours (at least for another day or two; I'd just agreed to give up a big chunk of real estate), but compared to the mountains of gravel and the projectile sofa I'd grown used to, it was a dream. The design was simpler than what Seth had come up with, but it was executed to perfection—no welcome circle, no woven bamboo, just beds of mulch divided by paved walkways. Crop yield obviously wasn't a driving factor here. Towering sunflowers and redolent lavender were just as abundant as tomatoes and cucumbers. At the center was a stately open-air greenhouse composed of wooden beams; as I walked by, a little girl was wandering through, awed to be inside and outside at the same time. Best of all, the garden was a good twenty yards away from the handball courts. Standing in one, you might not even know the other was there. I wondered who was in charge of taking care of the plants; I bet they enjoyed their work.

Before the renovation, the playground had been perfectly adequate, far nicer, in fact—cleaner, safer, better equipped—than Peter's Place. But the minute Park Slope's ruling class decided it was time for an upgrade, the city's political players lined up to sweeten the pot. Meanwhile, it had taken me and Elliot blundering in with our wheelbarrows for anyone with pull to even notice the Triangle. And let's face it: Jack's assurances were no guarantee that the decades of neglect were over.

I had a funny feeling that change was less likely to come from Jack installing a water feature than from John Cardini opening the floodgates. Sooner or later, a Rita's imitator would stake its own claim, followed by a single origin coffee shop, an artfully curated consignment store or a pop-up gallery. The buzz and cheap rent would attract more Sashas and Xanders, who would eventually get married and have babies (not necessarily in that order). Xander would realize that doing graphic design for a commercial firm wasn't so bad after all; Sasha would get her master's in education, start taking teaching seriously as a career. They'd still make art when they could find the time. Their friends who'd gone into law and finance would come to visit and see that something was happening in the Triangle; there were actually some interesting places to eat and hang out. They could afford to buy, maybe even one of those sweet little row houses with a front yard. And hey, look there's already a charter school in the neighborhood! A few years would pass, and this new wave would no longer think of itself as new. Once they'd taken advantage of the full range of fertility treatments and maximized their earning potential, the campaign to bring café seating and a wicked half-pipe to Peter's Place would begin in earnest. Maybe they'd even get someone to pick up the trash.

All that might happen or it might not. If it did, odds were that Contreras, Suzette, and the rest would be protesting rising rents and the displacement of local businesses, and who could blame them? Hell, if I truly cared about the Triangle, not just as the backdrop for a *Savory Brooklyn* photo shoot, but as a real place where people lived and fought and played, I'd be right there alongside them, manning the barricades.

I wanted to care that much. I knew I should care that much. But knowing it wasn't the same as feeling it. What I did feel keenly was that it would be wrong to fake it. The people I'd met were impossible, but they deserved better than that.

As hard as it was to admit to myself, it was even harder breaking the news to Tricia. The rhino-dung-enriched soil I'd tracked on the rug, the arguments over how much she spent on moisturizer—all for nothing. She listened patiently as I stumbled through an account of the meeting and strained to explain my decision. She grimaced once or twice during my tale; I hoped it was just prenatal heartburn and not an involuntary reaction to my failure. The only words that really mattered were the last ones: "I can't do this anymore."

The first thing she said when I'd finished was, "What about Elliot? You're not just going to leave him hanging, are you?"

Truth be told, I hadn't thought much about Elliot since the meeting. When I found out John had offered him a job at Crop Top, my first thought had been that I couldn't possibly run Raise the Roof without him. Would he feel the same way? Was I, in effect, making a decision for both of us, the result of which would be the end of the farm? And what if I was? Was that reason enough to tough it out?

"I won't leave him hanging," I said. "I'll do whatever he needs for as long as I can. I just don't want to be responsible for it anymore."

"Then you've got nothing to be ashamed of."

"You sure about that?"

Tricia laid her hand on my arm and gave it a pinch. "Refusing to admit defeat is for losers."

I wished I could believe her. For the time being, it was enough to hear her say it.

She got up. I figured she was making her twentieth trip to the bathroom for the day, but then I heard the air conditioner in the bedroom kicking on.

"So," she called over the rumble, "what are you going to do now?"

This was the part I was dreading most, but I had a family to think about, and there was no putting it off. I swallowed hard.

"I'm going to talk to Viv."

* * *

Elliot showed up at Peter's Place on Monday bearing a gift: a Pavement T-shirt. Mercifully, it had rained all weekend, so neither of us had to come out to water. I had called him, though, to report back on the meeting.

"You did good," he said. "I'd say we're definitely over the hump now. Or, you know, atop the hump. Astride the hump?"

Jack had followed through on the first of his many promises. The moving crew from Parks was there to greet us when we arrived at sun-up. We pleaded with them to go easy on the plants, but it was clear their mandate was speed not finesse. Within a couple of hours, the farm we'd built in the handball court was gone. The section of the parking lot that had been fenced off for our use with wooden posts and chicken wire was about half the size. The guys loaded the gravel we no longer needed onto a truck, no doubt to be repurposed for another of Jack's schemes. I pointed out to the foreman that he was making off with at least a hundred bucks worth of gravel; he shrugged and said that just one of the trees he was delivering was worth triple that.

Ah, yes, the trees. The second of Jack's promises come to fruition, so to speak. While the Parks crew reassembled the farm and rinsed the film of dirt off the handball court (they'd brought their own high-powered hose, complete with water tank), Elliot and I were put to work digging up the swale bordering the playground to make way for the new trees (one pear, one hawthorn, one Japanese dogwood). As manual labor went, it was actually fairly diverting. The swale was studded with buried junk: tin soldiers, pottery shards, a spoon. It was like history's least important archaeological dig. The work went quickly. Knowing I wouldn't be doing this much longer made me swing my shovel with a little more oomph.

By the time the guys were finished, most of Seth's precious seedlings were kaput. In their place, they'd planted a funky grab bag, the dregs, no doubt, of some godforsaken Parks Department stash house. There were bell peppers and...well, mostly bell peppers with the occasional misshapen cabbage and listing bean pole thrown in. The foreman, however, stood back with his chin propped on his knuckles, like the Picasso of landscapers, waiting for us to express our appreciation. The source of his pride wasn't the vegetables but rather the battery of decorative bushes arrayed in pots around the inner perimeter of the fence. The effect was weird, like the garden—I couldn't bring myself to call this version a farm—was a tiny country club we were trying to protect from view. Whatever. There was room for the new chili plant I'd brought, so I could live with the rest of it.

There was one more promise left to be fulfilled that morning. Before they clocked off, the crew backed their truck up to the entrance of the parking lot and rolled an enormous boulder down a ramp, blocking the open space. I assumed it had to be a prop, hollow inside, but a quick inspection confirmed it was a genuine hunk of rock. The guys deposited another boulder in front of the second entrance on the other side of Peter's Place. Now the only way in and out was a small gate adjacent to the school building. The parking lot had been reclaimed.

Elliot and I were taking an inventory of the new garden when I told him I was out. He took it calmly, like he'd been expecting it. The lack of protest just encouraged me to babble on about water features, trees, and loyalty. I promised I had no intention of leaving him in the lurch.

"You still need me to water, I'll be here. Until I get a job, I mean. Obviously."

"You talk to Viv?"

"She sent me a few names. There's an old crank at the Century Club looking for someone to ghost-write letters to the editor."

"Wow. That sounds, um…"

"It's temporary. I hope. Between you and me, I want to try to find the next thing on my own. Anyway, I mean it. You need me, just say the word."

"Cool. I appreciate it."

"And that five thousand from Gollick?" I went on. "Now that we don't have to pay Kat for the rest of the summer, you should pay yourself."

"Actually, I think I'm going to use it to hire Dante."

"Babyface?"

"He's been angling for a job all summer. Should be good for community relations."

Even now, after my Jack-brokered truce with the community, it would never have crossed my mind to entrust one of the ballers with plant care. That was the difference between Elliot and me. If he could replace Kat with Dante, he'd probably have Contreras taking over for me before the week was out. Maybe he'd have been better off with a different co-director from the start.

"I hope I didn't fuck this up for you," I said.

"Don't worry about it. Once school starts, we'll be golden."

"No, I mean from the beginning. If you had a different partner, someone with a better attitude, maybe things wouldn't have turned out like this."

"Dude, if I had a different partner, Raise the Roof wouldn't have America's Next Top Logic Model."

"That's me, the logic master."

"Not always. You're the one who said, 'no more meetings, let's build the fucking thing already.' That wasn't logical. In fact, it was pretty goddamn perverse. But if you hadn't said it, we'd still be running between community boards, trying to make everyone happy. You, kemosabe, brought this whole clusterfuck to a head."

He rapped his fists together, then spread his fingers—boom.

"And now you have to deal with the fallout," I said.

"That's the fun part."

"You should take the job with Crop Top. John said it himself. Everything he does succeeds."

"I told you, I'm not feeling the whole working-for-the-man thing anymore. As long as I can still get comped at Rita's, my relationship with John is right where it should be."

"If Dante's going to do the watering, I can still write grant proposals. Seriously, anything you need."

"I thought you didn't want to be stuck in the background writing proposals."

I did say that, didn't I? I was about to tell Elliot that was the old me—the old new me. The new me (the new old me?) had gotten enough dirt under his nails for the time being. I didn't have a chance, though, because just then Sal came charging towards us, his Playboy medallion swinging, his face red with sunburn, rage, or a mix of the two.

"What did you little fuckers do now?" he said, his hoary chest heaving.

"There a problem, Sal?" Elliot asked with what I took to be genuine curiosity. I wasn't sure what was eating the guy either.

"Don't get cute with me. What's with the fucking boulders?"

"Oh, right," Elliot said. "That's not us. The Parks Department's reclaiming the space."

"They are, huh? And where exactly am I supposed to park? Do you know what it's like trying to find street parking around here? Everybody and their mother is looking for a spot near the hospital. The one thing that made my working conditions tolerable was knowing I always had a place to park."

"You should go to the next community meeting," I said. "Better yet, volunteer for the steering committee."

Sal squeezed his fists as though he was imagining them gripping a couple of stress balls or, more likely, our balls. "I know you two are behind this. The hoods scared you off their turf, so now you're moving in on ours. But you listen close: I'm the union rep for this dump. By the time we're through, their little act of vandalism is going to seem like a love tap. You've been warned!"

With that, he scuttled off in a hurry; his eggplant-colored PT Cruiser was parked in front of the fire hydrant.

Elliot laid his hand on one of the new decorative hedges like it was the head of a loyal dog. "You sure you want to quit?" he asked me. "Things are finally getting good."

The Next Evolution

Fast-forward a year-and-a-half or so, and before me is a tableau of abundance: cucumbers, tomatoes, spinach, radishes, carrots, peas, beans, even melons—all being tended by a crew of tweens and teens with serious expressions. A girl—at least I think it's a girl—in full beekeeper's regalia inspects a frame of honeycombs. An older boy shows a couple of newbies how to turn compost; they wrinkle their noses but do their part without complaint.

It would warm my heart me to tell you I was making a return visit to Peter's Place, but alas, I wasn't. I was taking a tour of Miss Lorraine's Farm, a project of The People's Pantry of Bed-Stuy, in my capacity as a program officer for the Prometheus Foundation. It felt good to be outside again.

After months cooped up in the apartment ghost-writing for Vivienne's opinionated friend; cranking out policy briefs for my Career Center instructor Mr. Clark, who'd finally decided to run for City Council; making funny faces at baby Pete, the offer from Prometheus had sounded like just the ticket. Brad remembered me, of course, and while he was intrigued by my experience in city government, I'm pretty sure I wouldn't have landed the job if I hadn't spent the past year "in the field," building a nonprofit from scratch. Never mind that what I'd built had all but collapsed around me (and that we'd never technically registered as a nonprofit). My mistakes just served to prove I was entrepreneurial, that I could relate to the typical Prometheus grantee; hell, Raise the Roof was a Prometheus grantee. You'd think the scant return on that planning grant would have disqualified me, but Brad didn't see it that way; on the contrary, it was my logic model that sealed the deal.

Now I'd been sent to shepherd the People's Pantry through the Prometheus trial by fire. There was a lot at stake, this being the foundation's biggest urban agriculture award since In It Together.

The People's Pantry was founded by a local reverend in the '70s. It was a typical food pantry, distributing provisions to the needy, until a few months ago, when Pastor Leo received a call from a fired-up woman named Suzette who was deeply concerned about the lack of positive outlets for young people in Bed-Stuy. For years, she'd been trying to organize basketball tournaments and poetry slams on shoestring budgets, but recently a vision of the future had come to her: young people of color going back to the land, learning to nourish themselves and respect Mother Earth. She'd seen it happen in other communities. Why not theirs? Pastor Leo was sold; the People's Pantry would begin growing its own fruits and vegetables, with youth from the church's afterschool program doing the weeding and hoeing. The legendary Miss Lorraine had died earlier that year; naming the farm after her was a natural. As one of the largest neighborhood hunger prevention programs in the city, the pantry already had a grant from Prometheus, so it was just a matter of asking for an increase. Prometheus, however, had other ideas. It usually does.

Rather than adding a zero to the pantry's anti-hunger grant, Prometheus saw an opportunity for an innovative (dare I say disruptive) economic development project: the food grown on the farm wouldn't be given away to the poor; it would be sold. The kiddie farmers wouldn't be volunteers; they'd be paid employees, not only earning a fair wage but developing the first line on their resumes. It was the In It Together model with a twist: rather than setting up a farm stand or selling to local restaurants (a market Crop Top had pretty much cornered in that section of Brooklyn), Prometheus had brokered a deal with the finally open Whole Foods in Gowanus. The site had been scrubbed of every last speck of toxic waste, and the shelves were overflowing with local products, more than a hundred of them.

Many of those items, as it happened, came from the Broadway Triangle. Pfizer had finally sold the largest building in its old factory complex to a developer, the same developer, in fact, who hosted Crop Top. Apparently, he'd acquired a soft spot for the new breed of Brooklyn entrepreneur. The big idea this time: turn the factory into an incubator like the one in Gowanus where Seth hung his shingle. The Pfizer incubator would be a more exclusive club, though, leasing only to Brooklyn's pluckiest food start-ups—the granola makers, the jerky curers, the taffy pullers, each a likely candidate for a *Savory Brooklyn* centerfold. Where once antidepressants and laxatives had flown off the assembly line, now a new generation of wares was winging its way onto shelves: KomBushwick DIY brewing kits, Ashkenummy small-batch gefilte fish, three rival brands of pickle.

The goods hatched from the Pfizer incubator joined a cornucopia of similarly hyper-local items: Flake, our former haunt, now had its own cookbook, *Bake Like a Flake*. Rita's was hawking frozen pizzas, John's first foray into packaged foods. It was a crowded field (Tommy Brutti's line of products alone could fill an aisle), but John had a competitive edge: his pies were baked and then flash-frozen, sealing in the old-world flavor imparted by Nonno Arturo's brick oven (or, more likely, a reasonable facsimile thereof). I picked one up the other day when Tricia had her hands full with little Pete; I have to admit, it wasn't terrible.

Nestled among these wonders were the fruits of the People's Pantry farm. Their bestseller was the People's Pluot, a plum-apricot hybrid. Prometheus had hired a product research firm to analyze the market for locally grown produce and identify any gaps. Money well spent (at Prometheus, there's no other kind) because the data pointed Pastor Leo to the pluot. The wisdom from above is full of good fruits, as the Bible says. I asked the analysts about the market potential of locally grown *fraise de bois*, knowing full well that if there were any, John would be all over it.

Actually, John had handed off the day-to-day decision-making at Crop Top to Greta. There were even rumblings that Crop Top may cut ties with Rita's and become a 501c3 after all. One rumor was that John had lost interest when it failed to turn a profit; another was that it *was* turning a profit, and he was seeking a more favorable tax arrangement. Either way, it was clear the farm was just one of many pots he had simmering on his crowded cooktop. The most intriguing of these was that John had quietly bought up the entire block around Rita's, lot by lot, and rather than expanding the always-teeming dining room, he was building the largest, most state-of-the-art kitchen in Brooklyn, a culinary laboratory to rival the fabled El Bulli in Spain. The kitchen would contain one table, where Francisco and visiting chefs from around the world would dish up their latest inventions to an invitation-only assemblage of trendsetters, string-pullers, and Page Six bait—hand-picked apostles of the legend of John Cardini. It would be the most exclusive table in the city.

The funny thing is that, even as he was ramping up his empire-building intrigues, John seemed to be losing interest in the hijinks that had been Rita's original *raison d'être*. Word was he only showed up at the restaurant once or twice a week, and only partied with the old abandon if there was a VIP who expected it. He spent the rest of his time holed up in the Rockaways where he'd bought a beach bungalow and (supposedly) opened a modest clam shack for local surfers, filing all the papers under an assumed name so no one in the business would catch wind of it. The subterfuge may have been for naught, though. The *Times* has reported sightings of waxed mustaches and kitchen implement tattoos on the boardwalk.

Meanwhile, Crop Top had established itself as the mecca of urban farming. Profitable or not, it was widely hosannaed for the many innovations it had introduced in its brief existence—everything from sunset yoga among the crops to the first mushrooms cultivated within city limits, a science project that started in one of the old Pfizer factory's abandoned chemical labs. As I understood it, many of these ideas came from Kat. She was like a shoot rescued from a withering vine and grafted onto a thriving one. Her latest stroke of inspiration was a program for refugees from war-torn countries. For the refugees, growing beloved foods from their homelands served as a kind of therapy. For the Crop Top team, the program was an opportunity to learn the refugees' native farming techniques and drum up a market for fruits and vegetables still largely unknown in the city. Genius. When I first heard about it, I got wistful about what might have happened if she'd come up with the idea while she was still working for me and Elliot.

I was getting wistful a lot in my first few months with Prometheus. The world, which is to say Brooklyn, had changed. Crop Top was just the most formidable in what had become a crowded field of competitors. All of a sudden, everyone was a farmer. In It Together was still around, though I'd heard rumors that Duncan was taking time off to write a book. Linda Light had cut the ribbon on the Living Classroom in Gravesend and was proud to announce plans for twelve more throughout the city. To help raise the funds, she was introducing a line of hand-forged egg-coddling spoons for $250 a pop. There were new organizations devoted specifically to beekeeping, poultry, and fish (Kat had been ahead of the tilapia curve, too). Every church, daycare center, and school—I mean every school—had a vegetable garden at least as big and well-designed as Raise the Roof's.

That urban farming was a boon to society was now considered self-evident. An article on the latest players and trends appeared every other week. Upstanding liberals were just as likely to donate to the vegetable plot around the corner as to the local animal shelter or soup kitchen. Elliot and I had never heard of Kickstarter when we were rounding up donors for Raise the Roof; just a few months later, it was an essential tool of the trade. Sometimes, when I was stuck at my desk, futzing with a PowerPoint presentation on "moonshots" and "strategic linkages," the knot of my tie pressing against my Adam's apple, I found it hard not to think of myself as a victim of bad timing. But then an intern would stick her head in my office to let me know there were croissants in the Cronus Room, and I'd remember I'm not a victim of anything.

I never went out to our farm again after the day it was moved to the parking lot. Whenever I asked if Elliot needed help, he and Dante and the usual neighborhood suspects seemed to have it covered. For a while, it looked like my absence really was going to prove the key to Raise the Roof's success. Then came the start of school. Sasha and Miss Marcella brought their classes out a few more times and gave Elliot's tricked-out curriculum a spin. But he was never able to rally the parents. The first round of standardized testing that semester was a bloodbath, and the Schlossers decided the time had come to oust Principal Jenner; there were factions for and against, and the ensuing tussle sucked up all the oxygen at the school. Elliot had to scrap his plans for a harvest festival fundraiser when it became clear no one was going to show. The money to pay Dante ran out. Vivienne was busy shaking down her friends for a new endeavor: VIV Academy Charter School. Marnie's idea, of course. Baruch was still dragging its heels on that endowed chair, so why not cut out the middleman and start a school of her own? Better yet, why not a chain of schools? The name stood for "Vision. Initiative. Victory."

On the bright side, Sal never made good on his threat of old-fashioned union action. Contreras and his bloc, too, kept their promise to leave the farm unmolested. By October, Elliot had a good two hundred pounds of bell peppers on his hands. The problem was what to do with them. He couldn't donate them to the Begin to Win cafeteria; it was too late to secure the necessary permissions from the Department of Education's Office of School Food. Distracted by all the drama with the handball court, we'd never gotten around to investigating the process. Nor had we tackled the paperwork to apply for a farmers market permit. So every morning for a month, Elliot showed up at the front office of Begin to Win and left a basket full of peppers for parents, students, and staff to take as they passed by. He brought another daily basket to the adjoining special ed school, but it was barely enough to make a dent. Sasha, Xander, Henry, and the few other card-carrying members of the farm each took home a share, and still Elliot was buried in peppers. He tried to sell off the rest to Rita's, but thanks to Crop Top, they were fixed for product.

Here at last was a chance to do my part. That fall, Elliot was our personal CSA. Every weekend, he'd bike over to our place with a crate strapped over his handlebars, mostly peppers with a few surprises mixed in: a smattering of lima beans, a bunch of basil from Henry's plant. We're still slathering our English muffins with the pepper jelly we canned for winter. I must say, it's delicious.

I was proud and a little jealous of Elliot for seeing the project through, but I suspect he was a little jealous of me, too. While I was hanging pictures above my desk (the only place Prometheus permitted personal decorations) and choosing a retirement plan, he was picking peppers, plotting a course out of the Triangle. He bided his time till Principal Jenner's last week on the job, then showed up to tell him how sorry he was to see him go. There was one piece of business he was hoping they could square away before the new principal took over, a formality really. Elliot needed his signature on the form that would transfer proprietorship of the farm from Raise the Roof to Begin to Win, legally recognizing its conversion from a community garden into a school garden. Principal Jenner's recollection of our first meeting was hazy, but Elliot assured him that this had been the understanding all along. Raise the Roof's model was to provide schools and communities with the resources they needed to start sustainable farm projects, then leave those projects in their partners' capable hands. Having built Begin to Win's capacity to manage the farm, Elliot's work here was done. Of course, if the school needed additional support, technical assistance was available; his consulting fee was negotiable.

Who knows whether Jenner bought this or just wanted to stick it to the Schlossers. Whatever the case, he signed. Elliot helped Sasha with the application for a three-year grant from the Pepsi Foundation (they were on a PR offensive in the city at the time, part of their campaign to defeat Bloomberg's ban on jumbo sodas). So began his career as a nonprofit farm consultant.

It was a masterstroke, really. Elliot had the ideal set of assets for a consultant in this brave new world. First, he had the curriculum—vetted by experts, piloted in an esteemed charter school—just the thing for a fledgling nonprofit farm looking to attract philanthropic dollars. Second, he had the connections. Need help securing a permit? He still had Vivienne on speed dial. Looking for an in with funders? His former partner just happened to be a program officer for the city's most prominent foundation. How about branding and public outreach? He was close with a leader in the field of strategic communications. That's right. He'd made nice with Marnie, for whom new business always trumped old beef. He'd even buried the hatchet with Seth—I gave him permission to blame me for everything—just in case a prospective client needed an architect. Other than Sal, not a single person who'd crossed Elliot's path was on bad terms with him.

That more than anything was what made him the perfect consultant. Everyone liked the guy. Clients were willing to pay just to have him around for a while. Pastor Leo was a believer. All it took was one conversation—and a recommendation from his friendly Prometheus program officer—to seal the deal.

There he was waiting for me by the pluot nursery, his beard trimmed to a professional length but his tan so deep now it seemed permanent. He had the look of a man who's gotten used to being his own boss. I finished up my confab with Pastor Leo and headed his way.

He picked a pluot and tossed it to me. "Like what we've done with the place?"

The bite I took was tart. The pluot wasn't quite ripe yet. "Could use some more strategic linkages," I said.

"We put them in the fertilizer."

"That sounds about right."

"Pastor Leo's going to ask for an increase on my budget line. We're just getting started with the education initiative."

"I could tell he was buttering me up for something. He kept talking about 'the next evolution in project-based learning.'"

"That's why I love Brooklyn. Even the pastors believe in evolution."

"I hope you realize what you're doing to me. It's going take ten meetings to get this approved."

"I just hate to think of you being bored. Hey, speaking of meetings, I was out at Peter's Place yesterday. Or should I say, TBD Place."

Elliot had taken my place on the steering committee. Even after he'd handed over the farm to Begin to Win, he stuck around, figuring it couldn't hurt to stay involved in a major neighborhood revitalization project. You never knew when the good folks of Community Board 3 might be in the market for a consultant. They still met regularly to tweak the plans (if the skate park included a full funbox, would there be room for the food truck court?), but according to Elliot, they were no closer to construction. Turns out, Jack wasn't kidding when he said he was putting in for retirement. His replacement was Winston, who seemed unmotivated by the distinctly bourgeois turn events in the Triangle had taken. On the rare occasion he showed up for a meeting, he just spaced out, biding his time till the revolution came. So, for the foreseeable future, the revitalization would consist of a few fruit trees and a parking lot blocked by boulders.

"Junior Contreras asks about you all the time," Elliot told me. "You really made an impression on him."

"I wrote 'keep in touch' in his yearbook, but, you know, he never did."

"Come on, be honest. You miss it, don't you?"

I did, of course, parts of it anyway—hanging out with Elliot most of all.

"You coming to Pete's birthday party?" I asked.

"We're going to try. I've got to deal with some league business in the morning."

Elliot had gotten one last favor out of Jack before he retired: a permit for use of the soccer field in the new waterfront sports complex alongside the Brooklyn navy yard. The permit was expensive, but the demand for space and playing time among the city's countless leagues made it a shrewd investment. The virgin field with its grand view of Manhattan quickly became the most coveted in the city. Elliot formed his own league and sold memberships for a tidy profit. I think all that time with John must have rubbed off on him. During the season, he devoted as much energy to managing the soccer schedule as he did to his consulting business.

"I just hope all the kids from daycare show," I said. "We've still got pureed bell pepper to unload."

The plan was to celebrate Pete's first birthday in the park by the Old Stone House, where I'd become a member of the board. Volunteering was Tricia's suggestion. That way, even as I re-acclimated to office work, I'd have a community project complete with garden to keep me from feeling like I'd given up too much—or just given up. Compared to Raise the Roof, it was a pretty staid gig, but between new fatherhood and the long hours at Prometheus, it was about all I had the energy for.

It's hard to explain why we decided to name our child after the place I'd felt such a desperate need to escape, but let me try. My one regret about the way it all went down is that the kid won't be able to say his dad's a farmer after all. Instead, if all goes well, he'll be saying, "My dad's a program officer for a foundation." Honorable enough, but not exactly the stuff dreams are made of. So I guess I wanted my son's name to be a small reminder of a time in his dad's life when he dreamt a little bigger, when he took a risk, tried to reinvent himself. If I have one lesson to pass down, it's that there are no failures, only learning opportunities. It's going to be hard to tell him that isn't true for everyone.

Pete's name is a reminder of something else, as well: a moment in the history of the city, his city, when Brooklyn became not just a place to live but a lifestyle. I imagine that will seem weird by the time he grows up and the Old Stone House is a thirty-story condo and Red Hook is underwater. I kind of hope it does.

ACKNOWLEDGEMENTS

A debt of gratitude to my parents, Lawrence and Judy Browne, and to my teachers, particularly Meg Medina, Keith Young, Alan Ziegler, and Mark Slouka.

Shout out to Tomas Hunt, my partner in not-for-profit crime.

Thanks to G.K. Darby, Katie Pfalzgraff, and Thomas Price for their thoughtful stewardship of the manuscript and to all those who gave suggestions, advice, and support: Julie Bissell, Vanessa Davis, Colin Delaney, Rory Evans, Mike Harvkey, Jon Hull, E. Tyler Lindvall, Matt Mittenthal, Martha Schulman, and Mark Woltman.

Much respect to all the people in government, schools, foundations, nonprofits, and communities who fight the good fight every day. I hope I've honored you by counterexample.

This novel is dedicated to Lisa, Theo, and Mabel, the light that makes my garden grow.